Winning the Cowboy's Heart

JEANNIE WATT

D1808225

⊚™ MILLS & BOON®
Pure reading pleasure™

*First published in Great Britain 2009
by Harlequin Mills & Boon Limited,
Eton House, 18-24 Paradise Road, Richmond, Surrey TW9 1SR*

© Jeannie Steinman 2007
(Originally titled *The Horseman's Secret*)

ISBN: 978 0 263 87360 3

38-0309

*Harlequin Mills & Boon policy is to use papers that are
natural, renewable and recyclable products and made from
wood grown in sustainable forests. The logging and
manufacturing processes conform to the legal environmental
regulations of the country of origin.*

*Printed and bound in Spain
by Litografia Rosés S.A., Barcelona*

To the Rays and Mr Stein,
the best principals ever,

To my headstrong children,

To my parents,
who raised their own headstrong children,

To my mother, a true horsewoman,

I dedicate this book.
Thanks so much for everything.

"Are you trying to keep me from buying a horse?"

Will tilted his black hat back, enabling her to see his eyes without the shadow of the brim. And they were nice eyes – not deep brown, like Kylie's, but blue-grey.

"That would be rather presumptuous of me."

Regan let out a snort. "Yes. I agree."

"Been talking to Kylie?"

"Yes."

Will's gaze shifted to the door of the room behind her. He paused before he brought his attention back to Regan.

"I am not trying to keep you from buying a horse. I am trying to keep you from making a mistake."

Incredible. "And who are you to decide whether or not I'm making a mistake?"

Dear Reader,

What makes a person a good parent? Love, patience, dedication, willingness to sacrifice… the list goes on. Being a good parent means making a commitment and sticking to it, even when the going gets rough.

Will Bishop is a good parent, raising his headstrong daughter without benefit of a wife or immediate family. He's doing the best he can, but he's facing mystifying teenage-girl issues and, in spite of his efforts, his daughter seems to be following a little too closely in his own hellion footsteps for comfort. What's a father to do? Persevere. Hang on. Hope for the best. Especially when his life is further complicated by a deep attraction to his daughter's teacher, and having to contend with the secret he's been keeping for so many years.

I wrote this story with the idea of exploring the difficulties of being a single parent – in particular, a single parent falling in love and wondering how to work a relationship into his already complicated life. I hope you enjoy *Winning the Cowboy's Heart*.

I would love to hear from you. Please contact me at jeanniewrites@gmail.com.

Happy reading,

Jeannie Watt

CHAPTER ONE

THE CALL Will Bishop had been dreading came at 2:45 in the afternoon, just when he was beginning to think he was home free. As soon as he hung up the phone, he grabbed his hat and headed for the truck. True to form, his daughter Kylie had started junior high with a bang.

Will knew the way to the office by heart—he'd visited the place a time or two during his own scholastic career at Wesley Junior and Senior High. He pulled off his hat and stepped inside.

"Hi, Will." The secretary was the same woman who'd kept him company years ago, only a little grayer now and sitting in front of a computer instead of a typewriter. "Long time, no see."

"Mrs. Serrano."

"You can go in."

Will wondered how many more times he

was going to hear those words over the next few years.

He pushed the door open. Four faces turned his way. Kylie, of course, looking defiant as only Kylie could; Mr. Bernardi, the principal; Pete Domingo, the PE teacher; and a lady he didn't know.

"Have a seat, Will."

At least Bernardi had refrained from making any comments about old times. The last thing Will needed was for Kylie to think she was carrying on a family tradition, even if she was.

"This is Miss Flynn," Bernardi said, indicating the dark-haired woman who was now regarding Will with an inquiring expression. "Miss Flynn is Kylie's science and social studies teacher."

Miss Flynn acknowledged the introduction with a nod and a smile that stopped short of her striking green eyes. She seemed cool and professional, exactly the kind of teacher that Kylie—and Will, back in the day—always butted heads with. In fact, Kylie was glaring at her now from under her lashes. Will sensed a long school year ahead.

"Will, Kylie has engaged in some questionable behavior that needs to be addressed immediately." Bernardi sounded as if he was reading from a cue card.

"I see." Will was an old hand at translating teacher speak. He'd heard enough of it over the years. "What did Kylie do that was questionable?"

Mr. Bernardi was about to respond when he was interrupted by Pete Domingo. "Let's let Kylie tell her father what she did."

"Good idea," Bernardi agreed. "Kylie?"

Kylie sent Pete a smoldering look. "I got caught."

No kidding. "Caught doing what?"

"Caught smoking after PE," Pete Domingo said, forgetting his intention of letting Kylie fess up.

"Smoking!"

Kylie nodded slowly. If Will hadn't been so utterly ticked off, he would have noticed his daughter trying to send him a message.

He glanced at Bernardi. "I'll be taking care of this at home. What happens here?"

"We know there are others involved, but Kylie won't name names."

"I was the only one," she said.

"We know that's not true." Bernardi sounded tired.

Kylie stubbornly shook her head, her

straight dark hair shifting over her shoulders. She was no longer meeting anyone's gaze. Instead, she stared down at the floor tiles.

Principal Bernardi let out a sigh. "We've already discussed this with Kylie. If she won't tell us who else was there, then she'll have to bear the brunt of the punishment alone."

Will gave Kylie a long look. Her jaw was locked and she looked so much like his ex-wife at that moment that it almost frightened him. But even if she resembled Desiree, she mostly took after him.

"I understand why Pete is here, but…" Will glanced over at Miss Flynn. She hadn't said a word and she didn't appear as though she particularly wanted to be there. Unlike Domingo. The little general was enjoying this.

"They were outside my room," she said. "There was a group of at least three, but Kylie was the only one I recognized."

Will gave Kylie one last chance, even though he knew it was futile. "Kylie?"

She shook her head. Will stood. "Unless she needs to stay now, I think we'll go home and discuss this."

"This means an automatic three-day suspension, Will. School-district policy."

"I understand," Will replied. "Come on,

Kylie. We're going home." Kylie got up from the wooden chair and headed for the door.

"If I get any names, I'll let you know," he told Bernardi, and followed his daughter out of the room. He was almost at the main entrance when he heard quick footsteps behind him. What now?

"Go to the truck," he told Kylie, who went out the door without a word. Will turned to face Miss Flynn, fast approaching with purposeful strides, the expression on her face that of someone about to give helpful hints on how to handle his child. Well, he'd had enough input from educators for one day.

"Don't worry," he said, "I'm not going to beat her."

"That's happy news," she replied mildly, and Will felt somewhat ashamed of himself. "I actually wanted to talk to you about another matter."

"Like…?"

"I'm looking for a horse. A pleasure horse, and I heard you have some for sale."

This was not what Will had expected. Not even close. He gave a slow nod of acknowledgment. "I did have some horses for sale, but they went fast. I only have one left at this point, and I'm afraid he won't do for you."

Miss Flynn's eyebrows edged upward. "Why? I'm an experienced rider."

"He's a man's horse."

She regarded him for a moment. "There's no such thing."

"He was abused by a woman and now he doesn't like women—not even Kylie. Some horses are like that."

She looked as though she'd like to argue the point with him, but she didn't. "Well, do you know of any other horses for sale around here?" She pushed her hair behind an ear, mussing the layers.

"Not right now." It was true. There weren't many suitable horses for sale in Wesley, Nevada, and he wasn't going to direct her to the Taylors, who always had a horse for sale at some ridiculously high price. "You might try closer to Elko."

One corner of her mouth tightened in obvious frustration and suddenly she didn't look so teacherlike.

"I'll let you go." She rubbed the back of her neck in a way that made Will think he wasn't the only one who'd had a bad day. "I knew this wasn't a good time to ask, but I really want a horse. And since I was going

to call about your newspaper ad anyway...."
She shrugged. "Bad judgment on my part."

She turned then, walked back down the hall, leaving Will staring after her. He felt like a jerk.

He debated for a moment, then decided to rebuild his burned bridges later. Right now he needed to nudge the truth out of his daughter.

"So who are you covering for this time?" Will asked as he put the truck in gear. Kylie waited until they were officially off school property before she answered.

"Mark. You know what his dad would do to him."

Will knew. Mark's dad was a bully, but somehow Mark not only survived, he was a likable kid.

"What happened?"

Kylie gave a brief description of events, which played out pretty much as Will had expected. Mark, the geek, had been proving he wasn't a geek by smoking, with Kylie watching his back. The part where Kylie had got caught and Mark hadn't was still hazy, but Will let that slide for the moment.

"If you're suspended, I can't exactly let you go to the horse show this weekend, can I?"

Kylie's jaw dropped. "But I didn't do anything."

"You were there."

"But…"

"Smoking is wrong, and you were there," Will replied, holding firm.

"I was there because of Mark. People pick on him because they can. It's not right." Kylie let out a huff of breath to emphasize the remark.

"Well, I really don't think smoking was the answer. Do you?"

"No, but I couldn't talk him out of it."

"Then you should have walked away. You can't go through life protecting people, Kylie. And I don't see Mark standing up for you. He left you twisting in the wind."

Kylie gazed at her father earnestly. "He doesn't know. They got me after science and I didn't have time to see him. I totally missed my last class while we waited for you."

"And now you're going to miss three days."

"And the horse show," she muttered sullenly.

"You aren't going to be riding or working with your horse, either. I need some help fixing the pole corral and I think there's some house-work that needs attending to. We'll stop by the school tomorrow and pick up your work."

They drove a few miles in silence and then Kylie asked, "How come the new teacher knew you?"

"What makes you think she knows me?"

"The way she was looking at you."

Kylie didn't elaborate and Will decided it was best not to ask. "She doesn't know me. She knows we have horses for sale and she's looking to buy a horse."

"But all we have left is the paint gelding."

"I know."

"He won't do for her."

Will smiled in spite of himself. "That's exactly what I told her."

"Miss Flynn?"

Regan turned to see Pete heading down the hall toward her, his whistle bouncing on his belly.

"Yes?"

"Look, I don't know how they handled things down in Las Vegas, but frankly, I'd appreciate a little more support."

"I'm not sure I follow you."

"A united front."

Regan frowned, wishing he'd given her enough information to enable her to respond. His expression shifted toward impatience.

"I really think you could have backed me when I pointed out the other two boys that had probably been with Kylie."

"But I wasn't sure it was them."

"Well, I was."

In spite of not having seen them.

Regan forced a smile and refrained from pointing that out to him, in the interest of maintaining a peaceful work environment. She liked her new school. A lot. It had a small staff, nice-sized classes and one of her best friends from college worked there. Actually, when all her carefully made plans had blown up in her face, thanks to Daniel, her former colleague and jerk of an ex-boyfriend, it had been Tanya who'd encouraged her to move four hundred miles north.

"I'll try to be more observant next time."

Pete gave a curt nod. "It would help."

REGAN'S NEW PRINCIPAL lasted less than a week.

Bernardi experienced chest pains on Thursday. On Friday it was announced he was taking an indefinite leave of absence. Pete Domingo, the only person on staff with administrative certification, would become acting principal in the interim.

"Pete Domingo?" Tanya moaned on the day of the big announcement. She flicked her smooth blond hair back over her shoulder. "Do you know what we're in for?"

"A united front, I gather." Regan perched on the edge of a student desk, waiting for her friend to finish her lesson plan.

"I'd rather have a monkey as an administrator. No, make that a baboon. Pete's ego is entirely too big and he's not concerned with learning. He's a do-or-die coach. He just wants to *dom-i-nate*."

"So do you, only in the academic sense."

"Yeah, yeah, yeah. Come on, let's go." Tanya closed her book. "I can finish up tomorrow. Oh, by the way, my landlord knows a guy who's selling a horse. Some kind of fancy quarter horse. He told me about it, but I can't remember much. I think it's female, has four legs and a tail."

"Funny, but that's exactly what I'm looking for."

Tanya reached for the phone book on the edge of her desk. "I'll find the number."

TANYA WAS BUSY ON SATURDAY, so Regan drove to the landlord's friend's place alone. She was greeted by a man in cowboy gear who introduced himself as Charley. He led her to a panel corral, where a stocky bay mare stood.

"Her name is Bonita Bar Santos, but I call her Broomtail."

"Broomtail?"

"She rubs her tail on the fence in hot weather and makes a mess of it," Charley explained as he entered the corral with a halter. The mare lifted bored eyes and stood, docile, while he slipped the halter over her head and buckled it. Regan opened the gate and Charley led Broomtail out.

"Did you bring your saddle?"

"No." Her saddle was English and it was still at her mother's house. She'd have to send for it.

He dropped the lead rope and went inside the tack shed without tying up the mare. She cocked a hind leg and waited, ears at half-mast. After much clunking and banging, the guy came out carrying a dusty saddle in his left hand. "Only small one I have." With his right hand, he put a blanket on the mare and smoothed it, then settled the saddle into place. He cinched it up. "Just let me get the bridle and you can take her for a spin."

Regan rode for almost an hour, happy to be back in a saddle after too many years out of it. The horse moved slowly—pleasure rather than performance material. But she knew her stuff. She sluggishly picked up her leads, turned on the forehand and side passed. As Regan worked her, the mare gradually became more responsive, quicker in her movements. She tossed her head impatiently a few times on the way home and started to jig, but after her slow beginning, Regan took it as a good sign. Maybe the mare had life in her after all. Maybe all she needed was to lose weight and get some exercise.

"I hope I haven't kept you from something," Regan said after dismounting and handing the man the reins. He'd been looking at his watch when she returned and she felt bad for taking so long.

"Not at all." He smiled hopefully. "Well?"

"I'll think about it and let you know."

His face fell. "Just a word of warning. There will be some people coming to see her tomorrow morning."

"I'll let you know," Regan said firmly. "Thanks for showing her to me."

IT WAS NOT A CALL Will wanted to make, but Zero Benson from the feed store had seemed pretty certain of his information. Zero wasn't exactly the sharpest person in the world, but Will figured he'd better check things out anyway. He dialed Charley Parker's number.

The conversation lasted almost a minute before Charley hung up on him.

"Is Charley trying to sell Broomtail?" Kylie asked without looking up from her math book. Her collie pup, Stubby, lay at her feet, his chin resting on her shoe.

"When is he not trying to sell Broomtail?" Will went to the old-fashioned enamel sink and rinsed the coffeepot, then wiped down the counter.

"Charley'd probably be happy if someone stole her, then he wouldn't have to feed her anymore." Kylie erased part of an answer, then rewrote a few numbers.

"That would only work if he had her insured, and I'm pretty sure he doesn't."

"So, did the Martinezes have insurance?"

"Hardly anyone insures their horses around here, kiddo, except for maybe the Taylors. Too expensive."

"So when their horses got stolen…" Kylie made a gesture with her pencil.

"They're out of luck, unless we find them." And it wasn't looking good. Most stolen horses ended up in an out-of-state auction within days of being taken. The Martinez horses had been gone for three days.

"Should have freeze-branded them," Kylie

murmured before turning back to her homework.

"Ever hear that saying about the barn door and the horse?"

"Only when you say it," she replied in a way that made him feel very old and out of touch.

Will settled in the kitchen chair across from his daughter and pulled his account books closer. He'd developed the habit of doing his paperwork while Kylie worked on her homework, finding that it kept them both on track. He now had a set of books he was proud of and Kylie was proving to be a much better student than he'd been.

Now if she could just stay out of trouble for a day or two.

THE MARE WAS no longer on the market. Charley called early Saturday morning to give Regan the news.

"Did you sell her?" she asked, thinking that if he had, he'd sold her within the past twelve hours.

"Not exactly. I just…changed my mind."

Regan hung up the phone with a frown. Weird. The guy'd seemed anxious to sell the horse less than a day ago. She decided to chalk it up to small-town eccentricity.

She gathered her purse and car keys, ready to start phase two of her horse hunt.

Madison White operated the indoor riding arena at the edge of town and, according to people at school, if she didn't have a horse, she at least had the connections to find one. Regan had already decided to see what the woman had to offer before making a decision on Broomtail, which was fortuitous, since the mare was now mysteriously off the market.

As it turned out, Madison had a horse for sale that was stabled at the arena. A nice, big horse with a nice, big price tag. A Thoroughbred that had been purchased as a jumper and had proven to be too hot for the girl who'd bought him.

Regan borrowed a saddle and mounted what felt like a bundle of dynamite. But once she got him moving, she found that he was smooth and smart. He just needed work, and Regan was looking for a project to fill her free time.

She did a quick calculation, decided to eat less for a few months and told Madison she wanted the gelding. She managed to dicker the price down by a couple of hundred dollars, but the purchase was still going to eat a hole in her budget. Regan didn't care. She had a horse.

She made arrangements to continue boarding him at the arena until she got her pasture properly fenced, and then drove home, feeling richer rather than poorer.

Now all she had to do was hire a fencer, buy a water tank, arrange a vet check, send for her saddle and watch her pennies for a few months. Okay, maybe a year. But it didn't matter, she had a horse.

CLAIRE TRIED TO BE EXCITED for Regan when she called to share her news. But since Claire had never owned an animal in her life, Regan knew her sister was having a hard time relating. Claire soon turned the topic to her primary concern.

"I can't believe you left me alone in this city with Mom."

"How're your classes going?"

"I'm not wild about them. I mean, they're easy enough, but…I don't know. Something's missing."

Only Claire would say that engineering classes were "easy enough." She was accidentally brilliant, according to their mother. She could do upper-level math with ease, but she found the things she was good at boring. She liked to dive into subjects she knew nothing about, learn what she could and then move on. An attention-deficit engineer. Probably not what the world needed.

"What's missing?"

"I don't know. Passion?" Claire must have sensed Regan's smile. "Hey, you feel passionately about your job. Why shouldn't I feel the same about mine? And you put your foot down when Mom wanted you to go to law school."

"Yes, and you can do the same."

There was a slow intake of breath on the other end of the line, followed by a long exhalation. "I'm not quite ready for that."

KYLIE STAYED LATE on the day she returned to school, making up the science lab she'd missed the day before. Regan attempted to initiate a conversation once the girl was finished—*attempted* being the key word. In the wake of the smoking incident, Kylie wasn't exactly warming up to Regan.

"Do you ride?" Regan asked after a string of frustrating monosyllabic replies to other questions. The conversation was becoming a battle of wills, but Regan wasn't ready to give up.

"Yes."

"Does your dad ride?"

"It's his job."

"Riding?"

"He starts colts for people."

"I see." Regan was beginning to feel as if she were starring in an episode of *Dragnet*.

"That's what I'm going to do, too."

Ah, progress. Two answers with more than two words. Regan decided to press on. "Has your dad always been a horse trainer?"

"Pretty much."

"What did he do before he started training horses?"

"I think he's always trained horses. He used to ride rodeo, before he got hurt. I do junior rodeo in the summer." Kylie pushed back the dark strands of hair that had escaped from her ponytail.

"You're a lot like your dad, then."

"Yeah." Kylie gave a wry twist of a smile. "Even in ways he doesn't get."

Regan cocked her head. "Like how?"

"Like he keeps telling me I can't be rescuing things, but he does it all the time."

"He rescues things?"

"Horses. People."

"People? How does he rescue people?"

Kylie shrugged nonchalantly. "He saved you from buying Broomtail, didn't he?"

Regan just managed to keep her jaw from dropping. That was the end of twenty questions and Kylie knew it. Regan gave the girl a tight you-win smile and went to tidy up the lab equipment. She would be discussing the Broomtail matter further, but it would be with the father and not the daughter.

About a minute later Will's big diesel truck pulled into the school parking lot. Good timing. Regan would just as soon get this over with while she was still annoyed.

"I'd like to talk to your father alone."

"I'll wait here." It sounded like a procedure Kylie was familiar with.

"We're not going to talk about you," Regan assured her with a half smile.

Kylie couldn't quite erase the "yeah, sure" look from her face.

Regan stepped out into the hall, pulling the door shut behind her, and met Will at the glass entryway a few feet from her room.

"Are you trying to keep me from buying a horse?" she asked without bothering to say hello.

Will tilted his black hat back, allowing her to see his eyes without the shadow of the brim. And they were nice eyes—not Kylie's deep brown, but blue-gray.

"That would be rather presumptuous of me."

Regan let out a snort. "Yes. I agree."

"Been talking to Kylie?"

"Yes."

Will's gaze shifted to the door of the room behind her. He paused before he brought his attention back to Regan.

"I am not trying to keep you from buying a horse. I am trying to keep you from making a mistake."

Incredible. "And who are you to decide whether or not I'm making a mistake?"

"I know the horses in this community. But more than that, I know the people selling them." His expression was impassive. "I know a mistake when I see one."

Regan narrowed her eyes. "And just why do you know so much?"

"Because I'm a deputy brand inspector. If it has four legs and eats hay, I'm probably involved in the sale." His eyes went back to the door. "Do you think I could have my daughter?"

Regan didn't budge. "Why was Broomtail a mistake?"

"She's a very unpleasant mare most of the time."

"Most of the time? But she seemed…"

Regan's voice trailed off as several aspects of her experience with Broomtail began to make more sense—the mare's lethargic attitude, followed by a display of impatience. Charley glancing anxiously at his watch....

Will saw that she'd caught his meaning.

"He gives her enough tranquilizer to make her less cranky and more salable. We had a chat the other night. I don't think he'll be doing it again in the near future." He gestured to the classroom. "My daughter?"

Regan moved to her door and pulled it open, her mind still working over the Broomtail issue. Kylie stumbled out a bit too fast, but the brand inspector didn't seem surprised by his daughter's sudden appearance.

"Let's go," he said. He met Regan's eyes for a brief moment as he pushed the glass door open. Kylie slipped out under his hand and Will followed, letting the door swing shut behind him.

Regan gave her head a slow shake. It sounded as if Kylie was right. Her dad had rescued her.

"WERE YOU EAVESDROPPING on us?" Will asked as he put the truck in gear.

"I couldn't hear through the door.

"I'll take that to be a yes."

"Dad," Kylie said seriously. "I like to know what's going on, if it concerns me."

"It didn't concern you."

"Yeah. I figured."

"How?"

"You guys didn't even look at me when I went by."

Will told her to knock off the eavesdropping, but he was impressed. His kid was observant, which was why she was good with horses. She could read cues. It was a valuable skill, one she seemed to be more talented at applying to people than he was. A bit of her mother coming through there.

"Something wrong, Dad?"

Will shook his head, keeping his eyes on the road.

"What are we eating tonight?"

He gave the standard answer. "Beef…"

"It's what's for dinner." They spoke in unison, mimicking an old ad slogan from the Beef Council.

One of these days she'd probably grow tired of the games and routines they'd started when she was younger, but he still had a few years left. He hoped. Kids seem to grow up so fast.

"Anything else?"

"No," he said facetiously. "Just beef."

"Good. I was tired of vegetables, anyway."

"How was school?"

"You didn't hear from anyone, did you?" It would have been funny, if she hadn't been serious.

"No."

"Then it was fine."

"Kylie."

She grinned. "Gotcha."

He rolled his eyes, wondering if he was ready for the approaching teenage years. Somehow he didn't think so. He was still debating how to handle certain matters that would have to be cropping up soon. He wasn't squeamish about girls' growth issues, just uninformed. Okay, maybe he was a little squeamish. He was hoping he could get Beth Grant, Kylie's best friend's mom, to help with that part of Kylie's upbringing. It wasn't exactly fair, but neither was growing up without a mother. Father and daughter both had to do the best they could.

He pulled to a stop in front of the house and reached over the back of the seat for the bag of groceries.

"I see carrots."

"There's worse stuff below that. Spinach, beets, spuds and corn."

"I liked the just-beef plan better."

"I'm sure you did, but veggies are a fact of life."

A STORM WAS MOVING IN. A full moon was in the offing. In Regan's experience, those were usually the best explanations for the off-the-wall behavior of her classes on such a day.

Jared, the new guy, Pete's long-term PE sub, stood in the hall with her. "I'm whipped," he said. "I usually teach elementary. Now I know why."

"This age grows on you."

"When?"

Regan smiled at his comeback and he returned the smile crookedly. The bell rang and Jared exhaled and headed for his class.

Regan managed to keep a lid on things until sixth period, near the end of the day. Kylie's class. Regan was teaching observation skills and since kids love nothing better than something gross and slimy, she'd invested in several calamari. The lesson was good—she'd simply picked the wrong day to teach it.

The trouble started as soon as the students were released to start their lab.

"Hey, Sadie," one of the boys called, holding up his squid. "Doesn't this look a lot like a *spider?*"

The girl immediately turned pale and stared straight down at the table. The boy wiggled the squid and a few students laughed, until they saw the look of death in Regan's eyes. It had been a long day and she was not going to put up with this. She walked over to the offending student, took his books, led him to a desk and told him to read chapter two of his textbook, outline it and then answer all questions at the end.

She moved back to Sadie, who was still staring down at the floor with Kylie beside her, and discovered that the girl did indeed have a major fear of spiders. Regan assured her that the squid was not a spider and that she could observe it from a comfortable distance. *"No one will bother you."*

A quick look around the class told her that everyone had gotten her message—or so she'd thought—until the students filed out after the quietest lab of the day and she realized that one of her specimens was missing.

She didn't need it—her final class was social studies—but she couldn't have an unauthorized squid floating around the school.

She hated to think of what might happen if it fell into the wrong hands. She had to find that cephalopod.

Then a shriek in the hall gave her a good of idea of where to look. She hurried to the door and pushed her way through a throng of kids to see three people in the center of the hall—Pete Domingo, Sadie and Kylie. The missing squid lay on the floor near Pete's feet.

"Pick it up." He was talking to Sadie.

Sadie's face was ashen. She shook her head, looking as if she was about to be sick. Domingo's face grew red.

"I. Said. Pick. It. Up."

The girl was close to tears. She didn't move.

"Joseph threw it at Sadie. So Joseph should pick it up." Kylie said hotly. Sadie was Kylie's best friend and Kylie was bent on protecting her.

"I distinctly saw it in Miss Grant's hand just before it hit me in the face."

"I was just getting it off me." The girl's voice was shaky. Her entire body was trembling, but Pete didn't seem aware of that. He'd just been hit in the face with a squid. The world was about to end.

"I'll pick it up," Kylie snapped. She started to reach for it, but Pete stopped her.

That was when Regan stepped into the center of the circle, calmly stooped down and grabbed the slimy creature. "I was wondering where this had gotten to," she said evenly, looking Pete in the eye. "I'm glad you found it." She turned and the crowd parted as she walked back to her room.

There was a silence and then— "Anyone who is not in class when that bell rings will have three days' detention."

The crowd broke up, leaving Kylie and Sadie standing silently in the center of the hall, uncertain whether they were supposed to go or stay. The bell rang and Regan paused at her door to see what was going to happen.

Domingo shook his head. "Three days, ladies."

His voice was clearly audible in Regan's classroom. She let out a breath and, knowing the kids were watching her reaction, carefully kept her face expressionless as she walked to the front of the class and started taking attendance. Inwardly she was seething.

Tanya was right. A baboon would be better.

CHAPTER TWO

"DAD, do you think you'll ever get married again?"

Will managed to flip the hotcake he was cooking without muffing it. "Not anytime soon."

"Good."

"Why?"

"Mark's dad and stepmom are breaking up. He says it sucks."

It did suck. No argument there. "Marriage is serious business, Kylie. Not something to be entered into lightly."

"How about you and my mother?"

My mother. The shadow figure. Kylie rarely spoke of her, although she did keep a photo of her in her hope chest. The last Will had heard, Des had hooked up with a rodeo stock contractor and was living in Florida. He hoped she'd finally matured enough to try to stick it out in a relationship.

"We were young."

Kylie speared a hotcake off the plate her father had set in the middle of the table. "That matters?"

"A lot of times it does. You can't have a grown-up relationship if you're not grown up."

"Marriage must be a lot of work."

"A good one is," Will said as he poured more batter into the pan.

"Then how do parents have time for kids?"

Will didn't know, since he'd never had a wife and a child at the same time. He winged it. "They work together to raise the kids."

"How do they have time for each other?" Kylie slathered butter on the hotcake and started to eat, not bothering with syrup.

"They make time."

"Mark's parents didn't."

"How so?"

Kylie gestured with her fork. "He said his stepmom was always complaining that his dad paid more attention to Mark than to her."

"So Mark's feeling guilty?"

"He doesn't like his stepmom, but he feels bad about his dad being so unhappy."

"Well, I don't think you have to worry. There aren't any women knocking down my door."

The phone rang. Kylie answered it and

then wrinkled her nose as she held out the receiver. "It's Madison… I think *she'd* like to knock down your door."

Will took the phone with a mock scowl.

"Will? Madison here." Madison always spoke as if she were slightly out of breath. "Did you get the contract for the clinic?"

"It came this morning."

"Thanks for stepping in."

It had been the third time in a year and a half he'd "stepped in." He was beginning to suspect she wasn't getting cancellations, "Are you sure you're really booking a second trainer for these clinics?"

Madison laughed. "Honest, I am. Del cancelled the first time and Mike the second. I'm just lucky you're close."

"And agreeable."

"That, too." She still had a smile in her voice. "Think of all the good you're doing for those horses whose owners don't have a clue."

"Hey, you already have me. You don't need to sell me."

"Actually, I'd like to get you to present on a regular basis. Two, three times a year—it wouldn't be that bad."

"I'll get this contract signed and back to you tomorrow."

Madison was enough of a trainer herself to know when to stop pushing. "Just think about it, Will."

"Goodbye, Madison."

Will turned down the burner under the pan and poured the last of the batter. He hated crowds and he hated talking, but Madison had a point about the horses. Most people who came to a training clinic were genuinely concerned about their animals, although there were always a few who thought bigger bits and spurs would solve most of their problems. Which was why Will often had more work than he could handle rehabilitating damaged horses.

REGAN HAD SUSPECTED her sister's four days of phone silence were a sign of impending disaster and she'd been correct. Claire called early Saturday morning with a classic case of stress overload. She'd had an argument with one of her professors, followed by a fight with her boyfriend, then her roommate had spilled wine on her new cashmere sweater. *But,* Claire assured Regan, the biggest problem was their mother, who was having a hard time butting out of Claire's life. Arlene had already lost one daughter to public service, and now the other one was damn well going to live up to her potential.

Regan listened patiently for almost fifteen minutes, letting Claire talk herself out. Finally, her sister wound down and asked Regan how she was doing.

Regan responded with a simple, "Fine." It seemed easiest. "Do you want me to call Mom and see what I can do?"

"Would you?"

Regan always did, but she had been hoping when she put some miles between herself and her family that Claire and Arlene would somehow learn to deal with each other without getting a mediator involved.

Regan called her mother a few minutes later, negotiated a truce and then parried a few thrusts aimed in her direction.

Yes, she did like the smaller community she'd moved to. No, there wasn't much opportunity for advancement in this school district. No, she wasn't going to keep in touch with the Education Development Authority (EDA), a private curriculum-development company that she'd hoped to work for only months before. There was no way she would work for them now that Daniel had taken a job there. Besides, she had a job she liked.

Unfortunately, Arlene was not convinced. By the time Regan hung up, she was exhausted. And she was thinking about Daniel again. She made herself stop. It was bad for her blood pressure.

THE MUSTANG MARE circled the round pen at a floating trot, her nose high in the air, her attention outside the rails, on anything but Will, who stood near the center. Her objective was fundamental. Escape.

Will kept her moving, using his body language to propel her forward, to control her direction. Finally, she shifted an eye toward him as she trotted by, flicked an ear back. Will's gaze immediately dropped from her head to her hindquarters and he took a backward step. She slowed, uncertain, then decided she would rather ignore him and escape. Will upped his energy, moving the mare forward again.

A few circles later, another glance, another ear flick. Will stepped back. The mare slowed, both eyes on him now. He took another step back, rewarding her attention by reducing the pressure on her. She slowed still more, eventually coming to a stop, her eyes on Will. They stood and studied one another.

Will took a single slow step forward and the mare made her decision—no one was going to control her. Will set her moving again.

Will had made some major headway with the mare by the end of the session. Sometimes with mustangs, especially older ones, it took almost twice as long to teach a concept, but once they got it, the knowledge was deeply engrained. He had yet to saddle her, but he *had* been able to rub her all over, desensitize her body, pick up her feet. He'd start again tomorrow and see what she remembered.

It had been a good day, made better by a phone call from the head brand inspector late that evening. Trev's laid-back voice actually held a note of excitement. "We located Martinez's horses."

"You're kidding. Where?" Kylie, who was settled at the kitchen table with her homework, glanced up, a hopeful expression in her dark eyes.

"Idaho. A total fluke, but, hey, we have them."

"How about the thieves?" Will gave Kylie a thumbs-up and she grinned.

"We don't have them."

"Does Martinez know?"

"He's already on his way north. I thought

you'd want to know that we're no longer batting zero." No, but they were close to it. Six incidents of horse stealing in the past six months and this was the first recovery. Trev filled in the details and then said, "Heard about Kylie today. Pretty funny."

"Yeah." Funny if it wasn't your kid who'd popped the school bully in the eye. Fortunately, she'd lived to tell the tale. Kylie'd always been a pretty good sprinter. "Hey, I need a favor. I'm looking for a pleasure mount. Would you let me know if you hear of anything?" Will scuffed his boot along the floor as he spoke. Kylie'd forgotten to sweep again.

"For Kylie?"

"No. I have a friend who's looking." Or, more accurately, he wanted to make peace with his daughter's teacher and this seemed like a good way to do it.

"I'll let you know. I think McKirk might have some horses for sale. He was talking about reducing his herd, now that his kids are in college. What price range?"

"Not a clue. Just let me know if you find anything." Will hung up a few seconds later and turned to face an incredulous daughter.

"Is it *Miss Flynn?* Is she the *friend* who's looking for a horse?"

"It's an expression."

"Good. I don't want you to be friends with my teachers." Kylie gave a shudder.

"I'll try and be careful about that."

ALL OF THE SQUID WERE MISSING.

Instead of creating a hot-weather biohazard in the school Dumpster, Regan had stored them in the staff freezer on Tuesday, planning to throw them out on trash day. And now they were gone.

Regan shut the freezer and tried to ignore the sinking sensation in her midsection. Perhaps the custodian had seen the gross creatures and disposed of them. Or Pete had found them and tossed them before another one hit him in the face. There could be no other explanation.

Regan caught sight of Tanya's distinctive blond hair through a crowd of students moving down the hall to their class. With some careful maneuvering, she managed to catch up with her friend.

"Do you think eight missing squid are a problem?"

Tanya stopped dead, forcing the current of students to flow around them. "Here at school?" Her blue eyes widened. "No, Regan. No problem at all."

But the morning passed without any strange incidents and Regan was able to convince herself that the custodian had indeed cleaned out the freezer. Kylie had initially aroused her suspicions by being uncharacteristically subdued, but as the class wore on, Regan decided that the girl was merely distracted.

"Are you all right?" Regan asked after the bell.

"I'm fine." Kylie's expression was not friendly. "Did you know that my dad is trying to find you a horse?"

"He is?" If Kylie had thrown out the statement to sidetrack Regan from thinking about squid, the strategy had worked beautifully.

"Yeah. But I don't think you should read anything into it."

Regan cocked her head at the kid. "What could I possibly read into it?"

"Maybe that he was doing it because he likes you. That isn't why he's doing it."

Regan managed not to laugh and say, *I'll try not to get my hopes up.*

"I expect he's doing it because he knows the horses around here," she suggested instead.

"Yeah. And he doesn't like it when people get horses they can't handle. That's how horses get hurt and ruined, you know."

Regan gritted her teeth. *Thank you for the vote of confidence, Mr. Bishop.*

She drew in a sharp breath. "You can tell your father that I'm buying a horse from Madison White and that I'll do my very best not to ruin him."

Kylie nodded gravely, missing Regan's irony. She picked up her books and left the room.

Regan gathered her materials for the next class. She wasn't going to think about Will right now. No sense taking her frustrations out on an innocent social studies class.

At the end of that class Regan discovered her overhead projector was no longer working. A quick investigation revealed that the bulb was missing.

A strange day was getting stranger. Someone had stolen it, and quite recently, too, since she'd used the machine just before lunch.

Who would want to steal an overhead projection bulb?

Regan rushed to the office between classes to get the key to the supply room. The student aid looked at her with surprise. "Mr. Domingo doesn't give out the key. He opens the supply room himself."

Regan let out an exasperated breath and set

off to find Mr. Domingo, the supply Nazi. He was in the gym, counting uniforms.

"There's only one more period," he said when she explained that she needed a projector bulb. "Can't you make it?"

"No. I need my overhead to teach the lesson." She stared at the uniforms. "Are you putting those in numerical order?"

"It's easier to keep track of them that way," he muttered. "Come on." Pete marched out of the gym and down the long, dark hall that led to the supply closet. He turned the final corner ahead of her and then let out a sharp cry and swatted wildly at something that appeared to be attacking his head.

Regan gasped as Pete reeled backward, cursing and thrashing, until he finally tripped over his own feet and ended up flat on his butt in front of her.

Several of the…things…seemed to fly off him as he landed, and then a familiar smell hit Regan's nostrils. Squid. Quite possibly freshly thawed.

Domingo glared up at her. A limp tentacle was stuck to his shoulder. Another was attached to his back. Several other squid parts were suspended from the doorframe above him.

He flicked the tentacle off his shoulder, radiating fury. Regan tried to think of serious things—SATs, mortgage payments, the nightly news. It wasn't working.

"Who had access to these squid?" he demanded, wiping a smear of slime from his face.

"I don't know. I was keeping them in the staff freezer and planned to throw them out on trash day, but…they were missing this morning."

"Why didn't you report this?" His face was dangerously red.

"You want me to report missing squid?"

"This wouldn't have happened if you had. *You* are responsible for this."

The bell rang. Regan pulled in a deep breath. "No, Pete. I'd say you're responsible. Maybe if you weren't so over-the-top with your discipline policy, you wouldn't be covered with squid parts right now."

"You can't talk to me like that."

Regan flicked a piece of slippery cephalopod off the wall. "I need to get to class. Are you all right?"

She was rewarded with a furious look, which she took as a yes.

"There will be no more seafood in this school!" Domingo shouted as she rounded the corner without her lightbulb. She decided then and there she'd bring shrimp salad for lunch every day for the rest of the month.

The next day, the Wesley staff and students discovered that hell had no fury like a principal who'd been punked.

Pete Domingo had no evidence, no suspects. All he had was a head full of possibilities, a school packed with smirking students and staff who'd heard about what had happened and had thought it funny, too.

Student after student was called down to the office to be grilled. All had returned to class looking shaken, but also vaguely satisfied. Kylie and Sadie were subjected to a longer inquisition than the other kids called from Regan's class, but they came back unscathed. No one confessed and, at the end of the day, Pete was no closer to solving his crime than he'd been when he was sitting on the floor in front of the supply-closet door, flicking tentacles off his clothing.

The staff avoided being seen gossiping in groups. No one wanted to be accused of conspiracy and no one wanted to relight Pete's very short fuse.

"You've been a good sport about this," the librarian whispered, late in the afternoon, as she scanned Regan's reference book. "I hope you didn't get into too much trouble."

"I'm fine," Regan whispered back. "But I wish I knew who did it. I'd kind of like to shake their hands."

The woman winked and then nodded toward a table of three geeky eighth-graders who had been thoroughly reamed out by Domingo a few days before for some petty infraction.

"You're kidding," Regan mouthed.

The librarian gave her an arch look and disappeared into the stacks.

A few long hours later Regan was in her kitchen making tea, peppermint tea, to help combat the stress headache she'd acquired.

A windstorm had started brewing late that afternoon and was now in full force, bending the trees and rattling the windows, and at first Regan thought the noise at the front door was a blast of wind. When she heard it again, during a lull, she realized someone was knocking.

She glanced down at her after-work wear—a tank top, sweat bottoms and fuzzy socks. Short of ignoring the door, there wasn't much she could do about her appearance and she couldn't exactly leave someone standing outside in a windstorm.

Or could she?

Will Bishop was out there, his shoulders hunched as the wind whipped at his clothing.

A gust caught the storm door as she pushed it open, and Will caught it just before it hit him. "Do you want to come in?" She raised her voice to be heard.

"For a minute."

Okay. She could deal with a minute. He'd barely gotten inside when another blast hit.

"Does the wind do this a lot?"

"We get some good storms here."

She wondered if she should ask him to sit down, offer him something to drink. Then she glanced at him and decided no. He had some reason for coming and it wasn't social, so she'd skip the niceties.

"I'm sorry to barge in like this," Will said, getting right to the point, "but I'd like to know... Do you think Kylie is involved in this squid thing?"

Those damned squid again. She'd had it up to here with squid—especially when they brought parents to her house.

"Have you asked her?" she asked with a touch of impatience.

"She says she's innocent." The *for once* went unspoken.

The house shook with the force of the wind. Twigs and pebbles bounced off the windows, but Regan's attention was focused on Will and the deep concern she saw on his face. This man was worried about his daughter and she owed him an honest answer.

"I don't know if she was involved, but my gut feeling is no. I've heard that it was actually some eighth-grade boys, but I'm not sure."

Will put a hand on the back of Regan's recliner. "Domingo harassed Kylie twice today. The second time he came on pretty strong, trying to force her to confess." His expression became stony. "If he starts again tomorrow... Well, I wanted an independent opinion before I went in to have a, um, chat with Pete."

"Everyone's a suspect, including the staff."

Will let out a breath and dropped his hand, ready to leave now that he had his answer. "Thanks. This helps."

"Would you like some tea or something before you go?"

He'd started for the door, but now he turned back, looking surprised. Regan was a little surprised herself. Her mother had hammered manners into her, but she hadn't realized to what degree. "Since you're here," she said lamely.

"I need to be getting home. Kylie's supposed to be starting dinner and I need to make certain the vegetables don't get burned mysteriously. But thanks. Especially after, well, everything."

She followed him to the door. He stopped before going out. "I would have called, but you don't seem to have a number."

"Unlisted. I like to avoid irate parents at report card time."

"Irate parents tend to show up on the doorstep around here."

She smiled. "I noticed."

Their gazes held for a second and then he smiled. And, oh, what a smile.

Regan blinked and then Will ducked his head and stepped out into the bad weather. Regan grabbed the storm door, fighting the wind to latch it shut. It shook, making an odd noise, but it held.

She settled into her chair with her luke-warm tea and unsettled thoughts, listening to the house try to blow down around her, hoping she would remember her vow to stay away from damaged men.

APOLOGIZING had been the right thing to do.

Realizing that his daughter's teacher was

attractive was a guy thing to do. But it had been a long time since Will had felt such a gut-level draw toward a woman and it perplexed him. Well, it didn't matter, because he wasn't going to do anything about it. Wrong time. Wrong circumstances. Probably the wrong woman.

Will propped a foot on the lower rail of the pole corral and watched his horses graze as his daughter rode bareback at the far end of the pasture. The windstorm had blown out as rapidly as it had blown in, leaving the air oddly still. Will had zillions of branches to collect around the place, but he'd start tomorrow while Kylie was at school. It was a good way to stay close to the house and the phone, in case that jerk Domingo called.

Kylie started cantering a pattern, practicing her flying lead changes and probably winning big trophies in her head. It was almost dark and a school night, but Will was glad his daughter was enjoying the things a kid should be enjoying, things he'd never gotten enough of at her age. He'd been too busy dealing with his old man. The phone rang and he jogged to the house, scooping up the receiver on the eighth ring.

"Hey." It was Trev. And he sounded stressed.

Will made a guess as to what was coming next. "More livestock stolen?"

"No." There was a silence, and then he said, "I saw your brother in Elko today."

Will stilled. "Brett was in Elko?"

"Yeah. He's working for the Friday Creek Ranch. I thought you'd want to know."

"Thanks." Will pressed his lips together. He couldn't think of anything else to say. He was having a hard time thinking at all.

"I didn't talk to him, but I thought you'd want to know," he repeated.

"Yeah, Trev. Thanks again."

CHAPTER THREE

THE NEXT MORNING Will drove Kylie to school in a haze. She'd missed the bus, but he'd skipped the usual lecture on responsibility and simply told her to hurry so he could get back home and start working the horses. He was fully booked and it took a good part of the day to put in his contracted time on each animal; after which he still had to clear the windfall branches and conduct a brand inspection for a horse sale.

"You okay, Dad?" Kylie asked when they reached the school. "I mean, you didn't yell at me about the bus."

"I'm fine. Just tired. I didn't sleep very well."

"Too much coffee, probably."

"Probably. Behave, kid. *And don't miss the bus!*"

She grinned and got out of the truck, oblivious to the fact that her jeans were getting too short and totally unaware that her father's heart was squeezing tight as he watched her join a group of friends.

He pulled out of the lot and drove at the posted snail's pace to the end of the school zone. He passed Kylie's bus going in the opposite direction. The driver waved and Will forced himself to wave back, although he didn't think it would have killed the driver to wait a few seconds while Kylie found her history book.

Right behind the bus was Regan's small car.

So Kylie wasn't the only one having time issues that morning.

He accelerated as soon as he was out of the safety zone, then made a conscious effort to slow down. With only a couple hours of troubled sleep, he wasn't as alert as he should be.

Couple of hours? Probably more like thirty minutes. He'd finally dozed off just before the alarm rang. And then he'd been instantly awake and the worries had come crashing down on him.

Why the hell was Brett back?

It had been more than ten years since he'd last seen Brett and it had not been a happy parting. In fact, someone had had to call the sheriff and Will had barely escaped a night in jail. Brett had not.

They hadn't spoken since that night. Brett had left town the next morning and that had been the last Will had seen or heard of his brother.

Now he was back. Why?

The thing that really set Will on edge was that he wasn't quite sure about the legalities of his situation. He might be better off if he did know, but looking into those things meant opening a can of worms he was inclined to leave firmly closed. He wouldn't do it—not unless he absolutely had to. Brett was a good eighty miles away at the moment and he'd better *stay* eighty miles away. If he didn't, he'd be a sorry man.

REGAN PARKED in the only available staff space, some distance from the back door. She grabbed her work bag off the passenger seat and made a dash for the teachers' entrance just as the bell rang. Flinging the door open, she ran smack into Pete.

"Ah, Miss Flynn," he said, looking a bit like a satisfied bullfrog.

"Sorry I'm late." She tried to speak calmly, even though she was winded from her sprint.

"I had a problem this morning." As in, an enormous elm branch on top of her new fence had stretched the wire and popped the staples; another large branch lay across her driveway, too big for her to do anything about. It had taken her almost fifteen minutes to work the first leafy monster free of the drooping fence wire. Even then she could have made it to work on time by driving around the branch that was blocking her drive, if her mother hadn't called just as she was walking out the door. Claire she could put off, but not her mother.

"You do know it's district policy to phone when you're going to be late?"

Regan nodded and refrained from telling him she had called, but Mrs. Serrano had been away from her desk. No sense having Pete jump all over the secretary, too.

He gave Regan a stern look, then abruptly turned and stalked off on his standard morning hunt for marauding pranksters. Regan secretly wished the pranksters success as she unlocked her classroom.

It might have been the aftermath of the squid inquisition, or it might have been that the students were hoping for the appearance of new slimy specimens to use for various nefarious purposes, but, whatever the reason, they paid close attention to Regan's lesson on classification. And she'd wisely opted to use an utterly benign material for this lab: leaves.

At first the kids seemed disappointed, but as the lab progressed the general mood became lighter—to the point where Regan began to wonder if Pete was going to find his car full of foliage when he left work that day. Once the thought had occurred to her, she issued a stern warning about the misuse of lab materials. The kids looked as if they were listening and a few even nodded after she spoke, but she'd taught for long enough to know that kids could look as if they were listening attentively and still not hear a word she said. All she could do at this point was hope for the best.

"Regan, what are you doing?" Tanya asked as she walked into the teachers' lounge several hours later.

"Watching Pete's car."

"Do I want to know why?"

Regan turned back to the copy machine, which was happily churning out ninth-grade history work sheets.

"I'm trying to avoid trouble not of my own making."

"I knew I didn't want to know." Tanya, a one-woman cleaning machine, went to the sink and started rinsing and drying coffee cups. "So why were you late this morning?"

"The wind blew a branch down on my fence and I had to get it off."

"It couldn't wait?"

"I needed to call the fence man, if it was damaged. He's kind of a slow worker and I want to get Toffee home this weekend."

"Was there that much damage?"

"Yes. I can't tighten the stretched wire myself, so I called him. He's going to try to get out there before the weekend." She tightened one corner of her mouth. "Emphasis on *try*."

Tanya gave her a sympathetic look just as Karlene, the girls' PE teacher, came in and flopped down in a chair, blowing a few of her short brown curls off her forehead. "Ever have the feeling that you wanted to kill your boss?"

"Shh." Tanya said. Pauline Johnson walked into the room just then, her high heels clicking on the tiles with metronomelike precision, the hem of her skirt hitting exactly midknee and her pale hair carefully lacquered into a French twist. She gave her colleagues a professional smile and went to check her mail. After sorting it, she marched over to the copy machine.

"Do you have many more?" she asked, indicating the masters Regan held in her hand.

"Two more sets."

"We really need to have a schedule for this machine."

"We pretty much have one," Tanya pointed out. "We're supposed to use it during our prep periods."

"I'm talking about before and after school." She gave a sniff as Regan positioned another master copy in the machine. "I'll talk to Pete about this. I think it's important."

Regan stubbornly went on with her copying, in spite of Pauline's impatient gaze boring into her back. Every school seemed to have a Pauline on its staff and Regan had plenty of practice dealing with them—her last school had had no fewer than three. One Pauline was no problem at all.

WILL DIDN'T GET ANY SLEEP that afternoon, though he'd promised himself he would. The day was simply too jam-packed. He put in an hour on each of the horses he was starting and he got the biggest branches piled up and ready to burn, the smaller ones left for Kylie to stack after school. Then Will got his inspection book out and headed to the Taylor ranch.

The Taylors had sold yet another overpriced horse, this time to a first-time horse buyer from Elko. The buyer seemed pleased as punch to pay double what the animal probably was worth. Will silently documented his inspection, noting the horse's brand, sex, age, color and markings. He handed the book to Todd Taylor to sign, then peeled off the copies.

At least the animal was well trained, so the new owner wasn't buying trouble. Todd paid the inspection fee, grumbling about the recent increase, which amounted to about one fifth of a percent of the purchase price. Will felt bad for him. Especially when he watched Mrs. Taylor drive up in her gleaming new SUV, waving as she eased the big machine into a three-car garage.

"So, how does Kylie like her teachers?" Todd asked after the garage door had closed.

"So far, so good."

"Great." Todd smiled. He continued to smile until Will gritted his teeth and asked the question he knew Todd wanted him to ask. "How's Zach doing in football?"

Todd launched into a ten-minute spiel. Will nodded. A lot. And then finally managed to sidestep his way to his truck and reach for the door handle.

"Oh, you probably have to be going. Well, anyway, be sure to go to the game next Friday. Zach will be starting and I think you'll see what I've been talking about."

Will gave a noncommittal nod and got into his truck.

On the way home he took the loop, even though it added a couple miles to the trip, passing by Regan Flynn's house to see what havoc the windstorm had wrought, wondering if she had a hole in her roof or other major damage that had caused her to be late that morning.

He didn't see much wind damage—just a few scattered branches—and then he wondered just what the hell he was doing driving by her house in the first place.

Looking at the wind damage. Right.

He was curious about Regan Flynn.

Shit. As if he didn't have enough trouble without adding to it in a way he'd promised himself he wouldn't—at least not while Kylie was still living at home.

REGAN LIKED WORKING in Madison's arena, even if it was a little pricey. It was well kept and in addition to the large covered arena there were several paneled work areas outside.

Today she chose to work inside, since the wind was starting to blow again. She'd managed to drag the big branch off the drive before she left and was hoping there wouldn't be another branch in its place by the time she got home.

"That's quite an improvement," Madison called almost an hour later, after Regan finished her last training pass of the day.

Regan eased Toffee to a halt and dismounted as Madison walked toward her, carrying a sheaf of papers in one hand and a cell phone in the other.

"He's coming along," Regan agreed, rubbing the gelding's forehead. She'd spent a good forty-five minutes working him over both ground poles and a series of foot-high jumps, talking to him with her hands and her body and teaching him to yield to her cues.

"He likes the work," Madison commented. "You used to show jump, didn't you?"

"How'd you know?"

"After watching you ride a few times, I figured you had to have been in competition somewhere, so I Googled you."

"I see." Regan wasn't sure that she liked being Googled.

"Do you have any plans to compete again?"

Regan smiled as she slipped the reins over

Toffee's head. He pushed her with his nose, nearly knocking her off balance. It was getting to be a habit. She put her hand on his nose and firmly pushed his head away before turning her attention back to Madison.

"Those days are long gone. I just want to ride for my own pleasure." She started leading the horse toward the gate as she spoke, fighting to keep him from crowding her space. "Kind of a sanity saver, you know?" she said through gritted teeth, wishing Madison wasn't there to witness the power struggle. When she was on Toffee's back, there was no question as to who was in control. On the ground, he had both the height and the weight advantage, and he used them. He was very disrespectful.

"You might consider teaching a jumping class," Madison said, eyeing the horse as she opened the gate for Regan, but saying nothing about the obvious. "People would be interested and I like to offer a variety of classes here at the arena."

Regan gave a brief nod. She wouldn't mind teaching a class, once she was settled into her real job. It would be a good way to meet people who didn't have kids in school.

"All you have to do is book the times

with me, charge the fees set on the arena rate chart and give the arena thirty percent of the proceeds."

"Is that all?" Regan replied, thinking it sounded like highway robbery, since she'd seen the rate schedule.

"You'd have access to the jumps and all the other equipment, and I'd put you on the calendar of events, which goes out in the newspaper and over the radio."

"I'll think about it."

"You know," Madison said as they reached the stall, "I'm putting on a training clinic next weekend. You've seen the advertisements, haven't you? Del Gilbert and Will Bishop?"

It was impossible not to see them. They had appeared that morning and were plastered all over town—the grocery store, the post office, even the school.

"You, uh, might consider going." Madison shoved the cell phone into her pocket and handed Regan yet another paper advertising the event. "I give a ten percent discount to people who board with me. All you have to do is bring this paper with you. There's a discount code stamped on the bottom."

"Thanks," Regan said. "I had planned on going." She'd never seen anyone start a horse from the ground up and she'd heard enough about Will's abilities to be curious.

"It's worth the fee," Madison replied. Regan had a feeling she could have said she'd like to watch the tractor till the arena and Madison would have told her it was worth the fee.

"There's something else. I was wondering how much longer you plan to board Toffee here. I'm getting calls from people who want a stall and I'm full up."

"The fence was finished yesterday—just in time for the windstorm to bring a big branch down on top of it. I need to have the wire tightened again before I can bring him home."

"Well, it shouldn't take long to do that." Madison spoke confidently, making Regan believe she'd never worked with contractors. "I'll call Trev or Will about doing a brand inspection and make arrangements for one of them to haul Toffee to your house whenever they're available." Madison waved at a person who'd just walked in the stable door and then turned her attention back to Regan. "You don't have a trailer, yet. Right?"

"Not yet. Do you think they'd mind hauling for me?"

Madison shook her head no.

"Great. I'll pay them, of course. But I

won't be available on a weekday until after school hours."

"When is that? Three o'clock?"

"Better make it four." She knew Pete wouldn't bend the rules for her and let her leave a little early.

"I'll give you a call."

"Thanks."

Madison smiled a nice-to-do-business-with-you smile before walking down the aisle between the stalls, slipping clinic discount flyers under each of the nameplates.

Regan pulled her stall door open and Toffee all but walked over her in his hurry to get to his hay. She firmly smacked his chest with the flat of her hand. "No," she told him. He stopped and let her take off the halter. As he walked away, Regan leaned against the edge of the door frame, admiring his lines and gleaming coat and wondering how on earth she was going to get him to respect her. She'd never handled a horse with no manners before and she knew she needed to do something about it.

With luck, the clinic would give her a place to start.

BY THE NEXT DAY it was obvious that, although Pete hadn't fully given up on his squid-related prankster hunt, he was winding down. He stalked around the school scowling, almost a defeated man. But then, just after lunch, he received an ego boost of such massive proportions that it had to be shared with the staff in an emergency after-school meeting.

"This feels bad," Tanya murmured behind Regan, as they entered the meeting room.

Pete did look remarkably smug, rocking on his heels at the podium and waiting for the staff to straggle in, most of them showing signs of irritation at having been pulled away from their after-school prep time. And most of them seemed to have an idea of what was coming.

Mr. Zeiger, the school superintendent, stepped to the front of the room. "I wanted to tell you, in person, that although Mr. Bernardi is doing better, he has decided to retire. The board met last night and rather than commence an employment search now, we're going to continue with the current situation. Mr. Domingo will continue as acting principal until the end of the school year."

Karlene raised her hand. "When will you advertise this job?"

"We'll fly it in February and interview in March. The position officially begins in July. That'll give the successful candidate a chance to tie up loose ends." Zeiger gave Pete a small nod. "Unless, of course, he's local."

Pete's chest swelled so much that Regan began to wonder how his buttons held. "Thank you, Mr. Zeiger."

The superintendent smiled and then turned his attention back to the group. "On a more serious note, the Renshaw family is still dealing with some huge medical bills and they're trying to avoid bankruptcy. Our schools are in good shape, financially, so the board has agreed that a percentage of the proceeds from our independent fall fund-raisers can be donated to this cause. Also, the high school's FFA club is organizing an auction to be held in October, and there'll be various bake sales and car washes, too. I know you'll support these events as best you can."

There was a general murmur of approval. Even Pete looked supportive.

"Who are the Renshaws?" Regan asked Tanya.

"They work for the district. Mr. Renshaw in the bus garage, and Mrs. Renshaw in the district office. Their daughter had to have a kidney transplant, and the insurance hasn't covered everything."

"I'll want the individual faculties to vote

and decide what percent of their fund-raisers, if any, to donate. And now I'll turn things over to your principal."

Pete took his place behind the podium as the superintendent stepped away. "That'll be all for this afternoon," he said, "but we'll be having another short meeting tomorrow at 8:00 sharp, to discuss our own fund-raiser."

"Scary." Regan said to Tanya, as they walked back to their classrooms. "He looked orgasmic."

"He was orgasmic. He's wanted this for a long time."

"Maybe he'll relax once he has the position." Tanya rolled her blue eyes and Regan sighed. "I guess we'll just muscle through this year and hope the board is smart enough not to make the appointment permanent."

"We can hope, but never discount the good-old-boy network. I think Pete has a shot at this. Heck, I wouldn't be surprised if they'd already decided to shoehorn him in."

"Because of his charismatic personality?"

"Because of the eight state football and basketball championships. School boards and ex-athletes in positions of power like that kind of stuff."

WHEN REGAN ARRIVED at the arena on Friday afternoon to pick up her new horse, she found Madison preoccupied, anxious about some problem with the upcoming clinic and ready to take it out on the first innocent person who crossed her path. And then, as if that wasn't enough, Toffee made it clear he had no intention of getting into a small two-horse trailer.

Regan had just spent a long day trying to keep more than 150 adolescents under control and she was in no mood to deal with either of these two. Fortunately, though, the brand inspector, a man named Trev Paul, had a way with both horses and women.

He was a good-looking man, dark and lean, with an easy smile, but it was his patience and the sense that he saw more than he acknowledged that most impressed Regan. Both Madison and Toffee responded well to his combination of easy humor and quiet determination, and in a surprisingly short amount of time, Regan was following his truck and trailer back to her place.

Once they were there, Trev unloaded Toffee and led him around the house to the pasture. It was obvious the gelding had no more respect for Trev than he did for Regan, but Trev was big enough to do something about it. He elbowed the horse out of his space more than once on the walk from the trailer.

"This boy needs some groundwork," Trev commented, as he released the horse into the knee-high grass.

"Amen to that," Regan muttered.

"Are you going to Madison's clinic?" Trev pushed his ball cap back and Regan found herself staring into a pair of stunning hazel eyes.

"Sure am."

"You might talk to Will or Del. I'd suggest Will, since he lives here and you won't have to skip a rent payment to pay him."

Regan laughed. "Speaking of payment, you're sure you won't take anything for hauling Toffee?"

"Nope."

"Are you sure you can get your trailer out of this narrow driveway?"

"Yep." He grinned. "See you around."

Trev effortlessly reversed down the drive and made the tricky backward turn onto the county road in one shot. Regan hoped she'd be that competent once she bought a trailer, which would be in two years or so, the way things were going.

She had grading waiting for her, but

instead of doing what she was supposed to be doing, she walked to the pasture to take another look at her horse. After all, how many times did a person get her first horse?

Her horse. Not a leased horse or a borrowed horse or a schooling horse.

He stood almost exactly where he'd been released, pulling up big mouthfuls of fresh grass, his dark coat shining in the late afternoon sun. Every now and then he would raise his head to look around, as if he couldn't believe he had all this space, all this freedom—all this grass!—to himself.

With the exception of the grass, Regan knew exactly how he felt. She loved her mother and sister, but she was glad to be several hundred miles away from them and no longer required to act as a handy referee. And although dating Daniel had not put a crimp in her freedom, the aftermatch of their relationship had given her an an even deeper appreciation of independence.

Too bad it had been such a hard lesson.

Regan settled her forearms on the gate, telling herself to focus on the present, forget about the past, but she hated the fact that she'd been conned so masterfully—personally and professionally. She'd even broken a number of personal rules for him—don't date a colleague, don't let anyone get *too* close.

But after working with the guy for a year, team teaching a math and science pilot program at a middle school, she thought she knew him well enough to break those rules. They'd started dating and it had seemed a perfect relationship. They were close both personally and professionally, yet Daniel understood and respected Regan's need to have her own space. He was supportive and attentive, generous. Almost perfect. Or so she thought.

Her professional goal at the time, heartily endorsed by her mother, Arlene, since it involved getting out of the classroom and into a power suit, was to secure a position with the Education Development Authority.

Over the course of that school year, she developed a package of innovative interactive lesson plans, which both she and Daniel used in their classes. With Daniel's input, Reagan had fine-tuned the material. When EDA had announced a job opening, Regan was ready. But so was Daniel.

He'd been up front about the fact that he was applying for the job, as well. Regan had been a bit surprised, but she knew that was the way things were in the professional world.

She convinced herself she didn't have a problem with it. However she did have a problem with the fact that when it was her day to be interviewed, to present her materials and teach a demonstration lesson, it soon became apparent the interview committee had seen quite similar material before. The day before. During Daniel's interview.

Maybe, if life was fair, neither of them would have gotten the job. But life wasn't fair. Daniel had set the stage nicely, talking about his junior teaching colleague, Regan, who'd helped him tweak the lessons he'd spent so much time developing. It was only fair, after all, that she get a tiny portion of the credit.

At least Daniel had been smart enough to know that Regan would no longer be sharing his life after he'd accepted the job, so there had been no nasty breakup. Just a painful case of self-recrimination for trusting him, for almost convincing herself that she loved him.

She wouldn't be making that mistake again.

WILL WENT THROUGH his equipment, setting aside the few things he planned to bring with him to the clinic. He didn't need much. The horse would be there. All he needed was a sturdy halter, a rope, a saddle and a clear head. Three out of four wasn't bad.

"Hey, Dad." Kylie strolled into the barn, yawning but fully dressed and ready to go. The only time she got up willingly was when the day involved horses.

"Hey."

She had on her good black cowboy hat, her T-shirt with a barrel racer emblazoned on the back and her new jeans, which were already getting too short. Shopping time again. He'd have to see if Sadie's mom had a trip to Elko planned in the near future. No, maybe he'd take her himself. He didn't want her in Elko without him just now.

"You look ready."

She grinned at him. "So do you. Are you up first today?"

"Nope, second." Del liked to go first. He was the headliner.

"Can Stubby come?" Both Kylie and the young border collie looked at Will hopefully.

Will shook his head. "Not yet."

"He'll behave."

"He'll eat the interior of my truck."

"He didn't eat much the last time."

No. Just the gearshift knob, but Will wasn't taking any chances. "Not this time."

Kylie bent down to explain to the collie that he had to stay home, then she got into the truck as the pup slunk to the porch steps to watch them leave without him.

Will waited as Kylie fastened her seat belt and the surge of protectiveness he felt as he watched her small hands work the latch was almost overwhelming. He knew logically there was probably nothing to worry about, that Brett had been in the area for more than a month and he'd made no attempt to contact them, but paternal instinct and logic did not always jibe. In fact, in Will's experience they rarely did.

"Ready?" Kylie's dark eyes were shining with excitement. She loved any and all horse events—especially those that involved her dad. He smiled.

"Ready as I'll ever be, I guess."

Kylie gave him a patient look. "I know you hate having all those people looking at you, but just imagine them in their underwear."

"That's a frightening thought, considering some of the people who will be there."

Kylie grinned. "I'd never thought of it that way. Do you think old Grandpa Meyers wears boxers or briefs?"

"Stop now."

Kylie started giggling and Will put the truck in Reverse. The day was actually off to a decent start.

REGAN WAS THERE.

He'd been scanning the crowd, while Madison introduced Del, looking for his brother, just in case, when he spotted her on the opposite side of the arena. And then, since it kept his mind off his upcoming performance, he continued to watch her. He'd never seen her in jeans before, but they suited her. And he liked the way her chestnut hair was pulled back in a haphazard non-teacherish ponytail.

She had a notepad balanced on one thigh and from the moment Del stepped into the ring with his horse, her attention was focused on his performance. She jotted notes every couple of seconds, it seemed.

Will watched her as she wrote, wondering if she'd take notes on him, too. He told himself he'd check, but he knew that, once he was in the round pen with the mustang, all his attention would be focused there. It was the only way he ever got through public performances—by pretending the audience wasn't there. Kylie's classic underwear strategy didn't work, primarily because of people like old Grandpa Meyers.

Lunch was the usual free-for-all, with the high school's FFA club flipping burgers and people hustling Will and Del for free advice.

Just before it was Will's turn to begin his afternoon performance, he eased away from the person he was talking to and approached Kylie and Sadie in the audience.

"Hey, would you guys do me a favor and stay here during the demonstration? In the front row?"

"Why?"

"I need some feedback and I want you to watch in order to give it." He pulled the reason out of thin air, but it sounded good and he could see that Kylie liked it.

"Okay."

"You won't get bored and wander off?"

"Nope."

"Good. I expect something constructive."

"Be careful what you ask for," Kylie quoted one of his favorite sayings. Will reached out, tapped the brim of her hat down and she laughed.

"Stay put," he repeated.

WHEN MADISON ANNOUNCED the start of the final demonstration, Will walked to the center of the arena, his short chaps flapping just below his knees, his gaze down, so that it was impossible to see his face under the brim of the cowboy hat. But when he reached Madison, he

tilted his hat back, gave a tight-lipped, well-
here-I-am smile and looked as if he'd dearly
love to be anywhere but where he was.

Madison talked about Will, his background
and training strategies, but Will's eyes were
on the chute through which the mare would
enter the round pen. There was some banging
on the rails, as the horse was pushed into the
paneled runway, then she emerged, her eyes
round and wild.

She circled the round pen at a full gallop
several times before coming to a stop at the
side farthest away from the crowd. The rails
were too high to jump, but she bunched up
as if she was going to try. She continued to
dance at the edge of the pen, desperately
looking for a way out.

Will stood quietly until the mare threw him
a wild glance over her shoulder and snorted.
He took a slow step forward and the mare
took off, galloping furiously around the pen,
her hind feet kicking up divots and her attention outside the rails. Will moved to the
center, pivoting as she circled, keeping his
eyes on her, waiting for her to slow. When she
did, he stepped forward quietly to get her
moving again. This time her canter wasn't
quite as wild and every now and then she

looked at the man in the center of the pen, trying to read him.

"What Will's doing is controlling the mare's movements—showing her that he is the lead animal, the boss," Madison explained. Will also had a microphone clipped to his collar, but Regan wondered if he even had it turned on. "Horses want to know their place in the hierarchy of the herd and that's what Will is establishing now. He'll keep her moving, then give her an opportunity to stop when he wants her to stop."

The demonstration continued, the crowd watched attentively as Will eventually approached the mare and then touched her. When she turned away from him, he set her moving again, repeating the pattern until she understood that he wouldn't hurt her but if she didn't hold still for him she'd have to run. And running was work.

Will continued approaching and backing off, asking her to allow him to do as much as she could tolerate, then releasing pressure by backing away for a moment. In the end, he was able to rub her all over, halter her and saddle her. Madison kept up a running commentary throughout the entire procedure.

Finally, Will stepped away from the mare

and walked to the edge of the round pen. The mare followed. He ran a hand over her neck when she stopped, facing him.

"I'm not going to get on her," he said, speaking for the first time since the start of the demonstration. "She's done enough for one day. I hope I've been able to show you guys something during this demonstration. If there are any questions…?"

Several hands shot up and Regan leaned back in her seat as Madison began fielding the questions.

After the demonstration, Will was surrounded by people—mostly women, Regan noticed as she gathered her notebook and purse—and although he was polite, she had a feeling that like the mustang mare, all he wanted to do was escape.

WILL WATCHED REGAN LEAVE the arena over the head of a woman who was outlining her horse's behavior in a rather long-winded manner. He redirected his attention and listened, thinking that this woman's only problem was that she babied her animal. When he told her that, she wasn't happy with the answer. She wanted her horse to mind her because he loved her, not because she was the boss. Will opened his mouth to tell her that horses were not wired that way, but instead he just nodded. If she'd sat through both his and Del's presentations and hadn't yet picked that up, then she was only going to hear what she wanted to hear. Some people couldn't understand that affection and boundaries could actually go hand in hand.

When he'd answered his last question, he found Kylie in the front row where he'd left her. Sadie was gone, but another girl had taken her place.

"Honest," she was saying to Kylie as Will approached. She suddenly noticed that Will was there. "I gotta go. See you tomorrow."

"What's that all about?" Will asked after the girl left.

Kylie frowned. "She said that she saw a guy who looked just like you in Elko yesterday."

Will felt an instant tightening in his midsection, but before he could think of something to say, Kylie screwed up her forehead and said, "Gee, Dad. You don't suppose it's Uncle Brett, do you?"

CHAPTER FOUR

"WELL, do you think it was him?" Kylie repeated a few seconds later.

"Might have been."

"Aren't you curious?"

Kylie was certainly curious. She always had been and the older she got, the more curious she'd become. He didn't blame her. The kid hardly had any relatives and the few she did have were not part of her world. So far, they'd only had a few brief discussions about Brett and the fact that Will and his brother hadn't been in contact for more than a decade. She'd eventually stopped asking, but he knew she still wondered about her uncle.

"Get your stuff together."

"Dad." He frowned down at his daughter's perplexed expression. "Don't you ever want to see him again? I mean, was what happened really bad?"

"It wasn't good." Will made an effort to sound matter-of-fact. "And maybe someday Brett and I will get together and hash things out, but I don't think it's going to be any time soon."

Kylie bit her lip and let the subject go, even though Will knew she wanted—deserved—answers. He couldn't give her answers just yet. And he didn't know if he ever could.

They started toward the truck, Will carrying the saddle and blanket and Kylie carrying the halter and rope.

"You know, Dad, you did really good in your demonstration."

"Thanks, kid." He appreciated her changing the subject, but he knew they'd be facing it again one of these days.

"You might try talking a little, you know, like Del does. Madison does all right, but I think people'd like to hear you explain more of it."

"All right," he said. "I'll try. Anything else?"

"Nope." She flipped the end of the rope as she walked. "Sadie was kind of weird today. She kept looking around, instead of watching the performance. And she asked me if I wanted to buy makeup with her when we go to Elko. I said okay, but," she puckered her forehead, "whenever we put on her mom's stuff, I forget and rub my eyes and it gets all over."

"You're pretty just the way you are," Will said gruffly. "And I'm thinking maybe I'll take you to Elko myself. All my jeans are worn out. I need to replace them."

"All right," Kylie said hesitantly.

"Come on." He took the halter and rope from her. "I'll buy you a milkshake."

"You're on." Kylie scrambled into the truck. "And maybe a hamburger?"

"And maybe a hamburger."

PETE BREEZED INTO Regan's room on Monday just after the final bell rang, dismissing the students. "A moment, Miss Flynn?"

"Sure." She'd seen this expression before. It was his taking-care-of-business face and it had yet to bode well for her.

"I'm concerned about some of your students' grades."

"Really?" Regan'd had a feeling this was coming. Some of her ninth-grade football players were not meeting their academic commitments and therefore were flirting with ineligibility.

"These three, in particular." Pete held out a short list of names.

"Those boys owe makeup work from last Friday. It was an important assignment, but they can still turn it in. I'm accepting it until tomorrow."

"They have practice tonight."

"So does everyone else on that list."

"Most of those kids could have finished their work on the bench at last Friday's game. But these three," he flicked the paper for emphasis, "are starting players."

"The assignment is due tomorrow."

Pete sucked in a breath, obviously taking issue with her attitude, but Regan spoke before he had a chance to. "Look, I'm not heartless. I don't mind giving a student a break, but it bothers me when they expect it."

"How so?" Pete asked.

"Those three didn't turn in last Friday's makeup work, either. I excused those assignments and now look at the result. They expect me to do it again."

"Miss Flynn…"

"At what point do these boys learn responsibility?" Regan asked, shaking the pencil she held at Pete.

"They are learning that on the football field."

"Life is not a football field."

"The lessons apply," Pete replied sternly.

"These boys will do their makeup work, but if they require extra time, I expect you to give it to them."

"Yes, sir."

Pete eyed her, trying to decide if she was being insubordinate or properly respectful. Finally, he gave her a curt nod.

"Thank you. Have a good evening, Miss Flynn."

"Same to you," Regan muttered as he left.

She pressed her lips together as she shoved homework papers into her tote bag. Damn, but she hoped those three would turn in their work tomorrow. This was not an issue she wanted to press, but if she had to, she would. The boys were more than capable of getting their work done *and* attending football practice. They weren't doing their work simply because they thought they could get away with it.

The phone was ringing when Regan walked into her house, half an hour later. Her sister. What now?

"Mom is driving me crazy!"

"Don't let her, Claire."

"Oh, very helpful, Reg."

"What's she doing?"

"You name it."

"Let's narrow it down to one or two specific issues."

After listening to her sister unload, Regan waited a moment to make certain Claire was finished and then said, "Just do what you want."

"And listen to Mom harangue me?"

"Claire, I've seen you stand up to everyone else in authority. You may as well give Mom a shot."

"I'd like to give Mom a shot," her sister said darkly.

"You're going to have to do this on your own or it isn't going to work, you know. You can't keep depending on me to run interference."

"It's so much easier when you do."

"Just ask yourself, what's the worst that could happen if you did take a stand with Mom?"

"She could move in with me as a punishment."

"DAD, she is s-o-o-o pretty."

"Yeah," he said and she had a look in her eye, too.

Will knew, the minute that Kylie had dragged him over to the holding pen outside the auction barn, that he was in trouble. The mare was poor, but her conformation was excellent and she had that dark gold palomino coat that Kylie particularly favored.

"She looks so much like Skedaddle. Maybe we could stay and see what she goes for."

Will had already bought a two-year-old roping prospect for one client, a brood mare for another and a Welsh pony that Kylie was going to tune up for a younger neighbor kid. He'd also spent the day on the edge of paranoia, wondering if Brett would show up at the sale, and he was not in the best mood because of it.

"We only brought the three-horse," he said, referring to his trailer.

"You know that we've put four in there before."

"They knew each other. These are strangers."

"Hey, I bet Trev would haul her home. He hauled Miss Flynn's horse to her house just a few days ago. She told the class. And he didn't buy any horses today, so his trailer is empty."

"Kylie, this mare has not had a good life." It showed in the way she was watching them.

"I know," his daughter said softly. She reached through the panel bars. The mare moved away. Kylie pulled her hand back and leaned her forearms on the panel.

"Maybe we could just give her a try. You said I could get a new horse pretty soon." She smiled up at him. "You've turned some really scared horses into good horses, Dad. Couldn't we just try? And if she doesn't work out, we can sell her."

Will felt himself bending and he had to decide fast whether to keep going or not.

"Just because she looks like Skedaddle, it doesn't mean she'll act like her, you know." Kylie's beloved first horse had died the previous summer, and Kylie still hadn't quite gotten over it.

"No one will ever replace Skedaddle," she said firmly. "But I like this mare and I have money saved up. How about we go halves?"

Will looked the mare over. She had the potential to be a stunning horse—one that show judges would give a second look. And it was late in the day, raining to boot. The sale prices had been low across the board and it was possible she wouldn't go for much, unless someone wanted a palomino bad. "What's the most you can afford, without draining your account?"

Will knew exactly how much she had and

was surprised when the price she named was half her money, instead of all of it. He gave a slow nod. "But, if it turns out that she's too much for us to handle, she goes. Right?"

"Right." She suddenly waved. "I see Trev. Let's ask him to haul her."

"We might wait until we see if we've actually bought her."

Kylie gave him a "details, details" smile and hurried off to talk to Trev.

"This may not have been your wisest move," Trev said later, as they stood in the drizzling rain next to his horse trailer. The mare had been terrified when they loaded her, and she obviously expected to be beat when she balked at the trailer door. When she finally went in, it had been with a huge bounding leap and then she'd immediately tried to back out again.

If he'd been at home, Will would have let her exit and that would have been the beginning of a lesson, but in the rain, miles from home and late in the day, he'd shoved his shoulder against the door, absorbing the impact of the horse's hindquarters as he latched it shut. The mare immediately stepped forward and started pawing the front wall.

"I think Dad will be able to do something with her," Kylie told Trev in a serious tone, as the banging grew louder. "He's handled worse."

Trev grinned. "He's handled you, I guess."

"Yeah, and look how good I turned out."

THE BRASS BELLS tied to the feed store door jangled as Will walked in. He'd seen Regan's car outside and he figured she was buying things for her new gelding. Sure enough, there she was reading labels on nutritional supplements for horses. She looked up at the sound of the bells and their gazes connected for a moment. She smiled briefly, impersonally, before she looked down at the label again.

Every time he saw her, Will was struck by how pretty she was, with her delicate cheekbones, wide green eyes and chestnut hair. It was the kind of pretty that crept up on a guy, but then, once it hit you, there was no going back. And surprisingly, the day he'd realized just how attractive she was, was the day her hair had been tousled by the wind and she'd been wearing big, fuzzy socks.

Will headed for the order counter, where Maggie Benson was going over invoices.

"I need senior equine food. Better make it four bags."

"Have you taken in an old horse?" she asked as she wrote the ticket.

"Nope. More of a starved horse. I'm supplementing."

"Should do the trick. I'll have Zero load you."

Will tucked his change into his wallet while Maggie called her husband on the intercom. Regan came to stand behind him, a rope halter in one hand and a vitamin supplement in the other. She met his gaze squarely, the way teachers tend to do, but she didn't look at all teacherish today. Her hair was pulled back in a short ponytail at the nape of her neck, but most of it seemed to have escaped around her face. He noticed for the first time that she had freckles. She looked nothing like the polished educator he'd first met in Bernardi's office. He moved aside so she could put her items on the counter.

"I liked the clinic. I learned a lot. Do you do many?"

"Madison usually has me do two a year."

"Do you ever give clinics elsewhere?"

He shook his head.

"You don't like the crowds, do you?"

"Is it that obvious?"

"Only to the trained eye."

Maggie rang up Regan's total. As Regan dug through her purse for her checkbook, Will heard the distinctive growl of a hungry stomach. She gave him a sheepish grin. "I'm starved."

"So's his horse," Maggie said, cackling at her own joke. Regan frowned at Will.

He shook his head. "I'll explain later." The last thing he wanted to do was to encourage Maggie—especially in front of an audience.

"You want to explain over pizza?" Regan asked, gathering her purchases. He must have looked startled, because she gave him a wry look. "Come on, Will. Live dangerously."

"Yeah, Will," Maggie chimed in. "When's the last time you…" Her words became a cough as he shot her a quick look.

"You don't have to," Regan said mildly. "I had some horse questions, but I can catch you another time."

"I'll come."

He saw Maggie smirk out of the corner of his eye, but he ignored her. A few minutes later he and Regan left the feed store together.

"How about this?" he said as he held the door open. "We could pick up the pizza and go someplace where we could talk in private."

"Afraid to be seen with me?"

"No, but…."

"But what?" she asked.

"You're Kylie's teacher." *And I haven't been seen out with anyone in about a hundred years—even for pizza.*

"Let's make people talk," Regan said as she started across the parking lot to the pizza place. "I'm too hungry to wait."

Will hesitated, then jogged a few steps to catch up. He had to admit he was intrigued by this side of Regan—open, totally human. And he had to admit he'd like to see more.

"Pretty good for a guy in boots," she said.

"I'm a man of many talents."

Heads turned when they walked into the busy restaurant.

"What's with these people?" Regan whispered as they took a seat in the back booth. A thirtysomething woman had been craning her neck to watch them.

"I, uh, don't go out too often."

It took her a second to get his drift.

"What? Are you like a monk or a hermit?"

"Not exactly." *Yes, exactly.*

"Not *exactly?*" She regarded him for a moment; when he didn't clarify, she slowly shook her head. "That's sad, Will."

"I think it's important to keep my life on an even keel while Kylie's still at home, so I just focus on being a parent." To Will, the words came out sounding as if he'd practiced them in front of a mirror, but they must have been okay because Regan nodded.

"I wish more parents put their kids ahead of their social lives," she said, pushing the napkin-wrapped cutlery aside to lean her elbows on the table. She rested her chin in her hands. "I think we'd have a more stable population of students."

"Uh, yeah." And if she'd known the real direction of his thoughts at that moment, she'd have called him a damned hypocrite. Here he was expounding on putting parenthood first, while he was pretty much undressing her in his mind. Damn, how long had it been since he'd really been attracted to someone?

A long time. And it had not ended well.

The waitress showed up then to take their order. She took her time and wrote it out word for word, taking little peeks at them over the top of her order pad. Finally, after the third furtive look, Regan folded her hands together and spoke in her teacher voice.

"As I mentioned earlier, Mr. Bishop, I think Kylie would benefit from the accelerated-tutor program. Every student who's been on it has jumped at least one grade, usually more…" She grinned at Will after the waitress trudged off to the kitchen a few seconds later. "There. Your reputation is safe."

He knew she was underestimating the determination of the local gossips, but he felt his mood lifting for the first time in days. "What horse questions did you have?"

"Okay, first of all, where can I buy hay? I cannot afford to keep getting it at the feed store."

"It's pretty late in the season, but Charley Parker is your best bet."

Regan let out a breath. "Will he cheat me?"

"Not if you have him weigh the truck and bring you the slip."

"All right." Two Cokes plopped down between them. Regan gave the waitress a quick nod of thanks, then focused on Will. "Statistics show that students who do online studies outperform their peers by…"

"Anything else?" Will asked with a grin as the waitress disappeared. He leaned back, stretching his arm along the top of the seat, feeling surprisingly relaxed. Regan dropped a straw into her glass. She took a long sip and it occurred to Will that it had been a long,

long time since he'd done anything so, well, spontaneous.

As it turned out, there was plenty she wanted to know: from techniques for correcting Toffee's rolled-out hoof—call Trev, and he'll show you—to his opinions on specific nutritional supplements, including the one she had just purchased.

"There's one more thing…." She sounded as if she was about to make a guilty confession, which instantly piqued Will's curiosity. "I'm having some trouble with Toffee. I thought maybe you could give me some advice."

"What kind of trouble?"

"He's pushy—he walks on me. Neither of my previous horses did that." She stirred the ice in her glass. "I don't put up with it, but he keeps doing it. I'm tired of elbowing him. And if I drop my guard he walks right up over the top of me."

"I *can* help you with that," Will said. "You want to ride him over to my place on Saturday and work with him?"

"I won't be able to pay you until payday, so maybe we should wait until then."

"Or maybe I could just help you."

She cocked her head. "Really?"

"You've never had anyone just help?" he asked.

She shrugged. "Of course I have." But there was something in her expression that made him wonder if she was telling the truth.

"Will Saturday work, then?"

"It would work fine." She gave him a smile that made the volunteering feel worthwhile. "Should I bring anything other than the horse?"

He shook his head. "I have everything you'll need."

The pizza arrived a few minutes later. "I was wondering," Regan said, as she carefully lifted a slice onto a paper plate, "what exactly a brand inspector does?"

"I'm a deputy brand inspector, so I only work part-time. We deal with livestock sales, making certain that an animal being sold doesn't belong to someone else. Or that animals in someone's custody actually belong to them."

"Kind of like an animal cop?"

"Exactly. We've been having a rash of thefts in the northern part of the state and we're the guys who deal with that, too. It's mainly Trev's headache, but we're all involved."

"Is it dangerous?"

"It can be, but I've never seen any trouble. I pretty much look an animal over, record markings and brands and collect a fee for the government. Trev actually stops vehicles transporting animals and looks at the paperwork."

"Interesting. So what's this about a starving horse?"

"Kylie and I went halves on a horse yesterday. She resembles Kylie's first mare and, well, the kid wanted her and I caved."

Regan's lips curved, but she didn't say anything.

"What?" he asked with a half smile.

"I don't know many dads who would cave on a horse. A new phone, maybe. An iPod... but a horse?"

He shrugged. "It's kind of in my line of work."

"My dad never caved. I had to lease my horses. I hated not owning them. I'm so glad to finally have a horse of my own." She bit the edge of her full lower lip as she gave him a conspiratorial look. "Someday, I'd like to have two horses. Toffee is already lonely being by himself all day."

"Well, I know a cranky palomino mare you can go halves on...."

It was six o'clock when they walked back to their cars. Regan smiled at him over her door. "Thanks for the pizza, Will."

"Anytime," he replied and, surprisingly, he wished they *could* do it anytime. Too bad real life had that way of rearing its ugly head.

CHAPTER FIVE

"I CAN'T WAIT for you to see her."

Regan clearly heard Kylie whispering during what was supposed to be silent reading time. She sent a warning glance in Kylie and Sadie's general direction, hoping it would be enough to quiet Kylie down. But she had a new horse and she was excited. The girl probably wouldn't believe it, but Regan knew exactly how she felt.

"I named her Skitters, because she's skitterish right now, but Dad is working with her."

Obviously, the warning glance was not enough to stifle Kylie's enthusiasm.

"Uh, Kylie?" Regan said in her no-nonsense teacher voice, "would you mind saving this for later, so other people can concentrate?"

"Yes, Miss Flynn." Kylie's shoulders slumped in frustration and she rummaged through her notebook for paper. Regan had a feeling the girl was about to commit her excitement to paper and pass it along. She decided not to notice. Sadie had been absent earlier in the day due to a doctor's appointment, so this was Kylie's first chance to see her, but something was amiss. Sadie wasn't as engaged in Kylie's whispered asides as usual. She smiled politely, but she didn't offer any comments in return.

Regan sensed Kylie's frustration. Especially when Sadie looked away from Kylie midsentence, shifting her attention to a boy who sat two rows over, smiling shyly when he glanced her way.

Hoo, boy.

Kylie looked as if smoke was about to come out of her ears. Regan focused on her papers. Junior high dynamics were exhausting and she was glad when the final bell rang and she no longer felt compelled to watch Sadie simper and Kylie fume. As soon as the kids left, Regan gathered her materials and headed for the teachers' workroom.

The copy machine was clear, for once. Regan figured Pauline must have just finished, since the top was still hot.

"Please, baby, just eighty copies of each," she murmured to the machine, which had a penchant for jamming when it was overheated.

"Miss Flynn, can I have a word?"

"Certainly, Mr. Domingo." Regan adjusted her face to be pleasant and turned around. She'd been trying, really trying—in spite of the athletes' grade problem—to maintain a professional attitude around Pete. It soothed his ego and made life easier for both of them. And he was her acting principal, technically her boss, even if he didn't have a clue about what he was doing.

"I'd like you to speak to the Taylors. They seem to think that Zach is ineligible for this week's football game."

"Right now, he is." Because in spite of being warned last week that she would not accept work at the very last minute again, he still hadn't handed in his makeup assignments. Regan had learned through the grapevine that Zach was a football marvel—a freshman starting quarterback—and apparently that made him feel that rules didn't apply to him. And Pete wasn't helping matters.

"No. He's not. His missing work will be handed in before the game."

"That's fine. And I'll accept his work, just like I told you, but until I get it, it's automatically a zero in the computer." Which made him ineligible.

"I told you—" Pete fought to maintain his composure "—his work will be in before the game and that's good enough for me. You take that zero out of the computer and mark the assignment excused."

"Fine." The word slipped out from between clenched teeth, as she tried hard to maintain a professional demeanor. This was not district policy. She'd read up on the matter.

"Now, let's go talk to the Taylors."

Oh, boy. Let's. Regan dropped her copying with a thud and followed Pete out of the room.

Pete walked, in scowling silence, as far as the office and then began to smile broadly as he opened the door.

"I've spoken to Miss Flynn. Zach needs to get his work in by tomorrow morning, then he can play."

"My concern is that this will happen again," Mrs. Taylor said. Regan felt a surge of relief, at least the mother understood that her son needed to be held accountable. "Zach doesn't need this kind of *stress* on top of everything else he's juggling. It's just too much."

"And it's affecting his playing," Mr. Taylor added sternly.

So much for accountability.

Regan sat in a chair across from the Taylors and met their cool gazes dead-on. She made it a point to never show weakness in front of bullying parents.

"Zach is a very capable student. He's bright and personable. I enjoy him in my class." *When he's not looking down his nose at me.* "But school district policy is clear on this matter. Athletes have two school days to make up work they miss due to sports-related events. I believe the board made this policy with the students' best interests in mind." Regan paused. The Taylors did not appear to be impressed by her opening remarks. They stared at her stonily. She was afraid to look at Pete, so she simply didn't.

"It would be confusing to both students and staff if we had different policies for different students. Therefore, if I give Zach a week, I have to give everyone a week. And if I'm giving my kids a week, then other teachers would have to give a week. And then district policy would have to be rewritten. You can see what a can of worms this would open?"

"Yes," Mr. Taylor finally responded, but the look he sent Pete was deadly.

Regan plunged on. "Now, if Zach needs additional help with anything he misses in class, I'm available at lunch and before school, so it wouldn't interfere with football practice. In fact, he's welcome to come into my room at those times and work on his makeup."

She paused to draw in a breath before she hammered the final nail into her coffin. "I just want everyone here to understand that I will be following written district policy from this point on. Two days for makeup work. Regardless."

There was a heavy silence. Regan waited for a reaction. Any reaction. Mr. and Mrs. Taylor exchanged glances and then Mrs. Taylor spoke.

"Thank you for your time, Miss Flynn."

There was no doubt Regan was dismissed. Mr. Taylor's eyes were on Pete, who in turn was staring at Regan, his jaw rigid.

Regan stood and excused herself. She thought she heard Pete say her name just as the office door swung shut behind her, but she didn't slow down. She was officially off the clock and she needed time to think before her next confrontation with the man.

She wasn't going to get that time. He caught up with her.

"How dare you make me look like I don't know my job?"

"*Do* you know your job?" Regan snapped. Pete went scarlet.

"You do understand that I'll be doing your evaluations?"

Since she was a new teacher in the district, Regan would have the pleasure of not one, but two observation sessions with Pete.

"Yes, and I'm certain they'll be conducted in a professional manner, or you'll be looking at a grievance."

Pete narrowed his eyes. "Do you know who the Taylors are?"

"No. Who are they?"

"Todd Taylor's brother is on the school board."

"Then Mr. Taylor should know district policy and respect it."

"This isn't Las Vegas, Miss Flynn. We run a more 'personalized' district here."

"Are you saying that some people are exempt from rules and others aren't?"

Pete's face became even redder. "I am saying," he said in a deadly voice, "that we handle things on a case-by-case basis."

"I didn't see that in the policy manual."

"It's understood!" Pete looked as if he

would burst a blood vessel and Regan found she was holding her breath, possibly in anticipation of the big event. She slowly exhaled as he turned and stomped down the hall, apparently too angry to speak.

Keep breathing, Regan told herself as she went into the teachers' room to finish the copying Pete had interrupted. *Deep steady breaths.* She wanted to go home, but she knew she'd be dealing with a line at the copier in the morning. Better to do it now.

"Guess what?" Tanya said, when she walked in a few minutes later.

"Pete's been made superintendent," Regan replied without looking up from the jammed copy machine.

"You already heard." Tanya flipped her hair over her shoulder.

Regan carefully tried to ease a sheet of paper free from the interior, biting her lip as she worked. The paper tore and Regan dropped her shoulders in defeat. Now she would have to retrieve every little bit that had been left behind or the machine would remain inoperable.

"Hey, what's wrong?"

Regan knew full well that Tanya wasn't talking about the copy machine. "I made the mistake of trying to make the same rules apply to everyone."

"This doesn't sound good."

"Not good at all." Regan briefly described her encounter with the Taylors, as she pulled little scraps of paper from between the roller bars. "So," she concluded as she finally dug out one particularly stubborn piece, "I know what I did was right. Zach is intelligent and capable. He's working the system and feeling entirely too safe doing it."

"And that drives you crazy."

Regan glanced over at her. "Yes. It does. No one's doing this kid a favor by convincing him the world revolves around him. But maybe I should have ignored my conscience and played along. I don't know."

"Why should you have done that?" Tanya asked softly.

"I don't want to endanger my job and I am first-year probationary in this district."

"You did the right thing. I can't see anyone trying to punish you for following policy." She paused. "Except maybe for Pete."

"The Taylors didn't look all that friendly, either."

"Zach is their last child and their only boy."

"That explains things." Regan pulled out

yet another sliding drawer. "What were you going to tell me before I sidetracked you?"

"We're in charge of the dessert table at the school fund-raiser."

"We're what?"

"In charge of the dessert table at the Harvest Dance. No one ever wants the job so they always foist it off on the newcomer. And," she cleared her throat, "the newcomer's friend, which is me. Our first committee meeting is Thursday after school in the library."

Regan pulled out what was possibly the last sheet of misfed paper, shut various compartments and the main housing door of the copier. The control panel lit the all clear.

She checked her hands for toner smudges, then gathered up her copies. She was ten papers short, but she was not going to risk another tussle with the machine. She gave Tanya a weary smile. "Let's try to have fun with our dessert table?"

"Sounds good to me. Are you going to be all right? I mean, do we need to have a wine-cooler night?"

Regan shook her head. "I'm going home to ride my horse. And I am not going to think about a single school-related issue."

WILL WAS TIGHTENING the gates when the bus pulled up and Kylie trotted down the steps, skipping the last one entirely. He wanted to get all his pre-snow maintenance done early this year. In Nevada, winter was anyone's guess—early, late, warm, cold, wet, dry. He wanted to be ready for all possibilities.

Gravel crunched as Kylie marched toward him instead of heading to the house to drop off her backpack. Stubby met up with her and poked his nose into her hand.

"Did you and Miss Flynn go out?" she demanded before she'd even reached him.

Will's eyebrows went up in surprise. He hadn't expected this. "We ate a pizza."

"Why?" Kylie crossed her arms. In another second, she'd be tapping her toe.

"She needed answers to some horse questions."

Kylie's expression shifted, edging toward relief. "So you weren't talking about me?"

"Any reason we should be?"

"No," she responded quickly. "But it's kind of weird to hear that your dad was out with your teacher."

"I imagine that would be weird."

"You have no idea." She went to the edge of the corral, leaving her backpack next to

Will. Skitters moved closer and Kylie climbed up onto the fence to stroke her. "Hey," she straightened up so she was balancing on the bottom rail as she pointed toward the county road, "is that Miss Flynn?"

"Looks like it."

"She's riding English!" Kylie couldn't have sounded more shocked if she'd seen her teacher riding naked.

"Yeah. I see that." Regan had the horse nicely gathered as she rode past the house. Hard to believe this was the same horse he'd watched terrorize a jumping class at the 4-H horse show only a year ago.

"I don't like posting."

They'd had this discussion before. Kylie thought posting looked dumb and she really wanted Will to agree with her, but he stuck to his position that posting had a purpose.

"It's easier on your butt and the horse's back if you can't ride right," he reiterated.

"You don't post."

"I said if you can't ride right."

"Are you saying Miss Flynn can't ride right?" Kylie asked hopefully.

"No. Watch her." Regan was rounding the bend and almost out of sight. "She knows what she's doing."

Kylie's mouth twisted. "Yeah. I guess."

"If people can't sit a trot, they'd better post, whether they're riding English or Western. It's better than bouncing around, jarring the horse's back."

"Why do English riders always post?"

Will drew in a breath. "They don't." He cocked his head at an angle. "Maybe you should ask Miss Flynn some of these questions. She probably knows more than I do about English riding."

"I might."

"Don't misquote me." Will could only imagine what his daughter might do with the posting comment he'd just made.

Kylie smiled and jumped down off the fence. "I think I'll groom Skitters now."

She headed for the barn, whistling under her breath, leaving her backpack on the edge of the driveway.

Will kept on eye on the road as he finished tightening the cables that helped suspend the gate, but Regan did not ride back past him. She'd obviously taken the loop that ran past his house and ended near her own. Too bad. He kind of wanted to watch her ride by on that big horse again.

KYLIE WAS AT A 4-H MEETING when Regan arrived for Toffee's tune-up on Saturday.

"Hi." She pushed her dark hair away from her forehead as she looked down at him from atop her horse.

"Hi, yourself." He tipped the brim of his ball cap up. "Let's get the saddle off him and warm him up in the round pen."

"He's warm."

"No, I mean, get him used to being moved where I want him to go. Do you lounge him?"

"Yes," she said as she dismounted. "At least a couple times a week. More, if I can."

A few minutes later Regan's saddle was perched on a lodge pole rail and Will had Toffee circling the round pen at a relaxed canter. He stopped him, turned him, started him going again. As he'd expected, the horse was an old hand at traveling in a circle, picking up gaits on command.

Now to see what he did when he was on a lead line. Will snapped on the rope and started to lead the horse. In two seconds the gelding all but walked up the back of Will's leg. Will instantly turned, told the horse no and began vigorously shaking the lead rope.

Toffee took a few backward steps and looked

at Will curiously. Will started walking again and the horse was on top of him in an instant.

Will whirled around, only this time he started taking giant stamping steps at the horse as he shook the rope. Toffee quickly reversed, but Will kept coming at him until the horse had backed up a good ten feet. Then Will stopped. Toffee blew through his nose, but he kept his distance.

Will chanced a look over at Regan, who was watching with her mouth open. She quickly closed it.

Will quietly walked to the horse and rubbed his forehead and then his neck. "It's all right, son. You just gotta stay out of my way. Got it?" After a moment the big gelding began to chew, a sign that he was relaxing.

"Okay, let's try again."

It took several more tries before Toffee realized that Will was serious—he was not going to allow the horse to get too close. For a horse who had probably spent most of his life walking wherever he pleased, even if it happened to be on someone's foot, it represented a major shift in attitude.

Will gestured at Regan and held out the rope. "Your turn."

She took the rope. "I feel kind of bad scaring him."

"You aren't so much scaring him as you're teaching him respect. What do you do to control your classes?"

"I set boundaries," Regan replied, knowing that was the answer she was supposed to give.

"That's what you'll do here. When Toffee crosses that boundary, you want to make him so uncomfortable he doesn't want to cross it again, but you don't want to frighten him. When horses are frightened, they're not thinking. They're reacting, trying to save themselves. That's when people and animals get hurt."

"How do you decide how aggressive to be?"

"You take it horse by horse. Toffee's bull-headed. It's going to take more to teach him who's in control. Now that little filly over there—the tobiano?" He pointed to a young black-and-white pinto in a corral near the barn. "I barely have to make a move and she's trying to figure out what I want and how to do it. She's a much more sensitive horse."

"Well, here goes." Regan took the lead rope out of his hand, tightened her mouth in an expression of resignation.

He smiled a little. "I won't tell anyone if you don't do it perfect the first time." And the look she sent him told him he'd hit the nail smack on the head. Regan wanted to be perfect the first time.

REGAN WALKED A FEW STEPS and Toffee followed at a respectful distance until she turned toward the gate. At that point he crowded close, pushing against her in his hurry to leave the round pen.

Regan turned and tried to do exactly what Will had done, shaking the rope and stamping her foot as she moved toward him. She felt awkward, self-conscious with Will watching and, as always, she could hear her mother demanding a more accomplished performance. She forced herself to ignore it.

Her stamping left a little to be desired, but Toffee understood. He stood at the end of the rope and cautiously regarded Regan, as if to say, *Where did you come from and what did you do with the nice lady I could walk all over?*

"Good," Will said quietly. "Praise him and try again."

She moved close to stroke the horse, then started walking again. The gelding followed her without hesitation, keeping out of her space. She continued to lead him around the pen. He started to encroach again near the gate, but she gave a sharp, no, and flipped the rope. The horse immediately moved to the proper position.

"Good boy." She stopped after a complete circle around the pen and rubbed his neck. Then she smiled over at Will. "He holds no grudges."

"He shouldn't. He just needs to know his place. He's used to being the dominant animal. *You* need to be the dominant one. Once he understands who's boss, he'll accept his place."

"Hmm. I think that's what Pete's trying to do with me."

Will's expression was deceptively mild. "Is he bothering you?"

"Nothing too extreme," Regan replied. "Do you know Pete well?"

"We went to high school together. Graduated the same year."

Regan couldn't resist. "Did you get along?"

"No one gets along with Pete unless they're wearing a jock strap."

"So that's my problem," Regan said. "I left mine in Vegas. How about you? Were you a jock?"

"I was in high school rodeo, so, no, not in the traditional sense, anyway. We competed in the southern part of the state in the fall and the northern part in the spring. That took care of all the athletic seasons except for basketball, and I was never that good at dribbling." He grinned. "But Pete was."

"I bet he was. I hear he's a good coach."

"Yes, if you're all right with the win-at-all-costs philosophy, and a lot of people in this town are."

"I take it you're not?"

"I like winning." Will dropped the rope and started moving his hands over Toffee's body in a massaging motion. The gelding stiffened, but as Will continued, his head began to come down. Regan could almost hear an equine sigh as Will worked the muscles in the horse's neck. She found herself wondering what those hands could do to her.

"Tight spot," Will murmured. "Oh, there we go." He smiled a little as Toffee's head went even lower. He started toward the withers and shoulder area. "Anyway, I like winning and, yeah, Pete is good at putting together winning teams. But sometimes I think he loses sight of the big picture, focuses on the big names and ignores the less spectacular kids. Some of those kids eventually develop into reasonable athletes, but he's missing the boat with them."

"How do you think he'll be if he makes principal?"

"I wouldn't want to work for him if I wasn't one of his star players." Toffee suddenly shifted his weight and switched his tail as Will touched a spot on his hindquarters. "Little bit of a sore spot here."

Regan approached. "Where?"

"Here." Will took her hand and put it on the spot. "Press lightly." He kept his hand over hers as she pressed. "Can you feel the knot in the muscle?"

Yes, she could feel the knot, but she was more aware of the work-roughened hand that was covering hers. And of how close she and Will were to one another. She could feel the warmth of his body, smell sweat and soap and leather—a surprisingly heady mixture. Will suddenly seemed to become aware, too. He took away his hand, running it casually over the horse's rump as he stepped backward. Regan cleared her throat.

"What causes a knot like that?"

"Could be an old injury. Or overuse. Or compensating for some other injury. You might want to massage it every day and see if you can get it worked out. He'll move better if you do."

"I will." Regan moved toward Toffee's neck and started stroking his mane. "I guess I've neglected a big part of my equine education. I did a lot of work in the saddle, but maybe I ignored the groundwork." She smiled. "You know, the respect part?"

"How old were you when you started riding?"

"Older than Kylie. I was fourteen the first time I got on a horse."

His eyebrows went up. "You must have been a natural."

"I guess I was. Also, my riding teacher took me under her wing. She's the one who groomed me for competition. I rode for hours every day in the summer. She arranged to let me ride other people's horses for exercise and she took me on the jumping circuit with her." Regan twisted her fingers in the gelding's dark mane. "I never thought about it, but I guess she was my Pete. I was good, so she paid more attention to me than her other students." And she had quite possibly sensed that Regan needed to have ownership of something that had nothing to do with her mother.

"Maybe we all need a Pete in our lives," Will said sardonically.

"Easy for you to say when you don't have a Pete in your life." Regan pulled her saddle off the fence. "Well, I guess I should be heading home."

"All right." Will took the saddle from her and settled it on Toffee's back.

It almost sounded as if he didn't want her to go, which Regan found interesting. And what she found even more interesting was that at the same time she felt an impulse to stay—which was exactly why she needed to get on her horse and head home. Once Will had tightened the girth, Regan led Toffee to the fence and used the bottom rail as a mounting block.

"Thanks for the lesson, Will. I'll keep this big guy in line."

"If you need any more help, just yell."

She met his gaze and found herself getting lost in a storm cloud of bluish-gray. "I will," she said softly. "I promise."

CHAPTER SIX

REGAN GAVE CLAIRE a call after she'd returned home and settled a more respectful Toffee back in his pasture. It had been several days since she'd heard from her sister and she was beginning to wonder what the deal was. Claire never went that long without moral support.

"Wow, you must have ESP," Claire said in her best California-girl voice. "I was just going to call. Guess who I ran into?"

"Not a clue."

"Daniel. And," Claire's voice took on a gleeful note, "he asked me out! Just for coffee, mind you, but he actually had the gall to pretend that everything was peachy."

"He is such a jerk," Regan stated flatly. And he had such a need to look like a good guy.

"Well, if he wasn't aware of that fact before, he's aware of it now. In fact, I asked him if he was looking for a new job and needed some help getting ready for his interview. He turned red up to his ears."

"Good for you." Regan put the kettle on the stove. "Where did you run into him, anyway?"

"The, uh, UNLV College of Education."

Regan's hand stilled for a moment before she twisted the burner knob and lit the flame. She had an ominous feeling about this. Not for Claire, but for their mother, who was determined that at least one of her girls would follow the career path she'd chosen for them. "Why were you at the College of Ed?"

"Oh, just checking out options," Claire said quickly. "So how's life in Smallville?"

"Good." Regan recognized a blatant redirection when she heard one and she decided this was a good sign. Claire, in spite of her fiery nature, had always depended on Regan to steer her through the big decisions in her life. And the small ones. Claire would blithely tackle any and all problems with no thought to the possible consequences, then drag Regan in to help her clear up the mess. Teamwork was what Claire called it. A headache was what Regan called it.

Yes, the redirect was definitely a good sign and Claire was rather good at it. Regan was laughing by the time she hung up the phone ten minutes later. About the only reason she missed living in Las Vegas was her sister.

WHEN REGAN WENT INTO THE OFFICE first thing Monday morning, Jared-the-Sub was checking out the job board.

"Any luck?" she asked.

"Only if I want to go deeply rural. There's an opening in Barlow Ridge next semester."

Regan wrinkled her nose. "Where's that?"

"About seventy miles from here. I think the teacher is either pregnant or just coming to her senses."

"Would you take it?"

"I might. It would get me employed with the district, then maybe I could transfer to Pete's PE job here next fall."

Regan felt her stomach tighten. Jared was a Wesley native and he probably had a good sense of which way the wind was blowing. "You don't think the board'll put Pete in as principal, do you?"

He didn't answer out loud, but his expression told the story.

Regan blew out a breath as Jared walked away. She consoled herself with the thought that it hadn't happened yet.

"YOU RIDE ENGLISH, don't you?"

Kylie'd dropped by to pick up a notebook she'd left under her desk during sixth period and then, to Regan's surprise, she'd hung around, watching her redo the bulletin board.

"Sure do." Regan punched another staple into the cork as she hung photographs of the different biomes the class would soon be studying. She wondered if Sadie was off boy watching again, leaving Kylie at loose ends, because the girl rarely, if ever, stayed a minute longer in class than she had to.

"We saw you the other night."

Regan figured they might have.

"I think English saddles are weird."

"Do you think jumping is weird?"

"No."

"You need an English saddle to jump properly."

"I know." Kylie spoke with an air of wistfulness. "Do you jump?"

"I used to." A long time ago. She'd loved being involved in something that was hers and hers alone, with no input from her mother, but she was happy to just pleasure ride now.

"I jump low ones bareback. Dad won't let me jump in a Western saddle."

"That's because the horn will poke your belly."

"I know," Kylie said in a tone that made Regan think that she'd learned that lesson the hard way.

"You must be pretty good if you can jump bareback."

"I am," the girl replied matter-of-factly.

"Want to get better?"

"How?"

"I'm giving jumping lessons." She and Madison had firmed up the deal the day before. In fact, Madison had all but signed up three students before Regan had even agreed.

"Really?" Kylie's eyes widened and then she caught herself. "That might be interesting, but I don't have an English saddle and I don't think my dad'll buy one unless he knows I'm serious."

"Madison has a couple she'll rent."

"Does that mean you're giving lessons at the arena?" Kylie picked up a photo of the polar region and handed it to Regan, who stapled it next to the steppe region.

"That's the plan. I have to charge the arena rate for the lessons, but Madison has nice equipment and it'll keep us out of the weather." And the wind, which was blowing once again.

"How will you get your horse there?"

"I won't need him. I teach from the ground."

"You know, you really should buy a trailer. If your horse gets sick or something, you'll need to take him to the vet."

"Yes, well, I do have a trailer on my wish list." Right under a few other things, like something to pull it with. "In the meantime, I'll just have to find a vet who makes house calls."

"That'd be Dr. Martin," Kylie said. "He charges the least for mileage and he's a good horse vet."

"Thanks for the tip."

"No problem. When will lessons start?"

"I still have to iron out a few details, but it would be pretty soon. Two weeks maybe."

"I think I'll go and tell Sadie. She might want to do it, too, and I think her grandma has an English saddle."

Kylie practically skipped to the door and Regan hoped, for her sake, that Sadie was equally enthusiastic.

"Okay. It's all set." Pauline Johnson walked in as Kylie exited. Kylie gave the woman a wide berth and a look that Pauline fortunately missed. "We leave next Friday."

"We leave for where?" Regan asked, surprised to find she was going anywhere, much less with Pauline.

Pauline frowned and gave her head a small shake, as if she couldn't believe her ears. Her lacquered hair refused to move. "Standards training in Elko, of course. You're covering science and I'm covering math."

This was the first Regan had heard of it and she said so.

"Well, I don't know why you haven't. Pete met with me this morning and told me to handle the arrangements." She gave Regan a dubious look, as if she thought Regan was trying to pull a fast one—or worse yet, was kidding her. "We have reservations. government rate, of course."

"It's not that far." Regan closed the stapler she still held and set it aside. "Why don't we just drive?"

"It's more convenient and less expensive to stay at the hotel than drive both days."

"Government rate?"

"Exactly." Pauline held out a sheath of papers. "These are the materials we need to familiarize ourselves with prior to the training."

Regan took the papers, but didn't look at them. She'd been wondering if Pete would find a way to get back at her for the Taylor incident and now she had her answer. "Do I have any say as to whether I go or not?"

"We have to have a representative from both science and math. I volunteered to represent math," Pauline added importantly.

"But I didn't volunteer to represent science," Regan protested.

Pauline smirked. "No one volunteered from *your* department, so Pete decided to send the person with the least seniority. That's you."

No arguing that.

"I'll be picking up the car from the motor pool the night before, of course. If you'd like, I can pick you up at your house in the morning."

"That would be nice," Regan murmured.

"I'll let you know the time closer to our departure."

And since the departure was almost five days away, Pauline had plenty of time to figure it down to the minute. Regan looked at the stack of freshly copied papers, then back at Pauline. And she'd thought she was detail oriented.

"Thanks, I think."

First, the dessert table and now standards training. No doubt about it—Pete was getting his licks in. Well, Regan would go to standards training with Pauline and she would do her best to get something out of it.

Besides a headache.

THE DAY WAS PERFECT, as early October days tended to be. Warm and golden. Skitters had her ears pricked forward as Will guided her through the waist-high sage.

He rode the mare every day in the late afternoon. As soon as Kylie got off the bus, she demanded to know if the horse was ready for her. So far the answer had been "not yet," but Will was starting to think the day was getting closer. The mare'd been cranky the first few times he'd ridden her, shying and giving the occasional crow hop if she thought she had an excuse, but recently she'd settled a bit.

Kylie'd been spending extra time with the mare lately, grooming and bonding, and Skitters was beginning to show signs of affection toward the kid—so much so, that Will was thinking he'd let Kylie ride this weekend and see how it went.

The sun was warm on his back, the wind cool on his face and Regan Flynn was on his mind. Again. He wasn't paying as much attention as he should have been when a rabbit suddenly darted out of a bush at Skitters's feet. She shied violently and then began some serious bucking.

Will had ridden rodeo for years and he could ride a bronc, but Skitters'd had more recent practice than he had. She went high, flipped her hind legs to the right, twisted her body to the left, then lost her footing as she came down. Will kicked his feet free of the stirrups and managed to dive before she crushed his leg beneath her. He smacked his head pretty good on a big rock. The next thing he knew, the mare was a blur in the distance.

But at least she was headed for the ranch, so he didn't have to try to cut her out of the mustang herd, and because Kylie was in school, she wouldn't worry when Skitters came home without him.

He dusted himself off and tried to convince himself on the walk home that this was an isolated incident, but his gut was telling him differently. The mare had been waiting for him to stop paying attention, then had taken her opportunity.

Skitters was waiting calmly for him in the yard when he got home. She'd broken the reins, but other than that, his gear was unscathed. She let him catch her, as if nothing had happened.

He unsaddled her and was leading her back to her pen when the bus rolled to a stop at the end of the drive and his daughter emerged.

"Not yet," Will said before Kylie could ask her question.

"You sure?"

"I'm sure."

Kylie went to the edge of the corral and Skitters came over to her, nudging her with her nose. Kylie smiled as she stroked her.

Will watched for a moment, then decided to give Skitters a cautious benefit of the doubt. But he was going to spend a lot more time on her before Kylie got on her back. One more incident like today's and the mare was gone, no matter how much Kylie loved her.

REGAN GATHERED her newly acquired pile of materials and dumped them into the official State of Nevada educational standards tote bag that each participant of the class had received. She hoped that her substitute had had a better day than she had. Even Pauline was looking slightly cross-eyed from the pedantic blathering of the alleged trainer, but that didn't slow her down from organizing an evening fete.

"We'll meet for dinner at six o'clock," she announced on her way out the door.

"Um, all right," Regan said, but an hour later, when she met Pauline in the hotel lobby after a long, relaxing and well-deserved shower, she found that they were looking at a forty-five minute wait for a dinner table.

"There is some kind of a conference going on," Pauline explained with a frown. "I never dreamed we'd need reservations here."

"Do you want to go somewhere else?" Regan asked, trying to be a team player. "Or maybe we could have a glass of wine here while we wait. I'll buy." She had changed into jeans and a long-sleeved red T-shirt for a casual dinner, but Pauline was still wearing her dress-for-success conference wear. No matter where they went, one of them was going to look out of place, so she decided to let Pauline make the call.

Pauline considered. "Let's have a drink."

A few minutes later they were seated at a small table in the bar area waiting for their drinks—Picon Punch for Pauline and white wine for Regan.

"I've never had a Picon before," Regan said in the hope of starting a noneducational conversation. Maybe if she got to know Pauline, the woman would ease up a little. Become more human, less like Regan's overly perfect mother. Maybe. It was worth a shot.

"It's a Basque drink," Pauline explained with her customary touch of superiority.

"Are you Basque?"

"No. But I like to absorb the culture of the place I'm in and it's part of Elko's heritage."

Absorbing culture in Elko was a novel idea. Regan kind of liked it.

"How is it?" she asked.

"Interesting. It's a little strong, but interesting."

Pauline was practically sliding out of her seat half an hour and two Picons later. Regan finally convinced the woman to let her help her to her room.

"Yes," Pauline agreed, leaning heavily on Regan's shoulder. "I'm not very hungry anymore." She yawned noisily, bringing her hand up and accidentally popping herself in the nose. "I'm really more tired."

"It's been a long day," Regan agreed. She was glad she wasn't sharing a room with the woman. The suggestion had been made, in order to save the school district a little money, but Regan had shot it down. She'd do her part, but she was not rooming with Pauline.

"I think I'll just stretch out for a minute." Pauline crawled onto the bed on her hands and knees, her pink pencil skirt riding up around her thighs before she collapsed on her stomach. Seconds later she began to snore. Regan tiptoed out of the room, closing the door softly.

Her stomach rumbled. She was hungry and still had a dinner reservation. If she hurried.

Her table was ready. She ordered the special, without looking at the menu, and settled back to wait for her solitary meal. The table was at the edge of the bar area, so she amused herself watching the patrons as she sipped her lemon water.

And then she sat up a little straighter. Standing at the end of the bar was…Will Bishop?

No, it wasn't.

But the guy could have been Will's twin and he appeared to have radar, because he raised his head to look directly at her, catching her midstare. There was no graceful way to look away, so Regan didn't even try. A moment later she wished she had, because the man had pushed away from the bar and started across the room toward her table.

Now you've done it.

Regan pulled in a breath as he came to a stop. "You caught me staring."

He smiled, a carbon copy of Will's. "Well, now that you mention it…"

"I know this sounds lame," Regan bit the edge of her lip, hoping he'd buy her story, which was, after all, true, "but I thought you were someone else."

"Really." He didn't seem all that surprised.

"Are you related to Will Bishop?"

"I'm his brother."

"You'd almost have to be," Regan replied softly. So there were two Bishops. Both attractive, but this one was slightly younger, leaner, more chiseled. He swirled his drink, made no move to leave. Regan let curiosity get the better of her. "You want to sit down?"

"Sure." The pirate's smile came a lot easier to him than it did to Will.

"I'm Regan Flynn." She held out her hand in the automatic gesture of politeness that her mother had engrained in her.

"Brett Bishop." His fingers were warm, work-roughened.

"Are there any more of you? Bishops, I mean?" Regan asked.

"Just Will and me."

"I'm Kylie's teacher." She took a sip of water, then set the glass on the table, keeping hold of the stem. "Are you a horse trainer, too?"

"No. I'm a roving cowhand."

"I didn't know there still was such a thing."

"I spent the last ten years managing a ranch in Montana, but when the owner died the kids wanted to cash in the real estate, so I was out of work for a while. When I got a job offer here, I took it."

Regan tilted the glass, wishing the waitress would come and refill it, so she'd have something to do while she talked. For some reason, talking to Brett Bishop made her feel slightly unsettled. "Have you been here long?"

"A month or so."

"It's nice you could get a job closer to your family."

"Yeah." There was subtle irony in his voice.

All right. We'll leave the family issue alone.

"I moved to Wesley from Las Vegas," Regan said.

"That's a bit of a change."

"A good change." She smiled and let go of the glass, settling both hands in her lap.

"Not a big-city girl?"

"Born and raised there. But no. I'm not."

And she hadn't realized the extent to which she was not a big-city girl until she'd moved to the relative peace and quiet of Wesley.

"Good for you." He rattled the ice in his glass, then drained the last few amber drops. "Would you like a drink?"

Regan thought of Pauline and shook her head. "I'm waiting for my dinner." And she wanted to keep her wits about her, here with this guy who was so much like Will, yet wasn't Will.

"So what are you doing in Elko on a school night?"

"I'm taking a two-day class."

"I figured you probably weren't a pipe fitter." He nodded toward the raucous group shoving tables together at the opposite end of the dining room.

Regan smiled. "No. I bend young minds."

"Hi." The waitress set Regan's salad in front of her, then refilled her water glass. "You want to order?" she asked Brett.

He shook his head. "I'm good." The waitress smiled and moved to the next table. "Do you know Will well?" he asked as Regan mixed the dressing into her salad.

"I didn't know he had a brother," she pointed out.

"Well, we haven't seen each other in a while."

"You didn't come home much when you were in Montana?"

"No," he replied softly.

She smiled politely and then focused on her salad, wondering what was going on between the two brothers. Definitely a chasm there and she wondered if it was mutual or one-sided.

"So you're a teacher."

She glanced up. "Yes. And you're a cowboy."

"Roving cowhand."

"Ten years in one place doesn't qualify as roving."

"I was roving at heart." He idly tilted his glass, clinking the cubes against the side. "What made you go into teaching?"

"My mother didn't want me to," Regan replied, only half joking.

"What did your mother want you to do?"

"Oh, something high profile. Doctor, lawyer, CEO."

"What does your mother do?"

"She's a CEO."

Regan's meal arrived. She expected Brett to leave, but he didn't. They talked for almost half an hour while Regan ate. He asked her questions about her job, how she liked it, what kind of student his niece was, whether there was much of a difference between urban kids and rural kids. He laughed, disbelievingly, when she told him that Pete was her boss.

"I thought he'd be polishing trophies for the rest of his life."

"Well, we can all hope he goes back to it." Regan set her napkin on the table. "I need to get to bed, so I don't sleep through class tomorrow."

"Yeah, and I need to go and catch up with my friends." Brett got to his feet. He glanced down for a moment, frowning as though making a decision, then he looked back up at her. "I was wondering…if you're ever back in Elko, maybe we could have dinner or something. A real dinner. You know, where we both eat?"

"You had your chance," Regan pointed out with a smile.

"I didn't realize how much I'd enjoy the company," he replied sincerely.

Regan felt her color rise a little, even though she knew it was a line. Brett was obviously much more practiced with lines than his brother was. "Do you ever make it to Wesley?" She'd rather be on her home turf if she did see him again.

Again the subtle blanking of his expression. "Not often."

"I don't know if I'll be coming back to Elko anytime soon. It could be a while."

"Well, if I ever do get to Wesley, can I call you?"

Regan agreed and wrote her number on a napkin. Brett folded it into his pocket and buttoned the flap. As he walked away, Regan figured that was that. If he didn't forget her as soon as she was out of sight, he'd almost certainly wash that napkin the next time he did laundry.

CHAPTER SEVEN

ALTHOUGH WILL HAD GREAT FAITH in his daughter's abilities, he would have bet on substitute teacher Mary Burkey in a fair fight. And he would have bet wrong.

The first details were sketchy, but Will received an invitation by telephone to discuss the details at greater length with Pete Domingo, ASAP.

He wiped the corral dust off his face, refrained from checking for new gray hairs and took off for the school. Kylie'd been acting differently lately. She'd been quieter, more introspective and, to tell the truth, part of him was almost glad she was acting like her old self again.

Will entered Pete's office with his hat in his hand, as a token gesture of respect. A principal was a principal. Will was going to be polite and open-minded as long as both parties observed the rules.

There'd been changes in the office since the previous time he'd visited. The place was definitely Pete's, now. An ornate nameplate stood on the desk and pictures of Pete's winning teams hung on the walls. There was even a photo of Pete himself in his high school baseball uniform circa the early nineties.

"Where's Kylie?"

Will had expected to see her sitting on the uncomfortable straight-back chair next to the wall where he himself had sat a time or two while waiting for someone to come and pick him up—when someone *could* be found to pick him up.

"Washing desks." Pete leaned back in his chair. He was holding a spring-loaded hand-strengthening device, which he squeezed and released, squeezed and released.

Will watched for a few seconds, allowing the little general his wordless power play, before he said, "What's up, Pete?"

Pete leaned forward. "Your daughter is insubordinate."

Will took a wild guess. "She tried to take advantage of the sub?"

"Mrs. Burkey reported her for a disturbance in the hall, but that's not why you're here today." He leaned back and began to squeeze his athletic gizmo again.

Will waited. This time he'd let Pete break the silence. He counted the repetitions, wondering if Pete would end on a multiple of five. Gym teachers loved multiples of five. Fifteen push-ups. Thirty sit-ups.

Ten squeezes later, Pete spoke. "I will not tolerate disrespect."

"Neither will I. Kylie knows better." Will tapped the brim of his ball cap on his knee. "Out of curiosity, how do *you* treat *her?*"

"Like any other student."

"What about the squid incident, Pete? You threatened her."

When Will had found out about it, he had seriously considered challenging Pete on the issue, but then he'd decided that since Pete was temporary, it wasn't worth it. Now that Pete was looking less temporary, Will was rethinking things. "Did you threaten all the students?"

"She did it."

"She did not."

"How do you know?"

"I asked her."

Pete sneered. "And you believed her."

"Yes." Will could see Pete thought that was

part of the problem and it ticked him off. "She's never lied to me."

"Never?"

By omission maybe, but never directly— and Will had asked her point-blank about the squid. "What did my daughter do to you?"

"She was openly rude—in front of other people. I can't have that."

"I agree, Pete. She knows better than to disrespect adults." But he had a strong feeling that this adult must have done something to provoke her. "Would you mind telling me what she said?"

Pete waved the hand that held the exercise device. "That isn't important. What is important is that she receives a consequence for her behavior."

Will disagreed. He wanted to know what she said, so he could deal with it, but he decided for Kylie's sake not to press matters. He had other ways of finding out what was said. As he'd told Pete, Kylie had never lied in response to a direct question and she was about to be on the receiving end of some very direct questions.

"What do you suggest?"

"Working detention. After school. One week."

Will had a feeling Pete wasn't going to kick her out of school, because then he'd have to share whatever it was Kylie had said that so infuriated him.

"All right."

"I have an appointment in ten minutes, so I'll speak to her myself in the morning. You'll find Kylie with Mrs. Burkey."

"I'm sorry about this, Will," the substitute teacher said a few minutes later. They'd left Kylie washing desks in another classroom. "I had to report her because of the ruckus in the hall. I hadn't expected Pete to come down so hard."

"I think it has something to do with another incident."

"Well, she wasn't the only one involved. She was with that friend of hers, Mark, and that Taylor kid said something about Mark's weight—he is a bit pudgy, you know." Will was glad the school was empty. He was certain that Mark didn't want everyone to hear about his pudginess, and when Mary spoke in her normal voice, just about everyone heard.

"Anyway," she continued, "there was a bit of a tussle. Mark actually got a pretty good swing in at the kid before I broke it up. I marched everyone involved to the office, where Pete took over."

"Then what?"

"He gave everyone a good talking to, then when they were on their way out, Pete told Mark that he could stand to lose a few pounds—that there was no excuse for being heavy at his age. That was when Kylie said it."

"What did Kylie say?"

Mary looked both directions and leaned closer. "She told Pete that he shouldn't be picking on kids who were heavy, when he was such a lard ass himself."

Will almost choked.

"All of our jaws just dropped," Mary said, laughing merrily at the memory, "and then Mrs. Serrano, bless her heart, saved Kylie's life. She bustled in there, and while Pete was still doing his impression of a carp out of water, she took Kylie by the arm and hauled her out, saying, 'Well, I'll just get Kylie started washing desks to keep her busy, while you call her father.' That's when I called you. Good thing you got here fast."

"Thanks, Mary."

"Lard ass," she chuckled. "Where'd she pick up such a term?"

"I don't know," Will muttered as he started

down the hall, thinking it was time to give his fat, lazy stud horse a different name.

KYLIE MISSED the first of Regan's jumping lessons because she was grounded. Realistically, Will knew Pete had gotten what he deserved for picking on a kid like Mark, but Kylie could not spend her life disrespecting authority, even if she was standing up for someone else. Will wasn't doing her any favors condoning behavior that would only get her into more trouble.

In other words, Kylie needed to learn to choose her battles.

Father and daughter spent a mutually miserable Saturday afternoon cleaning out the tack shed during the time that Kylie should have been learning the basics of riding with an English saddle and Will should have been working with a horse. And Kylie had been quiet again. Not pouting quiet, preoccupied quiet. She'd been that way for more than a week and Will was starting to get concerned. Was this a passing stage or was it something he should be dealing with?

As soon as they were finished, Will sent Kylie in to do her homework and the dishes in whichever order she chose, while he saddled Skitters. He tossed a flake of hay into the feeder for Laredo—formerly Lard Ass— as he went by, then mounted and headed around the loop in the reverse direction to the one Regan usually rode. She rode on a pretty regimented schedule and by his calculations she should be coming around the far bend in a matter of minutes.

He was not disappointed.

"Hi," Regan said as she brought Toffee to a halt a few yards away from Skitters. "Is that Kylie's new horse?" Will nodded. "She's pretty."

"Yeah," Will agreed, but he wasn't thinking of Skitters. He turned the mare so she was pointing in the same direction as the gelding.

"What are you doing out so late?" Regan asked as she nudged her horse forward and the two of them started riding side by side.

"I was helping my kid do penance and it put me behind on my schedule."

"We missed her at jumping class. I hear she made a comment on Pete's physique while I was in Elko."

"Yes, and it didn't go over well. She'll be apologizing to everyone involved on Monday."

Regan laughed. "Well, she doesn't need to

apologize to Mary or Mrs. Serrano. They're both highly amused."

Will sucked in a long breath. "Yeah." He paused for a moment, then dived into the question he'd been hoping to ask Regan. "I was wondering. Lately, there's been something going on with Kylie. Something other than being in trouble with Pete. She's been quiet. Thoughtful. I guess I was wondering if you had any clues as to what's going on, because I sure don't." Which was hard to admit.

"She and Sadie have been having some ups and downs over the past week or two." She glanced over at him. "Were you aware?"

No. "Now that you mention it, there haven't been as many phone calls as before."

"Sadie has a crush on a boy and I don't think she and Kylie are communicating on the same plane."

"A crush?" Will let out a snort. "Her parents are going to love that."

"I don't think she's had any success yet. The boy is more interested in football than girls right now."

"I am not looking forward to the boy thing."

"No father ever does."

"How'd your father handle it?"

"From a great distance."

Will sent her a sidelong glance and Regan cleared her throat. "My father didn't have anything to do with my childhood, except for paying for my riding lessons and leasing my horse." Guilt money, her mother had always said. Regan knew she was probably correct. He'd also paid for the modeling and acting lessons that Claire had wanted. Claire had eventually grown tired of acting, but Regan had ridden right up until the time she'd had to choose between horse expenses and college expenses. Her mother had not yet hit the big time and money had been tight in those days.

"I think he got his money's worth," Will said.

"Thanks."

She focused straight ahead.

"How was the Elko class?"

"Not a lot of fun. But there was one interesting thing."

"What's that?"

"I met your brother."

Will's heart jumped, but he managed to ask offhandedly, "Did someone introduce you?"

"We ran into each other in the hotel restaurant. He was waiting for friends and I thought he was you."

Will was still waiting for the day when he

could hear mention of his brother and not feel a knee-jerk reaction of panic. Tentatively, he'd come to the decision that Brett really was in the area only for a job. It made sense. Jobs in ranch management were rare and Brett would have to take one wherever he could. And he'd made no move to get in contact.

"We talked for a while."

Will nodded, because he couldn't think of a reasonable response. Somehow, *I hope he keeps the hell away from here* didn't seem appropriate for casual conversation.

"He seemed like an okay guy."

"He is." Except in the ways that counted. Such as loyalty.

"Are you going to the Harvest Dance?" Mercifully, Regan changed the subject.

"We'll go if Kylie manages not to get herself grounded again. Are you going?"

"I'm working at the dessert table. I'll be serving pie for an hour and a half."

"You'll be busy."

She tilted her head curiously. "Why?"

"They only serve homemade pies and a lot of people go all out in terms of their pie consumption. Kind of a competition. Some people wait all year just to sample those pies."

Regan grinned. "How folksy."

"You'll certainly think it's folksy after you've spent a good hour shoveling pie onto plates." He pulled Skitters to a stop as they reached his driveway. "Thanks for letting me know about Sadie and Kylie. It helps."

She smiled. The breeze tousled the layers of her hair, giving her a just-tumbled-out-of-bed look that stirred thoughts Will knew he probably shouldn't have. But there was no denying the fact he was thinking them. And he was beginning to wish he could do something about them.

ZACH TAYLOR had drawn his final line in the sand. He'd fallen behind in his assignments again and Regan, fed up with his assumption that he was bulletproof, not only put zeroes into the computer, but called the athletic director and told him why Zach was ineligible. And the man backed her up. Two days later, Wesley lost its first regional football championship in eight years. Zach Taylor, starting quarterback, had not played.

Regan found herself in the unusual position of being in deep trouble with her boss, even as she approached folk-hero status with her coworkers.

"No one has ever taken on the Taylors successfully before," Karlene told her, with a look of awe, the morning after the game. "Way to go. Maybe he'll behave now, even if it is kind of a shame about the game."

Regan had not intended to cause the football team to lose. In fact, she didn't think she had. It wasn't her fault the second-string quarterback had been injured on the first play. Or that Zach was lazy and had a sense of entitlement. But Pete seemed to think so.

He didn't say anything to Regan. Not one word. But he glowered coldly whenever she was near. The reason was obvious. Zach's uncle was on the school board and had a lot of clout. The school board had the power to hire Pete. Pete had failed in his mission to keep Zach eligible. The team had lost.

Regan couldn't understand why no one on the board could see that Zach could have prevented all this simply by following through with his responsibilities. Her fellow teachers seemed to see it plain as day.

"Because they need a scapegoat and a new teacher is a lot easier to blame than a star athlete or a veteran athletic director," Jared told her over lunch.

Both Tanya and Karlene had assured her

the issue would blow over and the district would be better because of it.

Regan just hoped she'd be there long enough to see the improvement.

THE HARVEST DANCE was a big event—big enough that Will made certain Kylie wasn't grounded for it. She put her horse away early that day, got into her newest jeans, pulled her hair back into a ponytail and put a glittery doodad over the elastic. Will also wore new jeans, since they were the only ones he owned with no work-related wear and tear; a white cowboy shirt and his good belt with the trophy buckle.

They got there early and Kylie immediately started searching the crowd, as did Will. He told himself he was looking for Trev, but really he was looking for Regan. He thought maybe he'd go and give her a hand setting up the dessert table, when Kylie burst out with an incredulous, "Whoa."

At the entry, a pretty girl with long blond curls had just paused in the doorway.

"I don't believe it," Kylie muttered.

Neither did Will. The pretty girl was Sadie, wearing makeup, a short dress and heels. She looked about three years older than the last time he'd seen her. His daughter was staring opened mouthed at her friend.

"She didn't *tell* me," Kylie finally growled, her gaze following Sadie as she headed across the room to a group of eighth graders. The cool group.

"Maybe she didn't think it mattered."

Kylie sent him a look that said it mattered very much, then brushed past him, walking out of the gym.

Will followed, emerging into the hall in time to see his daughter disappear into the girls' restroom. He let out a frustrated breath. What now?

He had no idea how serious this was, but Kylie was definitely pissed.

He waited in the hall, trying to look non-chalant. He nodded at a couple of women as they emerged from the ladies' room. Neither looked concerned in any way.

Okay, that probably meant she was all right. Maybe he should just leave her alone.

If this was any other kind of emotional situation—a lost dog, a failed test, a white ribbon in a horse show—he would let her work it out and be available when she was ready to talk. But this was her best friend and it was new territory for both of them.

He needed advice.

Feeling a little desperate, he headed back into the gym and straight for Regan, the one person who might have an inkling about handling girl dynamics who wouldn't gossip about it with everyone in the county.

"I think I have a situation on my hands."

"I saw." She untied the official dessert-table apron she'd been wearing over her jeans and sparkly green top. "Where'd she go?"

"Ladies' room."

"You want me to check on her?"

Will nodded. "She was pretty mad. I don't want her heading home on foot or anything."

"Would she do that?"

"This is Kylie we're talking about."

Regan handed Will the apron and headed for the restroom.

KYLIE'S FACE was red, but if she'd been crying she'd managed to shut off the water-works before Regan entered the washroom.

Regan made no pretense as to why she was there. "Your dad is worried about you."

"Tell him I'll be out in a minute."

"He's afraid you might take off."

"Tell him not to worry."

"Kylie…" Regan touched her shoulder.

"I won't take off."

"Maybe you should talk to…"

"I'm not talking to her."

"I guess I don't blame you." Kylie glanced up, suspicious of empathy from a teacher and obviously wondering if this was some kind of trick. "But do you honestly think she did this to hurt you?"

"It doesn't matter, because she did. We've always told each other everything."

"There are other kids out there to be friends with, you know." Even as she said it, Regan knew it was lame advice. It didn't matter how many kids were out there if your best friend had just betrayed you.

Kylie gave a sullen nod.

A group of girls came giggling in and Regan turned away to the sink and started the water running. Kylie walked out as soon as Regan's hands were wet. Regan reached for a towel and followed, catching site of Kylie going back into the gym as she stepped into the hall.

Okay, at least the kid hadn't started walking home.

Regan returned to her post and tied on the apron Will had left folded over a chair. A few minutes later he casually made his way back to the dessert table.

"How is she?" he asked.

"Mad. Confused." Regan carefully peeled plastic wrap off the top of a pumpkin pie beautifully decorated with pastry leaves.

"I never saw this coming."

"Neither did Kylie. That's the problem."

"Excuse me…" Mrs. Serrano edged by the two of them to get some disposable coffee cups. "You might want to get out of here while you can, Will."

"Sure thing." He smiled politely at Mrs. Serrano and then leaned close enough to Regan that she could smell the spicy scent of his aftershave. "Thanks."

"Anytime." She fumbled with the latch on an old-fashioned metal pie carrier and Will automatically reached over to snap it open for her.

"Maybe I'll see you later."

"Maybe."

A line of people began to form at the dessert table, despite Mrs. Serrano's attempts to shoo them away until the coffee was ready. For the next hour and a half Regan wasn't aware of much of anything other than hungry people wanting to buy dessert.

By the time Tanya came to take her place, Regan was more than ready to hand over the pie server and apron. "Have fun," she murmured to Tanya, who grinned.

"The second shift is never as bad as the first."

"I love being the newcomer," Regan said with a grimace, but the truth was she didn't really mind.

Pete was holding court nearby, far enough away from the speakers and the dance floor that he could talk. From the number of mock basketball shots he took as he talked, Regan assumed he was reliving some championship game. The men surrounding him seemed fascinated by his story.

Kylie sat in the same general area, with Mark and a few other kids. Another girl joined them as Regan watched and Kylie said something to her that made her laugh. They all looked at Sadie, who was standing close to her crush and his friends, then they looked at each other, before laughing again. Sadie pretended not to notice, but Regan saw her back stiffen at the sound of Kylie's laughter.

Will was leaning against the wall several yards away, holding a glass of cider and looking as if he needed something stronger, watching his kid pretend not to be miserable. Regan went over to him.

"How're you doing?"

"I'm foreseeing a long adolescence ahead of me."

"It's only another five or six years."

Will made a face. "My gut instinct is to haul her away from all this right now."

"And protect her from everything that might hurt her?"

He nodded. "And maybe buy her a new horse, to make it all better."

"It would be nice if it was that easy."

"Hi, Miss Flynn." A seventh-grade boy suddenly appeared next to Regan, almost as if he'd been shoved, which Regan strongly suspected was the case. "You wanna dance?" he squeaked.

A group of boys were huddled nearby, nudging each other as they watched their friend.

"I'd love to," she told the kid with a straight face, letting her shoulders slump with disappointment, "but I don't two-step."

"Thanks, anyway!" The kid made his escape as his friends collapsed into fits of laughter. Will grinned at her.

"Welcome to my world," Regan said wearily.

"The next dance isn't a two-step. They play a slow one every fourth song. Like clockwork." Sure enough, a soulful country ballad came through the speakers a moment later.

"Thank you for not pointing that out to Romeo." Regan said dryly, then her eyes widened as she saw Pete heading toward her. "What now?" she muttered.

"Come on," Will said, gesturing to the floor. He held out a hand and Regan took it, liking the way it felt when his warm fingers closed around hers and experiencing a surge of satisfaction at the look on Pete's face as she made it onto the dance floor before he reached her.

"Thank you," she said, setting a light hand on Will's shoulder.

"I was going to ask you anyway," he said.

"Were you?" She looked up at him, surprised.

He shrugged. "I thought I might ease out of monk status just a little."

Regan smiled. "You'll probably want to take it slow, so you don't hurt yourself."

He held her with a chaperone-approved space between them. "I'm setting a good example." He said with a smile in his eyes. "This is the way I expect Kylie to dance when the bad days come and boys start asking her out."

"She's a very pretty girl, Will. It may not be too long."

"Her mom was pretty, too."

It was the first time Will had ever mentioned Kylie's mother and Regan found that she really didn't like it much. She wondered what their relationship was now, Will and Kylie's mom.

"Does Kylie have contact with her mom?"

"No." It was quite clear that was all that was going to be said on the matter, but Will pulled her just a little closer, as if to make up for the abrupt answer. Regan's hand tightened on his shoulder. It'd been a while since she'd touched anyone so rock solid. It'd been a while since she'd felt a deep physical attraction like this—and she was torn as to how to respond. She knew what she *should* do. And she knew what she'd promised herself she'd do. She just didn't know what she was going to do.

It's only a dance. With an attractive man. You swore off unhealthy relationships, not men. As long as you keep it light, as long as everyone knows what's what, there was no danger.

Yeah, and there's this bridge for sale in Brooklyn.

Will gestured toward his daughter with a nod of his head. Kylie was looking seriously unhappy.

"Any words of advice on how to handle a girl whose best friend has just abandoned her?" he asked softly. She wondered if he was aware of the fact that the chaperone-approved distance was slowly disappearing, that her thighs were now touching his. She didn't know how he couldn't be aware of it.

"Patience. It'll work out. The thing is, Kylie honestly doesn't get it. She doesn't understand why Sadie has suddenly changed on her."

"I'm glad she doesn't get it."

"She will soon enough."

"I know." He pulled her closer still and they danced without talking. Karlene and Jared-the-sub were also dancing nearby and there was definitely no chaperone-approved distance between them. Karlene's brown curls rested against Jared's shoulder and his arm was firmly clamped around her back. Regan closed her eyes, forgot about chaperones and enjoyed the rest of her dance.

When the music wound to an end, Regan eased herself away from Will. It was funny how safe she'd felt in his arms, as if nothing in the world could touch her. Speaking of which, Pete was trolling the edge of the crowd. He was watching her surreptitiously. But why?

"Thanks for the dance, Will." She nodded

in Pete's direction. "I think I'll head home now, before my boss has a chance to ruin my evening."

"I'll walk you to your car. You know, run interference, just in case."

"Thanks."

They wound through the crowd to the coat room. Regan found her jacket and then followed Will out of the gym, watching for Pete the entire way.

The breeze lifted her bangs as Will held the door and she stepped out into the much cooler night air, inhaling deeply. A few more people tumbled out behind them, laughing.

She felt like laughing herself. It was good to escape.

"What do you think he wanted?"

"I have no idea. I worked my shift. I didn't make any athletes ineligible. I left the squid at home."

Actually, Regan did have an idea. He'd been talking to Zach's father earlier and she had a feeling that'd had something to do with his interest in her. But she was surprised he was approaching her in public. Usually, he was sneakier.

Regan was parked around the corner of the building in her usual parking spot. It was darker there. The Vegasite in her was instinctively on the alert and she was glad Will was with her, even if she was only in sleepy Wesley. He was walking close beside her—close enough that their shoulders bumped companionably every now and then, but the feeling Regan was getting didn't exactly belong in the companion category. In fact, it was pretty much at the opposite end of the spectrum.

When they reached her car she unlocked it, but she didn't open the door right away. Instead, she turned and leaned back against it, looking up at Will, knowing she was probably going to regret her decision, but really wanting to see how this played out. She had a feeling that Will was venturing into uncharted territory with her and that he was as curious and conflicted about it as she was. He confirmed the suspicion a second later when he moved so close that she had to tilt her head back to look up at him.

Her eyes had adjusted to the darkness and she could see the intensity of his expression as his hands settled gently on her shoulders. And once again their thighs were touching.

"I haven't danced in a long time."

"It's that monk thing," she said softly, acutely aware of the pressure of his fingers as they stroked the curve of her neck and ran through her hair. "They don't dance much."

"They don't kiss people good-night, either."

"How long's it been for that?" she asked, trying for the casualness she kept telling herself she should be feeling. That's all this was—the causal flirtation of two lonely people.

"Long enough," he said, as he lowered his lips to hers.

His mouth was warm and firm. Inviting. Tantalizing. He didn't pull her nearer, but from the way he deepened the kiss, she suspected it had been a while since he'd kissed someone good-night. And from her response, he was probably thinking the same thing.

A loud hoot of laughter sounded nearby at about the time Regan thought her knees were going to buckle, followed by a car horn, bringing them back to earth.

Regan stepped back, putting some space between them, pressing her fingers against the cool metal of her car door so she wouldn't be tempted to wrap them back around Will.

"I guess I'll be going." Her voice was uncharacteristically husky.

"Yeah." So was his. He pushed his thumbs through his belt loops. "I'd better get back and collect my kid."

She nodded, but neither of them moved.

"I probably shouldn't have done that."

"It was just a kiss, Will." At least that was all it should have been. She couldn't figure out why it felt like so much more. Why everything with Will felt like so much more.

"I guess I was thinking more along the lines of, now that I've done it once, I'll want to do it again."

"And you can't?" Regan asked softly, almost hopefully.

"I want life to be stable for Kylie, so it's not so much that I can't, but rather that I need to proceed with caution."

Regan glanced down for a moment, choosing her words before she looked back up. "I have to tell you, Will, the last thing I'm looking for is anything resembling a relationship, so I think it's a good thing this happened."

"A good thing?" She sensed his frown. "How's that?"

"We were both obviously wondering what this would be like, with each other. Now we know and now we can move on." She sounded like a teacher conducting a lesson. Oh, well. Whatever it took.

"Just like that?"

She shrugged with an apparent nonchalance that she was far from actually feeling. "Just like that."

She had a feeling she'd just hit his male ego pretty hard, but after that kiss—which had been about a hundred times hotter than she'd expected—she wasn't taking any chances.

Will took a step backward. "You're right. Good night, Regan. I'll see you around." He started back toward the gym, leaving Regan wondering whether she'd just dodged a bullet or been hit by one.

CHAPTER EIGHT

ON SATURDAY, Regan rode Toffee cross-country, making a big loop behind Will's place and several other ranches. She'd been riding for almost an hour when she came to a fence. She followed it for at least a mile before deciding she wasn't going to find a gate and turned back. Toffee immediately pricked his ears and raised his head. A horse and a small rider topped the hill she'd just come down and headed directly toward them.

It was Kylie on an older sorrel gelding. Even though the girl seemed surprised to see her, Regan had an idea that the meeting was not quite as spontaneous as Kylie was pretending.

"Is there a gate in this fence?" Regan asked, pushing windblown hair out of her face. Kylie was wearing a blue ball cap that Regan had seen Will wearing a few days earlier. It was pulled low over Kylie's eyes, keeping her hair from whipping around her cheeks the way Regan's was.

"Not for a long way, but if you follow the fence far enough, you'll be close to the mustang hole."

"The mustang hole?" Somehow that sounded wrong.

"The place where the mustangs water."

"As in wild horses?"

"Mmm, hmm." The girl seemed pleased that Regan was impressed.

"How far?"

Kylie squinted her eyes. "About half an hour."

"I've never seen a mustang in the wild."

"They're neat and a lot of them are pretty but," the girl wrinkled her nose, "some of them are kind of ugly up close. Big heads and skinny necks. Not everybody likes them, but I do."

"I think I'd like them, too."

"You wanna see if they're around?"

Regan thought about the history tests she had to grade. "Yes. That sounds like fun." And she was still wondering how accidental the meeting with Kylie was. She wondered if the girl wanted to talk.

"How's your new horse?" she asked after almost twenty-five minutes of silent riding.

During that time they had crossed two low hills separated by half-mile-wide valleys, each with its own dry streambed. If Kylie had something to say, she was taking her time getting to it.

"Dad doesn't think she's trustworthy yet, but he's making progress. She bucked him off one day and he wants to make sure she's done with that before I get on."

"Has Sadie seen her yet?" Regan asked as she zipped her jacket the rest of the way up to her chin. The wind was getting stronger and the sky was clouding up.

"Who?" Kylie asked coolly.

"Is that the way it is?"

"It's the way it is now."

"Think it'll be that way forever?"

"Maybe." Kylie adjusted her ball cap as a gust of wind lifted the brim, keeping her attention firmly ahead of her as she rode.

"People grow up at different speeds, Kylie."

"I know all about that. We had that stupid video at school."

"I mean, some people like to stay kids longer than others and there's nothing wrong with that. If you're not ready to put on a party dress and hang out with boys, then fine."

"Who said I wasn't?"

"Are you?"

Kylie snorted through her nose.

"When you're ready, you're ready. Sadie feels ready. Maybe you don't. But one of these days you'll be at the same place again—for a while, anyway."

"What do you mean?"

Regan smiled. "I mean maybe you'll be ready to do some other things before Sadie, then she'll wonder what's up with you."

Kylie smiled a little, but it faded fast.

"You just might have to be patient with her for a while."

"I'll try." Her mouth tightened for a moment and then she said, "There's something else."

"Yes?"

"I think my Dad might kind of like you."

"What?" Regan unconsciously tightened the reins and Toffee bobbed his head in response. She let them slide back through her fingers a few inches.

"He kind of likes you. You know. As in, *likes you*." She spoke slowly, enunciating carefully, just in case Regan didn't get her drift.

"Um…"

"And I don't think that's a good idea."

"Oy," Regan muttered in a low voice.

Kylie pulled her horse to a stop at the top of the hill they'd been climbing. "He's been hurt before, you know."

Regan didn't know and she didn't want details from a kid. "Don't worry about me and your dad, Kylie. If he likes me, it's as a friend."

"You guys were looking friendly at the dance."

"Lots of people were looking friendly at the dance. It was a dance."

"My dad never dances much. He just goes to talk."

"And that's what we did. We talked while we danced." Except maybe at the end, when she'd let her imagination wander as she felt his hard body pressed up against hers. "Your dad and I are friends. That's all." Because she, for one, was not going to let the relationship move beyond that. For the first time in a long time, she was feeling at peace. In control. She wasn't going to jeopardize that feeling. Not even for a hot man.

Kylie regarded her for a moment, trying to decide whether Regan was being honest or just brushing her off. Regan could see the girl was on the edge of being convinced. She was about to reiterate her point when Kylie held up a hand, cutting her off.

"Look." She pointed to the bottom of the next valley. There, walking in a bunch through the grass, was a herd of fifteen or twenty horses.

The lead horse stopped suddenly and perked its ears, staring at the two strange horses on the horizon. For a long time the herd stayed stock-still, noses in the air, studying the riders and their mounts across the half mile of sage that separated them.

Toffee caught the scent. He put his head up and whinnied. The lead horse called back.

The herd went on alert and then the lead mare suddenly spun and ran. The herd followed and Regan had to fight to control Toffee, who had begun to dance.

"We should go," Regan said, shortening her reins even more.

"Yeah." Kylie turned her placid gelding and Regan managed to spin Toffee around.

"He probably wants to race them. Have you ever let him just run?"

"Not yet."

"I bet he's fast."

"Yes," Regan said through clenched teeth, fighting the reins until Toffee finally settled and started walking, "but I don't want to find out how fast he is today."

Kylie sighed and urged her own horse forward. "Boy, I would."

AS THE FALL LIVESTOCK GATHERS were completed, it seemed that a few more cattle were missing than usual. Strays were common, but strays concentrated in a certain area were out of the ordinary. Mountain lions and accidents took their toll, but when one of Will's neighbors ended up missing fifteen head, Will started to wonder if something was up.

There'd been a case of a kid stealing newborn calves early last spring. With beef prices up and a calf being easy to toss into a truck, Will understood the temptation. But that young thief had been caught and loading full-grown cows required a little more expertise than maneuvering a calf into a truck.

Will decided to take a wait-and-see approach and Trev agreed. There wasn't much else they could do except keep an eye out for unusual activity, which wasn't easy in a part of Nevada where there were plenty of cows and not a lot of witnesses.

"Helping with the Renshaw auction?" Will asked. Trev was pushing his chair back from the kitchen table. He'd stopped by to drop off some paperwork, then had stayed so long talking shop that Will knew he'd be working late that afternoon to make up the lost time.

"I'm shipping cattle that day." Trev set his empty cup in the old enameled sink. "But I'll be there when I'm done. I'm being sold."

"Me, too." Will was glad to do it. The Renshaws were nice people and it looked like this fund-raiser might help them finally get out from under their medical bills.

WILL BROUGHT KYLIE to her first jumping lesson on the day of Regan's first professional evaluation. She was not in the best of moods. She had a feeling that Pete had been waiting for the "proper" moment for his drop-in visit, and sure enough, he turned up during a lab that wasn't going well. One of her students had managed to spill vinegar all over Regan's new skirt and she'd looked up to see Pete smiling. Malignantly.

She'd smiled back, then helped the kid wipe the floor—just before the demonstration flask got knocked off the podium and shattered on the floor. Not a good day. Pete had loved every minute of it. He wrote so fast that Regan was pretty certain he'd have to ice his wrist that night.

But in spite of the stress of the school day,

in spite of the low-grade headache building between her temples, when Regan saw Will enter the arena wearing his canvas jacket and those old blue jeans that hugged his hips and legs just right, her pulse jumped.

"It was just a kiss," she muttered to herself. *A kiss that she'd dreamed about.*

Will started to leave after getting Kylie mounted, but Madison ambushed him—ignoring Regan's telepathic plea to just let him go—and he ended up staying for the entire session, leaning against the arena fence, watching, with Madison at his side.

Regan focused on her class, as she led her six students through a series of balancing exercises and then over low jumps, calling instructions and corrections. But she was acutely aware of the man by the fence, which was not helping her mood one iota.

For the most part, Will kept his eyes on his daughter—who was a natural at jumping—even when Madison was making a concerted effort to talk his ear off. Sometimes he smiled a little, but it seemed that whenever he did, his eyes invariably strayed to Regan and then the smile disappeared.

When the class was over, Regan decided she was going to face the situation with Will head-on and get it over with so things could settle. She'd liked their old relationship and she wanted it back.

She found Will sitting on the fender of his trailer, waiting for Kylie to finish cooling her horse.

"Hi."

"Hi," he echoed. He looked at her cautiously, maybe wondering if she was going to hammer his ego again.

She began by sidestepping the real issue. "I was wondering if Kylie had a peppier horse that she might be able to bring?" Kylie might be a natural, but the horse she was riding was not. He'd clipped his feet on even the lowest jumps.

"I thought we'd start with her old standby gelding, but, yeah, we'll bring something with more pep next time." He spoke politely, his expression distant.

Regan shoved her hands down into her pockets. "I also hope that what happened the other night isn't going to affect us."

"I think you made it clear that it was just a matter of curiosity."

"That's not exactly what I meant."

"Well, maybe…"

Kylie came around the trailer just then,

leading her horse. She scowled when she saw Will and Regan together, but her voice was polite as she said, "Good lesson, Miss Flynn."

She moved her gelding directly in between Regan and Will and tied him to a metal loop on the trailer. "Dad, we need to take the saddle back to Madison. She has to keep them here, because she has another class using them."

"I'll take it over while you load." He met Regan's gaze over the horse's back as Kylie undid the girth, then he pulled off the saddle and walked toward the arena office.

And that was apparently the way they were going to leave matters. Not quite settled— exactly the way Regan hated things.

"See ya, Miss Flynn," Kylie said in a flat voice, before getting into the truck.

Regan pulled her keys out of her pocket and walked around the trailer to her car. As she was unlocking her door, Will walked over. He checked to make certain he was out of his daughter's field of vision before turning back to Regan.

"Maybe you can tell me what you did mean the other night?"

"I meant that I like being friends and I'd like to stay friends."

"Me, too."

"And to be truthful, that kiss was a lot more than I expected—for friends."

"Not just a kiss, then?"

Her composure took a dip as he focused momentarily on her mouth before letting his gaze travel slowly up to her eyes in a way that surprised her. She forced herself to rally, to remember her purpose.

"No. But I wanted it to be just a kiss and I was annoyed with myself for letting things go too far."

"Why did you let things go too far?" he asked.

She hesitated for a beat, then her mouth twisted wryly. "Because I was curious. Why'd *you* let it go that far?"

He grinned back and the tension between them began to dissipate. "I guess I was curious, too."

"Gee, where have I heard that?" She bit the edge of her lip. "So what do you think now?

"I think I'd like to do it again, just like I said."

"But," Regan said, with a touch of cocky bravado, "will you ever have the chance?"

He took a step back and Regan suddenly knew what a horse in the round pen felt like when Will released the pressure. "I guess time will tell."

HER SISTER, Claire, hadn't phoned or e-mailed in almost five days, so when the phone rang late Sunday afternoon, Regan figured it had to be her.

It wasn't, however. It was Brett Bishop.

"You sound surprised," he said, in a voice very much like his brother's.

"A little." She was actually astonished.

"I'll be coming to Wesley in a week or so to look at some cattle, I was wondering if you'd like to go out? For dinner."

Regan pulled in a breath. She'd had enough one-on-one Bishop encounters for a while. They seemed to be ending unpredictably lately. "You know, Brett…"

"I thought we could talk," he said, when she hesitated.

"Talk?"

"Yeah. You know, as opposed to me hitting on you."

Regan laughed at his candor, but she wasn't entirely convinced. "Why don't you give me a call when you know for sure that you're coming?" That would give her some time to think things over and to decide whether she wanted to have another meeting with Brett Bishop or not.

"I'll do that," he promised.

Regan hung up after saying goodbye, only to have the phone ring again. Claire.

"Where were you a few minutes ago, when I needed you?" Regan said.

"What?"

"Never mind. How are things going with Mom?"

Regan could actually hear Claire's fingers drumming on some hard surface at the other end.

"I told her about some changes I'm making in my life. She's in a huff, but I'm weathering it. And I've made it a point not to call and ask you to be the referee." She stated this with exaggerated self-righteousness. "I'm going to do this on my own. I've been doing some Internet research and, according to what I've read, if I hold my position long enough, Mom will buckle. It's called extinction. Unfortunately, I don't know which of us becomes extinct first."

"What kind of changes?" Regan had a feeling they involved the College of Education, but nothing was ever certain with her sister.

"I'd kind of like to wait before I talk about them. See if I survive Mom. It'll be embarrassing if I'm the one who crumbles."

"Don't crumble."

"I'll try not to. And actually, I'm calling to give you a heads up."

Regan reached for a dishcloth and gave her counter a wipe. "What kind of heads up?"

"Mom's pulling in favors. She's trying to finagle an interview for you with the Department of Education."

"No." Regan crumpled the cloth in her hand.

"It's killing her that you're, and I quote, 'wasting your talents in some backwater town.' Unquote. She wants you back in Vegas, babe."

"I like it here." Regan returned to polishing the counter, trying not to let her mother's actions get to her.

"Why?" Claire asked, genuinely curious.

"There's a sense of community here."

"That sounds nice," her sister replied in a way that told Regan she wasn't all that familiar with a sense of community. That was what came of moving and changing roommates every few months.

"The staff at my school is very supportive. No one leaves until they retire."

"That sounds better than the thirty percent turnover rate at your previous school," Claire agreed. "What else have you got?"

"My rent is half what it was in Vegas for

twice the space, and I can take a walk at night if I want."

That seemed to impress her sister.

"Well," Claire said grudgingly, "I'm going to trust that you know what you're doing— even if you did abandon me to Mom. But I would truly love to know how you keep from dying from boredom on the weekends."

REGAN AND PAULINE were never going to be close friends, but after the Elko trip, Pauline had been much less prissy, which made Regan think she remembered more of her Picon adventure than she let on. Therefore, when Pauline flagged her down in the hall, wearing the same pink pencil skirt she'd had on when she'd collapsed on her hotel-room bed, Regan did not immediately assume the worst.

"I was wondering if you had anything you'd be willing to donate to the auction to help the Renshaws."

"Sure," Regan said, even though her bank account was still recovering from all the Toffee-related expenses. "How much?"

"Oh, no. Not money, unless you want to, of course. We're all donating goods or services. For instance, Millie Serrano is donating one of her crocheted tablecloths and the high school art teacher is contributing one of her paintings."

"I have an opal necklace I'll donate." Regan had been wondering what to do with the necklace Daniel had given her for her birthday. It wasn't as if she'd ever wear it again and now it would go to help a good cause.

"That sounds lovely." Pauline penciled a note onto her clipboard. "Thank you very much."

"Glad to help."

"The auction is next Saturday at seven o'clock at the arena. Quite a few people have donated livestock."

"I'll be there."

"One more thing. Mr. Domingo was looking for you the last time I saw him."

"Oh. I've been in the library."

"Don't worry about it," Pauline said. "If it was important, he would have called for you on the intercom."

Unless he wants to bully you in private.

She'd never found out why he'd been stalking her at the Harvest Dance. He'd basically avoided her after that night, with the exception of her first evaluation, which had been barely acceptable.

Regan thanked Pauline and headed for her

classroom. Pete was coming out as she was heading in.

"Can I help you?" she asked. She had the oddest feeling that he'd been on the edge of saying no before he said yes.

"I want to set up our next evaluation session."

"We just finished an evaluation."

"My schedule will be full, with wrestling and basketball, so I wanted to plan around the games and matches. I have a lot of evaluations to get through, you know."

"I understand."

They settled on a date in January—two months away—then Pete snapped his notebook shut and left without another word.

Regan stood staring at the door he'd just gone through. Something was up.

And then she noticed her computer screen. She'd left her e-mail account accessible on the bottom toolbar. Pete had probably been reading her e-mail. What a snake.

THE RENSHAW AUCTION was officially put on by the high school's agricultural club, but everyone in the community pitched in. Will spent most of the afternoon at Madison's arena, where the event was to be held, first setting up the auctioneering stand, then cataloging and tagging donated items while Kylie ran errands for Madison. Quite a few people donated livestock and the FFA club kids were kept busy setting up temporary pens and chutes just inside the doors at the far end. Soon the arena sounded like a petting zoo gone mad.

Will had gotten two cell-phone calls from Trev as he worked. Their horse thief was back. Or rather, *a* horse thief, but both he and Trev figured it was the same guy who'd been at it a few months before. This time the thefts followed the state highway, starting in Carlin and heading south.

Trev looked tired when he finally showed up late.

"Total of four thefts last night," he said, when he found Will behind the pens, making sure the numbers matched the animals. "Carlin, Eureka, Ely, Lund."

"Must be pulling a four-horse," Will commented darkly, handing his clipboard to the freckle-faced kid who was now in charge of making sure the right animal came out at the right time. "I'd love to know where he's unloading them. You know—meet him at the sale."

"Has to be some slaughterhouse. Have you…"

"Trevin." Madison's voice blared over the

PA system and Trev grimaced as his proper name reverberated off the metal walls. "We're ready to start the auction and you're first."

"Better go sell yourself," Will said.

"Ladies and gentlemen. To start the night, Trev has offered two free shoeings or resets. That's all four feet, right Trev?"

"Yep." Trev called, as he walked through the gate into the arena. He went to stand next to Madison's podium and smiled at the audience. Will decided he was going to try to smile, too.

"So what am I bid for this service? You guys know what a decent farrier charges and it's all for a good cause."

Will listened as Trev's services went for double what he normally charged. Maybe this auction *would* put the Renshaw fund over the top tonight.

"Oh, Will," Madison called. "Will Bishop is item number two in your programs."

Will stepped into the ring as Trev walked out. "Geri Winters bought me."

"She doesn't have a horse."

"I know." He sounded grim.

"Will has offered thirty days on a horse," Madison announced. "He'll start a new one or tune up an old one. Let's start the bidding at two hundred."

"MAYBE YOU SHOULD BUY HIM," Tanya murmured, close to Regan's shoulder. Will stood in the ring next to the auction stand, his hands on his hips. He was wearing jeans that had just the proper amount of fantasy-inducing wear and a plaid shirt rolled up over the elbows. He looked…good. And Regan was still processing their previous meeting.

"I don't need him. I can train my own horse."

"Pity." Tanya unfolded the auction list and perused it for the hundredth time, idly toying with the end of her blond ponytail. "I'm bidding on the housepainter."

"I'm bidding on the saddle rack."

"Regan, sometimes I worry about you."

"Sold!" Madison finally called, after a heated bidding war for Will's services, then Mrs. Serrano's lace tablecloth was brought out.

Regan and Tanya bid on a number of items, but the townspeople were feeling generous and after almost an hour, neither of them had ended up with anything. Regan's opal necklace had gone to a young newlywed, who happily presented it to his bride as soon as he'd paid for it. Regan hoped the girl would be far happier with it than she'd been.

Tanya excused herself to go to the concession stand just as a high school girl led a fat pony into the arena.

"Geri," someone called from the audience, "here's your chance to buy a horse to go with your farrier!"

Apparently the pony was a well-known fixture in the community, because no one met the starting bid. Madison grudgingly dropped the price by twenty dollars and Regan suddenly had a flash of inspiration.

She raised her card.

"I have one hundred." Madison pounced on the bid. "Now let's have one-twenty for this fine, um, piece of horseflesh." The pony swished his tail. "One-twenty? Anyone? Do I hear one-fifteen…one-fifteen? One-ten?" The crowd remained stubbornly silent. "Sold to number sixty for one hundred dollars."

Regan turned to see Tanya gaping at her, a drink in each hand.

"My horse is lonely," she explained.

"Your horse is lonely."

"Yes. And ponies don't eat much."

"Did you happen to notice that no one else was bidding on him? I mean, doesn't that worry you? A cute little pony and no one wants him?"

"I'm not going to be riding him, so, no." Regan picked up her purse. "I need to find some way to haul him, though. Madison will charge me if I try to keep him here overnight."

Four boys in FFA jackets came into the ring carrying a beautiful pieced quilt, which they unfolded for everyone to see. A gasp of appreciation sounded and the bidding was on. Tanya's card flashed into the air. Regan went to the sales table near the stands to pay for her purchase.

"I hope you know what you just did." Will's voice sounded behind her, just as she finished writing the check.

"What did I do?" she asked, taking her receipt and folding it.

"You bought Peanut Butter."

"I bought him to keep Toffee company," she said. "If he doesn't work out, I'll sell him."

"To whom?" Will asked innocently, leaning an arm on the arena fence.

Regan frowned. This did not sound good. "What…"

A whoop of excitement cut off her words. Startled, she turned to see Tanya jumping to her feet.

"I bought the quilt." Her friend was practically dancing.

"You could have got two ponies for that price," Regan pointed out.

"But quilts don't eat anything," Tanya replied smugly.

Two girls began dragging a bawling nanny goat into the ring as soon as Tanya's quilt was safely folded and taken away. All four of the goat's legs were locked, her splayed feet leaving furrows in the arena dust. As soon as the girls stopped, the nanny quit bawling, put her feet squarely beneath her and blinked at the chuckling crowd. The laughter grew louder when she gave her tail a few impertinent shakes.

Even Madison laughed. "All right, what am I bid for this fine animal? Goat tiers? *Cabrito* eaters? Anyone? Let's start the bidding at fifty dollars."

Trev strolled over and leaned on the rail next to Will, but his eyes were on Regan. "You bought Peanut Butter?"

Regan sighed at the doomsday note in his voice.

"How many people have owned old PB?" Trev asked Will.

Will pushed his hat back. "I can think of three sales I was involved in. No, four."

"I've seen at least that many."

"How would you feel about owning a goat?" Regan asked Will.

"I'd rather not."

"Then you'd better hope someone else bids, because I think your daughter is winning."

"What?" His gaze shot to the auction ring and then a colorful word escaped his lips. He pushed his way past Trev as Madison called "Going, going," but he was too late. The gavel came down.

"Sold to number seventy-eight."

Will quickly strode over to number seventy-eight and the two had a brief conversation. A few minutes later Kylie grudgingly approached the auction stand and whispered something to Madison.

"Ladies and gentlemen. Nanny is being donated back to us to auction again. Thank you, Kylie."

Kylie briefly stretched her lips into a good-sport smile before she turned and stalked back to her father, scowling the entire way.

She said something to him, he nodded, and the girl headed for the concession area.

Will watched her for a moment, then walked back to where Trev and Regan stood. Trev wore a wide grin.

"Yuck it up," Will muttered. "Here comes Geri to collect on her purchase."

Regan had to bite her lip to keep from laughing as Trev whirled to see a tall, curvaceous brunette striding toward him with a purposeful expression on her face.

"Geri," Will greeted the woman with a polite nod, as he edged past her. "See ya, Trev. I have to check the livestock."

"Regan," Trev said from between his teeth.

"I need to find a ride for Peanut Butter." And she did not want to get between a predator and her prey.

"Um, was it just me or was she licking her lips?" she asked Will as she caught up with him.

"I think Geri's had her sights on Trev for quite a while now."

"He doesn't seem too thrilled about it."

"Geri's known to be…hard on men."

"Oh."

Peanut Butter stood at the edge of his pen, looking adorable, his little ears tipped forward, his brown eyes wide and inquiring.

"So what's the matter with him?" Regan asked with a frown. "Is he mean?" He didn't look mean.

"No. He's smart. He's outwitted just about everyone who's owned him. People get tired of staying one step ahead of him."

"All I want him to do is to stand in the pasture and keep Toffee company."

"Well, since everyone else has expected him to either carry a kid or pull a cart, you may be all right—as long as he doesn't decide the grass is greener on the other side of the fence and figure out your gate latches."

"You're kidding, right?"

Will simply smiled. He leaned back against a pen, looking unaffectedly sexy as only a confident male could.

"I'd better go find whoever sold him and see if they'll drop him by my house."

"That'd be the Butlers. And if they can't do it, I'll haul him in the morning."

"I'd appreciate that," she said, stepping aside to let two kids with a rabbit cage go by. "Why'd you have Kylie donate her goat back?"

"Have you ever come out of your house to find a goat standing on the hood of your vehicle?" he asked.

"Just this morning as a matter of fact."

"Very funny," he muttered, but his smile was genuine.

"Why'd she buy the goat?" Regan went to lean on the rail next to him, smiling fondly at her pony.

"She was afraid someone would buy it to butcher."

"I hadn't thought of that."

"Kylie did, thanks to Madison. *Cabrito* means goat meat, you know."

She gave him a frowning glance. "I didn't."

"*Cabrito* or not, Kylie needs to understand she can't rescue everything."

"Isn't Skitters a rescue?" Regan asked candidly.

Will took his time answering. "When we bought her, I honestly thought I might be able to shape her up. Now it's not looking so good."

"What happens if you can't shape her up?"

"She'll probably go to the cannery."

"Oh." There didn't seem to be much else to say. She stared at her toes, thinking it was such a shame some animals got so beat up there was no saving them.

He reached out to tip up her chin, his fingertips warm, gentle. "Fact of life, Regan. Not all horses can be saved and few people can afford to feed a horse just because it's pretty."

"I'm curious. Why couldn't you just let her join the mustang herd, since it's so close?"

"Probably because it's illegal."

"Pretty good reason not to," Regan said softly.

"Yeah. I really wish I hadn't bought her, because I think I see heartbreak ahead. Kylie's getting too attached."

Speaking of whom...

"Dad. There you are. Ready to go?" Kylie gave Regan an I-thought-we-talked-about-this look as she approached. She did not seem pleased to see the two of them together.

"Any extra animals in the truck?" Will asked.

"No." Her mouth twisted and Regan could see the girl was in no mood to be teased. "I'm just glad the Andersons bought the nanny. They don't eat goats. They're going to milk her. I checked."

Regan wondered what Kylie would have done if their plans had been less goat friendly. A goatnapping, perhaps?

"Have you seen the Butlers?"

"They just left," Kylie said.

"Probably escaping while they can," Will said in a low voice.

Kylie looked at Regan with dawning understanding. "Did you..."

"Yes. I bought Peanut Butter."

Kylie gave her head a shake, as though trying to clear it.

"He's a *pony,*" Regan said. "I'm going to

see Madison and try to convince her to be charitable until I can find a ride for my pony."

"Give a yell if you need me to haul him tomorrow," Will called after her.

As it turned out, though, Madison was not only charitable, she was helpful. She arranged a ride from a couple leaving with an empty trailer. Fifteen minutes later Regan watched as Peanut Butter walked into the trailer, the picture of equine amiability. And he was so darned cute.

Will and Trev had to be exaggerating. He was just a pony.

How much trouble could one pony be?

CHAPTER NINE

KYLIE PULLED A booted foot up onto the seat and hugged her arms around her knee as Will turned out of the parking lot. "I can't believe Miss Flynn bought Peanut Butter."

"He is cute."

"Yeah." Kylie cast her father a sidelong glance. "What do you think of her? Miss Flynn, I mean."

"She's a nice lady."

"You act different around her."

Not exactly what Will wanted to hear.

"Do you ever want to, you know, go out with her or anything?"

Will had a feeling that even though she was making an effort to act nonchalant, Kylie was holding her breath as she waited for his answer.

"Would it bother you if I did?"

"Well," Kylie hesitated, then it all poured out. "I like Miss Flynn. She's pretty nice to me most of the time, but, it's kind of gross, you know? Guys your age. My dad and my teacher?" She made a face. "And when my friends' parents date something always goes wrong, then they're all unhappy. My friends say it sucks. They say I'm lucky that you don't do that. Mark's dad has been married three times! Mark says he's not ever getting married. And if he does, he isn't having kids."

"I get your drift," Will said.

"So you're not going to be dating her or anything? Even if she *is* nice to us?"

"I really doubt it."

Kylie sank back in her seat and stared straight ahead, but even in profile she looked relieved.

HOW MUCH TROUBLE can one pony be?

Regan discovered the answer the next morning when she got up just after dawn and found Peanut Butter standing belly deep in her neighbor's garden.

"Ohmigosh!" she muttered as she threw on a robe and shoved her feet into slippers.

She hadn't released the pony into the pasture the night before, since it was risky to put two horses together without giving them a get-acquainted period. So she'd tethered him on a picket line in her backyard, instead.

The pony was able to get close enough to Toffee so that they could familiarize themselves with one another, but not touch or fight. Once they knew each other, Regan would put Peanut Butter in the pasture.

That had been the plan, anyway.

"That your pony?" Her elderly neighbor, whom she'd hoped would still be in bed, called to her from his porch.

"Uh, yes." She attempted a smile as she picked her way through his half acre of pumpkins and gourds—now marked by deep pony prints—and into the corn, where Peanut Butter had taken refuge. "I'll pay for the damage he caused." Not that there should be much, since most of the garden had been harvested.

The old guy harrumphed. "I called animal control, you know."

Regan could honestly say she'd never had cause to deal with animal control before. So what was she supposed to do now?

It didn't really matter, because she knew what she was going to do. She was going to take her pony and run.

"I'll, uh, just take him back to my place until they come."

And then what were they going to do?

Impound Peanut Butter? Charge her with trespassing? Fine her?

She gritted her teeth as Peanut Butter tipped his fuzzy ears forward. "Cute isn't going to cut it this morning, bud. Come on."

She slipped the rope around his neck and pulled him out of the corn as carefully as she could. One of her slippers stuck in the muddy soil and water seeped through her sock. A colorful expletive escaped her as she took a backward step, slipped and fell flat on her butt.

The dry stalks of corn waved above her.

"You okay in there?"

"I'm fine," Regan said through clenched teeth as she got to her feet and wiped a muddy hand on her muddy robe.

She dragged Peanut Butter out of the corn with as much dignity as she could muster while wearing a robe with a wet, muddy butt impression on the back. The old guy started to cackle.

She could see a truck coming in the distance and decided to get Peanut Butter on her property ASAP, just in case it was animal control.

"Come on," she muttered. The little guy trotted companionably beside her. At any other time, it would have been cute.

She examined the halter, still snapped to

the picket line, expecting it to be broken, but it was in one piece and still buckled together.

Regan scratched her head. It fit him too well for him to have slipped it off, and there was nothing he could have rubbed against to get it off. Weird.

She debated, then put the halter back on the pony and snapped the line onto it, hoping he'd stay put while she cleaned herself up. She wanted to be wearing something warmer than a wet robe when she introduced her two horses to each other. If Toffee decided to stomp Peanut Butter—and she wouldn't really blame him at this point—she'd have to rescue the little guy.

She tossed Toffee a flake of hay, just as the truck pulled into her neighbor's yard. It was Will. She jogged to her house, knowing full well that her place would be his next stop, kicked off the muddy slippers and wet socks, sloughed off the robe and quickly dressed in jeans and a sweatshirt. She'd barely zipped up when she heard the knock.

Will stood on the porch, yawning. He had a five-o'clock shadow and his shirt was buttoned crookedly. She pulled open the door and tried to appear nonchalant.

"Yes?"

He wasn't buying it. "Dispatch called me because there was a horse at large."

"Animal control doesn't take horses?"

"They figured it was lost and, since I live close, that I'd know who it belonged to. It would have saved everyone a lot of time, if your neighbor had mentioned it was a pony."

"Am I in trouble?"

"Not if you pay for some pumpkins."

Regan swung the door wider. "You want some coffee?" She felt bad that he'd been dragged out of bed. And since he'd negotiated a settlement with her neighbor, coffee seemed like the least she could do.

"Sure."

But he seemed hesitant. Something had changed since last night.

"Good," she said. "You can keep watch."

"Watch on what?"

"Peanut Butter. Somehow that little…" her mouth tightened as she searched for a polite word "…bugger managed to slip his halter and I want to know how he did it."

Will went to the window while Regan measured coffee and poured water into the reservoir.

"Come here," he said. "I've never seen this before."

Regan clicked on the brewer and went to the window. "I don't believe it," she said. The pony had his head turned back toward his rear end and was methodically working the halter off over his ears with one hind foot.

Regan headed for the door, with Will a few steps behind her.

Peanut Butter looked up, the picture of innocence even though the halter was now only over one ear.

Regan put her hands on her hips. "What do you think?" she asked Will. "Should I tether Toffee and put Peanut Butter in the pen, or should I go for broke?"

"It's a big pasture. Go for broke. They've spent the night within sight of each other."

"All right." Regan freed the pony while Will opened the gate. "I just don't want Toffee to hurt him."

As soon as he was released, Peanut Butter made a beeline for the hay.

"Look at that," Regan said as the pint-sized equine snaked his neck and pinned back his ears, threatening Toffee. "He thinks he's going to scare off a sixteen-hand horse."

"He appears to be doing it."

Sure enough, Toffee whirled and retreated. He stopped a respectful distance away, his ears pricked forward as he studied the pony.

Toffee edged forward toward his hay and Peanut Butter turned his butt and cocked a back foot. Will laughed.

Regan glared at him. "This isn't funny."

"No. It's not." But his eyes were still full of amusement. Regan let out a huff of breath that lifted her bangs, wishing she weren't so aware of how good the man looked when he laughed.

He put a companionable hand on her shoulder and Regan had to force herself not to lean into it. "They'll probably settle in together just fine."

The two watched as Toffee approached cautiously from a different angle. Peanut Butter swung his butt around again and Toffee stopped in his tracks.

"At least Peanut Butter hasn't hurt him yet." Regan went to the haystack and threw another flake of hay a good twenty yards away from the first. Toffee moved toward it, but Peanut Butter headed him off and claimed it for himself. Toffee went back to the original smaller pile of hay.

"I guess I won't worry about him getting fat when I stop riding him this winter."

"Meanwhile, PB will be approaching coronary status."

"Hey."

They both turned to see Regan's neighbor stomping down the driveway.

"When are you going to pay for my ruined pumpkins?"

"Just as soon as…"

"She'll trade you fertilizer for them."

The old man's eyes widened. "Hey, yeah."

"Yes," Regan agreed, quite happy with Will's sudden inspiration. She never would have thought of a trade. "You can have all you want. Bring your wheelbarrow over anytime."

"All right. That would be great." He started back down the drive, then stopped. "I have some beds to work. Mind if I start today?"

"Just watch the pony when you go in and out. He's a slippery little guy."

"You bet. I sure don't want him back at my place."

The timer on the coffeepot beeped. "I never thought horse manure would make someone so happy," Regan said as she headed for the back door. "Thanks for thinking of it."

"No problem." Will stopped at the back step. Their gazes connected for a moment.

He hadn't bothered with the hat this morning. His sun-streaked hair was rumpled. He needed a shave. And Regan was no closer to forgetting how talented he was with his lips than she'd been right after he kissed her. The reckless part of her wanted to take him by the hand, lead him into the house and find out what else he could do. And the sane part of her wasn't protesting as loudly as usual, which concerned her.

"What's wrong, Regan?"

"I… What do you mean?"

"I mean I can practically hear the wheels turning in your head."

"I was just planning my day," she murmured.

He glanced at his watch. "I hate to do this, but I think I'll pass on the coffee. I should get back before the kid starts wondering where I am."

"Will she be up this early?"

"Maybe not, but I'd like to be back when she gets up." He tapped the toe of his boot against the back step, gave her an uncomfortable look. "Kylie's afraid I'm going to start dating you."

"We've spoken."

Will stared at her for a moment. "You've spoken?" Regan nodded and Will rolled his eyes. "I probably don't want the details, but do I need to apologize?"

"She's just worried."

"I guess it's because I've spent more time around you than any other woman during her life."

"She's not buying the friendship angle?"

"I'm not sure *I'm* buying the friendship angle," he said in a low voice.

"It's the only angle we have."

"I know." Yet Regan wondered if he did when he reached out to take a strand of hair behind her ear. His touch was gentle. She could see why the horses responded to it. She was responding, too.

"I have to go."

She gave a silent nod. No question about it. He did have to go.

WILL MANAGED to keep out of Regan's way for two weeks, thinking it would be beneficial to put some distance between them, to get perspective. It sounded good in theory, but in reality all it did was make him more aware of the empty feeling that had enveloped his life over the past several years.

Before he'd met Regan, he'd just lived with that feeling, never allowing himself to think about it too much. Now he not only thought about it, he wanted to do something about it.

But he had no idea what. Especially not when his daughter was so set against him dating—not that he blamed her for her attitude. His own father had brought a long line of women into his life after his mom had died, and it had seemed the quicker Will got attached to one, the quicker she took off. He never wanted Kylie to go through that. And she did have a tendency to get attached. Cranky, old Skitters was living proof.

But he was also damned tired of being alone.

Trev showed up at Will's house on a Wednesday morning, asking for both a cup of coffee and a favor.

"Are you riding the fence line for Meyers this weekend?"

"Sure am." Will cleared the kitchen table of his account books, then poured coffee into the last clean mug and set it in front of Trev. "I'm going on Saturday."

He usually checked the fence in the fall and spring for the older man, riding one of the young horses he had to put miles on and looking for stray cows at the same time.

"Would you, uh, keep an eye out for Geri's hound dogs? Two blueticks."

Will raised a brow. Trev looked away.

It was a long, solitary ride to the high country. Usually, Kylie went with him, but since she was doing volunteer work at the senior center with her 4-H group over the weekend, he was either going alone or… He debated briefly, then gave in.

He called Regan Thursday night.

"I have to ride out and check a fence on Saturday. I was wondering if you'd like to come along. It'll take most the day." The words seemed to fall out of his mouth without a lot of finesse. He was sorely out of practice.

There was a long silence and Will figured the answer would be no. It had been a long shot, after all; one he probably shouldn't have taken. She appeared to have had more common sense than he did.

"What time?"

A slow smile spread across his face. "Eight. You'll need to dress warmly."

REGAN HAD GIVEN UP on trying to keep Peanut Butter in the pasture when she rode. He always managed to maneuver himself under the bottom wire of the fence and would suddenly turn up at a dead gallop somewhere along her route, invariably spooking Toffee. She either had to tie him to the fence high enough so that he couldn't pull his halter-slipping stunt or let him come with her from the start. When she rode cross-country, away from potentially disastrous encounters with vehicles, she let him come along, telling herself he needed the exercise.

Will had obviously not expected the pony to join them. He tipped his hat back when he saw him.

"I can't leave him home alone. Where's Kylie?"

"4-H." Will was still frowning in Peanut Butter's general direction. And then he looked at Regan in that half-direct, half-guarded way he had. "Thanks for coming. Sometimes this makes for a lonely day."

"I'm looking forward to it."

But she had thought Kylie was coming.

They rode directly into the mountains across the valley from Will's house. Peanut Butter would stop every once in a while to eat dry grass as they climbed, then race madly to catch up, his little hooves thundering on the hard ground. It had been a dry fall.

It was Peanut Butter who first spotted the cattle. He was off on one of his mad jaunts, when he suddenly stopped on the crest of a hill and perked his ears. Will urged his horse up to the top and reached into the pocket of his heavy canvas coat for a small pair of field glasses. He bit the corner of his lip as he frowned into the binoculars. He gave his head a shake.

"Is there a problem?"

"They're haired up."

"Pardon?"

"It's hard to read the brands when cattle have their winter coats and I don't want to ride down there unless we have to."

It was a steep hillside and Regan wasn't wild about the idea of riding Toffee down, either, since she didn't know much about his hill abilities yet. Steep hillside could be tricky for a horse who wasn't used to carrying a rider downhill.

"Okay, there's a Bar P on the Angus, and a Rocking O on those two and… Come on, turn around so I can see you. A Diamond Bar… Definitely a mixed bunch."

"Now what do you do?"

"Contact the owners." His voice trailed off and she could see him frown as he moved the glasses.

"Something wrong?"

"Probably not." He put the binoculars back

in his pocket. "Are you hungry yet? I brought some food."

"You did?" Regan was starving and she'd been wishing she'd thought to throw something edible into a coat pocket.

"When you ask someone to work with you, you feed them."

"I didn't realize this was work."

He grinned at her. "Not everybody enjoys a long late-October ride."

"Do you?" She asked as he dismounted. She imagined it was second nature for him to spend long days in the saddle, regardless of the weather.

"When I have company, it's not bad." That surprised her, since Will struck her as a man who preferred his own company. "And I thought you might like to see some country."

He led his horse toward a granite outcropping and tied the gelding to a tree. Regan dismounted and followed, loosely looping Toffee's reins over the same gnarled tree, hoping the gelding wouldn't pull back and break them.

Will had already settled at the base of a cluster of big rocks, out of the wind, and Regan went to sit close to him. They ate the sandwiches he'd packed in his saddlebags, then shared a bottle of water. The horses moved together as the wind picked up and the pony slipped in between them, using the two larger animals as a windbreak. Regan took her cue from them and moved toward Will, borrowing some of his warmth. He didn't seem to mind. In fact, he settled his arm around her, pulling her even closer. Regan rested her cheek against the rough canvas of his coat and stared out over the valley, feeling warm and secure in spite of the wind. She liked this place, so wild and isolated. And she liked this man. Maybe more than she should.

A large hawk glided on the air currents above them, lofting before slowly spiraling down. They watched the bird until he finally spotted prey and dove. It must have been a successful hit because he did not reappear in the sky.

Regan figured it was probably a sign that it was time to go, but she was reluctant to move out of Will's embrace, away from his warmth. Away from him.

"You know," Will said, his eyes still on the spot where the bird had disappeared, "I think we're edging closer to one of those moments that'll give us pause later." His arm tightened around her.

Regan smiled at his phrasing. She'd been

doing some thinking and had come to some conclusions of her own. Will was a grown man. It wasn't her job to protect him from himself. Her only job was to set her own ground rules and pay attention to his.

"I can go with the moment just fine, as long as we understand that's what it is. Just a moment in time."

"Sweetheart, that's exactly what it is."

His mouth settled on hers, to punctuate the point. She sighed against his lips, wondered why she had expended so much energy trying to avoid this. His face was cold to the touch, but his mouth was wonderfully warm. Wet. Hot. For a guy who'd been out of circulation for a while, he had skills to be proud of. By the time they came up for air, she was practically lying on top of him. And she was not exactly in a hurry to get off.

"You've had me running scared, Will."

"Why?"

"Do you want the short list or the long list?"

"Your choice." He ran his hand up over her heavy coat, cradling her against him. His breath was warm against her face.

"Because we live in a small town and we can't exactly pal around without exciting comment. Heck, we couldn't even share a pizza without causing a stir."

"True."

"And because you have a daughter who doesn't want you to date just yet."

He nodded, his expression sobering a bit.

"And because I am serious about keeping my independence."

"So why is it you aren't looking to get involved with anyone?" he asked, lightly brushing her windblown hair away from their faces.

"I just don't want to deal with it."

"It's you or them?" he asked quietly.

She raised her head, her eyes widening a little as he put her exact sentiments into words.

"I have this habit of picking losers."

"I'm no loser, Regan."

"I know. That's why you kind of terrify me." But she didn't tell him the last man in her life hadn't looked like a loser, either.

He smiled, kissed her lips one last time, lightly, making her want more, then eased her off. "I guess that may be a good thing. Come on. We'd better get going."

They rode back along a different route, following the fence line toward the valley. There was a rutted dirt track running parallel and the horses plodded down it, side by side, with Peanut Butter taking up the rear, keeping out of the wind. Suddenly, Will raised his chin, his eyes narrowing.

"What?"

"There's someone coming up the road."

Regan glanced down at the ground. "What road?" And then she, too, heard the whine of an engine.

"Let's get off to the side a bit." He walked his horse several yards off the track, with Regan, Toffee and Peanut Butter all following.

"Dismount, would you?"

Regan did as he asked, wondering what was happening as he, too, dismounted.

"Come here."

She stepped closer, holding Toffee on a loose rein.

He reached out and took her hand. "Walk with me."

"All right." She wondered what was up, but did as he asked.

They walked hand in hand, slowly, leading their horses, Toffee staying out of her space like the good boy he now was and Peanut Butter poking along at the rear. Will's grip tightened as the vehicle, a beat-up dually pickup, came up over the crest of the hill, its engine roaring with the effort, then his fingers relaxed slightly.

"Do you know who it is?" Regan asked

"I recognize the rig, but not the driver." Will lifted their interlinked hands to his lips and kissed her knuckles in an old-fashioned gesture. And Regan felt an old-fashioned tingle start in her toes and move upward.

"What are you doing?" she inquired through her teeth.

"I'm trying my best to look like I'm here for pleasure, instead of business, and I hope I'm far enough away from those cows for them to buy it."

Her gaze strayed to the pickup, which was moving steadily past. Will lifted a hand in casual greeting, then dropped his arm around Regan's shoulders as they walked on. She leaned into him.

"Where does the road go?"

"To the next valley."

"To the cattle?"

"Yep."

The pickup rolled out of sight and Will slowly released her.

"I'd like to get to where I can talk to Trev. I won't have service on my cell phone here."

"You'll need to give me a leg up." Toffee

was so tall that the stirrup was too high for her to reach comfortably without a mounting aid.

"We need to get you a real saddle."

Regan smirked at him over her shoulder. He cupped his hands and she stepped into them, letting him boost her lightly into the seat. He mounted his own horse with that inimitably smooth motion that all good cowboys seemed to have.

"Forgive my denseness, but I don't understand what the big deal is. It isn't like they can steal a cow with a pickup."

"No, but they can feed them and hold them in one place until a trailer comes to get them. There were two bales of hay in the bed of that pickup."

"Oh."

KYLIE WAS ALREADY HOME by the time Will rode into the yard. He rubbed down his horse and put away the tack. He'd managed to get hold of Trev a few miles from his house and broke the bad news that he hadn't spotted Geri's hounds, then said that a few people needed to ride out to Munson Creek and collect their animals before they disappeared.

"I don't know who was driving, but it was that truck Charley keeps behind the barn."

"Well, Charley was helping us ship cattle today, so it wasn't him. Maybe I'll give him a call and see if he sold that rig."

"Sounds good."

Kylie had dinner going, including a pot of simmering green beans. A vegetable! Will assumed that meant she was about to ask for something she probably wasn't going to get, but it turned out that she was simply celebrating.

"Sadie and Chad broke up," she said conversationally, before heading back to her room with Stubby at her heels.

"Too bad," Will called after her, playing the game even though he knew Kylie wouldn't be too upset over the downturn in her friend's love life.

"Yeah. It is." She came back down the hall a few minutes later, pulling her hair into a ponytail. "Sadie said she was sorry she ignored me. I think she meant it."

"I'm sure she did." Will checked the spuds, then drained the excess water into the sink.

"We made this deal. We won't put boyfriends ahead of us being friends."

Will couldn't say he liked the casual way she dropped the *B* word, but he kept quiet. Boyfriends were going to happen. But they would be well screened and well managed. And if that didn't work, he'd invest in a porch and a shotgun.

"How was the ride?" Kylie asked, as she put the plates on the table.

"It was good." He took a breath, came clean. "You should probably know that I asked Miss Flynn to come with me." Her hand hovered for a moment, then she put the forks next to the plates.

"Why?" The single word tugged at his heart.

"Because she likes to ride and I thought it would be nice to show her some country."

"Okay."

But Will had a feeling it wasn't.

CHAPTER TEN

REGAN COULDN'T BELIEVE IT. She'd been called to the office. Again. And this time it had nothing to do with squid.

Pete Domingo handed her a policy manual. Regan frowned at the booklet, then at Pete.

"I know you have one of these, but there is something in it I'd like to point out. Would you please turn to page forty-eight and read subsection four?"

Regan knew that whatever she found on page forty-eight was going to make her angry and she was correct. After reading the vaguely worded policy, she looked up, her expression clear.

"I'm not certain I understand what you're getting at here."

"It's extremely clear, Miss Flynn. You are not to become involved with the parent of a student, while that student is under your sphere of influence."

"Define *become involved*."

"I think you know exactly what it means."

"You'd better give me some specifics."

"Will Bishop was seen driving away from your house very, *very* early in the morning a few weeks ago."

Regan's temper jacked up another notch. "So what? He was visiting." And just who had reported this incident? Her manure-shoveling neighbor? Someone who'd been driving by? And why would anyone mention this to Pete, unless he'd asked?

"At six a.m.?"

"He was there in a professional capacity."

Pete smirked. "You two were seen kissing at a community event. Was that also done in a professional capacity?"

Regan felt an unpleasant jolt of surprise, but fought to keep her expression serene. "By whom?" she asked pleasantly.

He smiled. "By me."

"Engaging in a little voyeurism, Pete?"

"No," he sputtered. "It was hard to miss."

It had been dark. He had to have been following them, which was more than a little disturbing. It sounded as if Pete was doing surveillance on her. Apparently standards training and the dessert table had not been punishment enough.

"What I do during my free time in my own business."

Pete tapped the manual.

"Oh, come on. The date on that is 1980 and I have a feeling that board attitudes have changed since then."

He placed both palms flat on the desk and leaned forward, his expression belligerent. "The important thing is that the policy is in writing."

Regan took a moment to study the framed photo of a much younger and slimmer Pete wearing a baseball uniform, and compared it to the older, more full-figured Pete leaning next to it. Not a happy contrast.

"Frankly," she said, "this smacks of desperation. I don't appreciate you spying on me and you're not going to intimidate me with an out-of-date policy manual."

"And I'm not going to have a teacher on my staff who is not a team player."

Ah, yes. The united front. She remembered the pep talk he'd given her after their first meeting with Will and Kylie.

"It isn't officially your staff yet," Regan reminded him softly.

"It *will* be my staff. If you keep trying to make trouble for me, you'll wish you hadn't." The veins were starting to bulge in his forehead.

"You're threatening me," Regan stated flatly.

"I'm informing you of school policy."

Regan turned on her heel and walked out of the office.

THE MEETING HAD MADE HER LATE for her jumping lesson. She went home and dressed in jeans and a heavy sweatshirt, fuming the entire time. The thing that really annoyed her was that she was taking such great pains *not* to get involved with Will, other than a little harmless kissing. It was like being accused of a crime she had yet to commit. Not that she thought Pete was actually going to follow through on the matter. If he brought the issue before the board he wouldn't accomplish anything other than making himself look foolish. Extremely foolish.

So why was he pursuing this?

Because he wants to get rid of you.

And then the second part of the answer came to her in a flash.

Because he's planting seeds.

If he put enough small things together,

well, it wouldn't do her professional reputation any good. That was a certainty. The question was, could he do any major damage? Regan had a bad feeling that he could. Especially with Zach's uncle on the school board.

Pete Domingo was not a man who shrugged off embarrassment—especially the kind Regan had caused. Instead, he got even.

Regan pulled into the arena parking lot ten minutes late. Her students were waiting, including a new one—Sadie.

"I hope you don't mind," she said to Regan. "I, uh, well, my mom borrowed my grandma's English saddle, because Kylie told my mom it was fun and Mom thought…"

"I'm glad you could come," Regan said, pleased that Sadie and Kylie's friendship was apparently on the road to recovery. "We'll just have you work on some basics for a bit."

REGAN HAD TO PASS Will's horse trailer on the way to her car and as she approached, she could see that Kylie was working on her father, trying to wheedle something out of him as she unsaddled her horse.

"Dad, maybe we could borrow Madison's saddle for the weekend?" Kylie was using her most persuasive voice. "She doesn't have a class and she says its okay."

"You mean rent a saddle, don't you?"

"I have allowance coming."

"You want to borrow my saddle for the weekend?" Regan asked. She wasn't going to be riding, due to an overload of grading. Kylie swung around excitedly.

"For real?" she asked. "Because Sadie and I were going to build some jumps of our own and practice. Low ones," she added with a glance at her father. "A whole jumping course out in the field. We could do different patterns."

"If you want to stop by my place on your way home, it's in the utility room. I'm going to meet Tanya—Miss Prescott—for dinner, but my back door is unlocked."

Kylie was practically bouncing. "Can we, Dad?"

Will met Regan's gaze over Kylie's head. Regan nodded and he gave her a half smile.

"Sure," he said. "And I imagine you'll have it oiled up, Kylie, before you return it?"

"You know I will. It's a long weekend. Can I have it until Monday?"

"I'll stop by Monday afternoon and pick it up."

"We'll drop it by your house," Will said.

"I have to shop sometime. I'll just swing by on my way home."

"Thanks for the loan," Kylie said, grinning broadly as she untied her horse. "This is going to be so cool."

Regan smiled and started for her car, glad at least one positive thing had come out of the afternoon. She waved at Will as she drove past the trailer, wondering how he'd react if he knew that Pete was spying on him, too. She had a feeling he might do something about it.

Brett phoned her early that evening, while Regan was still debating about Pete.

"I'm coming to Wesley this weekend. Are you interested in dinner?"

"That would be nice," Regan replied without hesitation.

"Great. Do you want me to pick you up or do you want to meet?"

"Let's meet."

"The Supper Club?"

"That would be perfect." Regan hung up with a feeling of satisfaction. There was no law against fraternizing with students' uncles and she hoped this might put a crimp in Pete's seed planting. How serious could she be about a parent, if she was going out with his brother?

A call from Regan's mother less than an hour later provided the perfect punctuation to the end of a weird day.

"Check your e-mail."

"Why?" Regan asked, instinctively cautious.

"I think you'll find something interesting."

"Mom…"

"I forwarded a job bulletin. It's perfect for you. Exactly like the job you applied for last spring."

"I like the job I've got."

"Regan."

"Mom."

"At least take a look."

"I will," Regan promised halfheartedly, then changed the subject to her mother's newest project. Arlene allowed herself to be sidetracked, but they both knew it had been her decision. If she'd wanted to discuss Regan's future further, they'd still be talking about it.

THE PARKING LOT of the Supper Club was close to full when Regan pulled in. Brett got out of an older model pickup truck and crossed the lot to meet her, walking with the easy gait of a natural athlete.

"I'm glad you decided to come." He reached out to close her car door for her.

"It's good to see you, too," Regan replied as they started across the parking lot. He had the same good looks as Will, the same rugged sensuality, but he somehow looked more careworn. Regan had a feeling that life had kicked him around a bit.

Brett opened the heavy wooden door of the club, ushering her inside. "This place used to have decent steaks."

"It still does. I eat here every now and then." As in twice. With Tanya. On payday.

When they walked into the dining area, people noticed. It reminded her of the night she'd gone out for pizza with Will. Did the Bishops *never* go out?

They had a drink while they waited for their menus and Brett pretended not to notice that people were checking him out.

"How long since you've been here?" Regan finally asked.

"A long time."

Regan smiled wryly. Brett ordered another beer.

The meals came just as a three-piece combo started to play. Brett seemed to relax a little as the drinks kicked in and the patrons who'd been watching him earlier either left or lost interest. He started to tell stories about working in Montana, his rodeo days, his hopes of going to college someday, which were rapidly fading now that he was thirty.

He asked Regan about Las Vegas, and although he seemed interested in her response, she sensed something just under the surface. Something that was keeping him on edge.

After the waiter refilled Regan's coffee cup, toward the end of the meal, she decided to find out what it was.

"Why'd you ask me out, Brett?"

He didn't even try to hedge. "I wanted to ask you about my brother."

Regan's fork hovered over the last of her cheesecake. "Your brother?"

Brett peeled a thin strip of paper from the label of his beer bottle, twisting it between his fingers. "I was kind of curious about how he's doing."

"Why ask me?" Regan asked, genuinely perplexed. There were many town gossips who knew a heck of a lot more than she did.

"Because if I ask anybody else, it'll get back to him."

"Do you really care if it does?"

"Yeah." And it sounded as if he meant it.

Regan placed her fork on the dessert plate and pushed it aside. "I think he's doing all

right, but I really don't know that much."
Except that he punched her buttons in a way
that Brett did not. "He's doing well with his
horse business."

The answer was basic, but Brett seemed
satisfied with even that small amount of information.

"Does he seem, I don't know… Happy?"

Regan thought this was an odd question,
but she answered him. "Yes. He does." *In a
lonely sort of way.*

Brett fiddled with the paper. "And Kylie?
I was wondering, what kind of a kid is she?"

"A great kid."

He grinned tentatively. "Is she?"

"Yes. She's smart, outspoken, loyal and
protective."

"Sounds like Will. Except for the outspoken part."

"I think she takes after him. A lot."

"Good grades?"

"Like I said, she's smart."

Brett was silent for a moment, as though
he was going over what he'd just heard and
was taking his time processing the information. Regan studied him over her coffee cup.

"So, what happened with you and Will?"
she finally asked.

"We had a falling out a long time ago."

Well, there was a load of information. Almost as much as she'd given him.

"And you don't think you'll ever work things out?"

"I doubt it, since neither of us is likely to try."

Regan opened her mouth. She honestly thought that if Brett wasn't interested in trying, he wouldn't be sitting with her, asking questions about his brother and his niece. But instinct told her to close her mouth and keep her thoughts to herself. She changed the subject.

"To be honest with you, I'm here for more than one reason myself." Brett looked up and she continued. "My principal thinks I'm carrying on with the parent of a student. I thought that having dinner with you would muddy the waters a little." And from the way people had been staring at them since they'd arrived, she was certain word would get back to Pete in no time. She just hoped there wasn't a section of the policy manual that dealt with this situation. It was a pretty thick book.

Brett leaned back in his chair, eyeing Regan with new respect.

"Who's the parent?"

"Will."

He started twisting the label again. "Are you carrying on with him?"

"No." At least, not yet. She set her coffee cup back on the saucer and waited for Brett's next question.

He frowned. "Then why…?"

"It's a long story, but it boils down to the fact that Pete doesn't like me."

Brett fiddled with the twisted bits of paper for another moment, then pushed them aside. "You want to dance?" he asked with a conspiratorial smile. "Give those muddy waters a swirl?"

Regan put her napkin on the table. "As a matter of fact, I do."

True to his word, Brett didn't try to hit on her. They danced, they talked and they laughed. Two hours later, he opened her car door for her, offered his hand, then kissed her cheek.

Regan gave him a light kiss back and then drove home thinking about the brothers. Brett, who seemed to want to reconnect with his family, but had no idea how to do it; and Will, who'd never even let his daughter meet her uncle.

What on earth had happened between the two of them?

WILL WAS WORKING a horse when Regan drove into his yard on her way home from shopping. He glanced over his shoulder, then refocused his attention on the mare. Regan parked and got out.

She watched for a few minutes, letting him finish. Finally, Will patted the horse, then walked to the gate, glancing at her only briefly.

"Hi," Regan said. "I came to pick up the saddle."

Will nodded, barely meeting her gaze. Something was up. Bad morning with Kylie, perhaps, or a bad morning with a horse. He headed for the barn and Regan followed.

The tack room was clean, well organized. Will walked to a wall-mounted saddle rack and pulled down her saddle. Regan reached for it, but he said, "I'll take it to your car."

"I can manage." She took the saddle from him and headed for her vehicle.

He opened the door and she settled the saddle onto the backseat.

"Bad morning?" Regan asked as she straightened up. Will closed the car door.

"I've had better."

"So've I," Regan said.

"How was your evening?"

Regan stilled.

Innocent question; not so innocent tone. In fact, a person could read a lot into a tone like that—especially with Will looking at her with a stormy expression she'd never seen before. And there was no doubt which evening he was talking about.

"What's it to you?"

"Nothing."

Oh yeah. She believed that. Regan drew herself up straighter. She'd had enough judgment, meddling and passive-aggressive nonsense to last a lifetime, and she wasn't going to take any from a guy who had no right to comment on what she did or didn't do. If Will had a problem with her dating his brother... Well, it really wasn't any of his business.

"I think I'd better be going."

"Did he ask about Kylie?" The blunt question surprised her.

"In passing. He asked about you, too. Maybe you should put him on your Christmas-card list. You know, keep him updated?"

"Hey, Dad!" Kylie yelled from the porch. "Trev's on the phone. He says it's important."

Regan gave him a tight smile, opened her car door and stepped inside.

The last thing she saw in her rearview mirror

was Will walking toward the house. She drove home with her jaw set so hard that it ached by the time she pulled into her own driveway.

WILL TOLD HIMSELF to stay home, to leave it alone, but he'd been a first-class jerk and he needed to explain—as much as he could, anyway. Or apologize. Or both.

He rapped on Regan's screen door.

"What?" she said, as soon as she opened the door.

"I came to apologize." But his tone did not sound apologetic. Even to his ears it sounded harsh, stressed.

"Thank you. I accept." She stared at him stonily, obviously waiting for him to leave. But he wasn't ready to go.

"We all have our knee-jerk responses, Regan. Brett just happens to bring out mine."

"Brett?" She said his brother's name with surprise.

He frowned. "Yes, Brett. What else?"

"Oh, I don't know. Maybe you thinking you had a right to comment on my life, because we've kissed each other a couple of times. I don't do well with possessiveness— or control."

She glanced away, but Will gently reached

out to cup her chin in his hand, bringing her focus back to him. He was surprised she didn't pull away; her eyes were cold.

"This was about Brett, Regan."

"Maybe to you." She shifted her chin so that his hand fell away. Apparently, he'd hit a hell of a nerve.

Finally, she spoke. "Is there some reason I shouldn't go to dinner with your brother? I mean, is there some problem I don't know about?"

It was his turn to remain silent. He couldn't tell her the real reason going out with Brett bothered him and "I'm jealous" wouldn't cut it, either.

"So where do we go from here?" he asked. It had become more than evident he wasn't going to talk about Brett.

"I think, for right now, it would be a lot less complicated if you were a parent and I was a teacher."

"Regan…"

She started back inside the house. "Oh, and one more thing. If I want to go out with your brother, I will."

It was all Will could do not to kick something on his way to the truck.

IT REALLY WAS a dream job.

Regan had finally opened her mother's forwarded job bulletin at school. It was a curriculum-implementation position with an independent educational consulting firm, Learning Tech. She'd be able to go into classrooms, demonstrate curriculum, lead seminars, train teachers.... And one of her college friends, Cheryl Riscal, was the human resources director.

She couldn't believe how good it looked.

Kylie and Sadie walked into class together as Regan closed down her computer. They were whispering, and Regan watched as Sadie walked by her former beau without even noticing that he was now talking to another girl.

"Okay," Regan said to her class, "I hope you did your genetic trait charts last night, because we're going to use that information today."

Teenagers loved anything that had to do with themselves, so Regan always started her genetics unit with a lesson on dominant and recessive traits and had the students record some of their own characteristics.

Regan collected the papers, then pulled out two charts at random. "Names will be withheld to protect the innocent," she said.

"I'll read the traits of parent A and the traits of parent B and, assuming that they are not hybrids, you tell me what traits the offspring will have. First we have tongue roller and non-tongue roller."

Hands shot up. Regan pointed at Sadie.

"Tongue roller," Sadie replied, with a smirk at Tyler, who always tried to answer every question.

"Why?" Regan asked.

"Tongue rolling is a dominant characteristic."

"Next, parent A has blue eyes and parent B has blue…"

"Blue eyes!" Tyler blurted out.

"What makes you so sure?" Regan asked.

"Two recessives cannot produce a dominant characteristic. Blue is recessive."

"All right, let's shift the rules a little—and no yelling out the answers, Tyler. The parents *are* hybrid, both having one brown eye gene and one blue eye gene. What percentage of offspring will have brown eyes?"

Pencils scribbled across scraps of paper and then several hands went up.

"Seventy-five percent," Tyler announced.

Regan gave him the death ray.

"Sorry."

"Does anyone agree with Tyler—who will be in the hall, if he yells out again?"

Most of the hands went up, except for Kylie, who was still scribbling on her scratch paper. She reached for her science book and opened it up to the chapter they'd just read.

Well, at least she was on subject, Regan thought. She read the next two characteristics and the class continued to chart the imaginary offspring of hypothetical parent A and parent B. Tyler managed to keep his mouth shut, thus remaining in the classroom, and Kylie eventually put away her book and joined in the discussion, but by that time Regan was practically done with the exercise. She handed out worksheets and started the students working in pairs. Kylie and Sadie not only paired up, they spent more time whispering than working.

And for once Regan just let it go.

REGAN'S MOTHER called that evening, to see if she'd applied for the position with Learning Tech.

"Not yet," Regan replied, balancing the receiver on her shoulder as she shoved clothes into the dryer.

"Regan, you're crazy to let this slide by. You

were the one who wanted out of the classroom and here's the perfect opportunity. *And* you're acquainted with the person who'll be hiring."

"I'm not so certain I want out of the classroom any more. I'm enjoying the kids this year."

There was silence on the other end of the phone, then her mother said, "At least apply, Regan."

"I'll think about it. No promises."

Regan held her ground for five more tiring minutes before her mother abruptly changed the subject—something she always did when she was losing. "Did Claire tell you about my holiday plans?"

"No," Regan replied, relieved to be on a different topic.

Arlene drew in a breath. "Stephen and I are going to Vancouver, British Columbia, for Thanksgiving."

It was obvious from her brittle tone that Arlene was not happy. She'd never been one to travel for pleasure, so Stephen must have given her a heck of an ultimatum.

"I'm glad you're going to be able to relax instead of working."

"Yes," Arlene murmured with dose of

sarcasm. "We'll stay in Las Vegas for Christmas, though. I'll see you then."

WILL HAD TO ATTEND two peace-officer training sessions during the month of November. The first was an overnighter in Ely. Thankfully, Kylie and Sadie had made up, so Kylie had a place to stay. But she didn't seem all that excited to go.

"You do want to go to Sadie's, right?"

Kylie nodded, but something was off. He'd sensed it for a few days now and was wondering if she and Sadie were having trouble again.

"Honestly."

"Honestly, Dad. I think I'll go brush Skitters."

The mare had developed a real bond with Kylie—possibly because, while ignoring Sadie, Kylie had spent a lot of time with her. But Will still didn't know if he would ever let Kylie ride the mare outside the round pen or arena. She was simply too unpredictable— quiet one moment and explosive the next. At least with him. He'd sacked her out in every possible way, worked at teaching her to shy in place and she could do it. When she chose to.

She'd pulled her buck-and-roll stunt on Will again, letting him know she hadn't accidentally lost her footing the first time. Kylie assured him it would be different with her, but Will wasn't ready to take a chance with his only child. A rolling horse could kill someone.

Will packed his duffel and even though he told himself that everything was fine with Kylie, he couldn't squelch the nagging feeling that something was wrong.

He hated leaving under these conditions, but he finally gave in and called Sadie's mom. The nice thing about Beth was that she'd already raised Sadie's two other sisters and she knew when to panic and when to step back.

Beth assured him that all was well between the two girls and hinted that maybe it was just hormones kicking in.

Hormones. Great. Well, he'd better get used to it. Hormones were pretty much a fact of life, and from what he'd seen, they were likely to get worse before they got better.

But Beth wasn't so positive about her hormone theory by the time Will came to pick Kylie up again.

"You know, Will..." There was something in her voice that alerted him. "You're right. Kylie is...well, distracted seems the best way to put it. She's not herself."

He absorbed her words. "Any idea?"

"She and Sadie seem to be thick as thieves again, but she's quieter than I've ever seen her. We had to make a trip back to your place to get a few things she forgot and— I don't know if this means anything, but she brought back her picture of Desiree."

"She did?"

"I saw it in Sadie's room." She tilted her head. "This might just be part of not having a mom at a time when a girl kind of needs a mom."

Will let out a breath. "Not much I can do about that right now."

"No. But maybe you could talk to her. I know it's hard for you to talk about Desiree, but Kylie might have questions and maybe she's afraid to ask."

"Kylie afraid?"

"Maybe."

"All right. I'll, uh, see what I can do."

Kylie was quiet on the way home. Too quiet. Usually, when Will picked her up after a trip she was bubbling with excitement.

He started to ask if everything was all right, but stopped himself. He'd asked that before and it had gotten him exactly nowhere.

He waited until they were in the house. "Hey, I'm feeling like popcorn. What do you say?"

"Okay."

"I'll make it. Why don't you take your stuff to your room? Grab an ice-cube tray from the back refrigerator on your way."

"Sure."

When they were settled at the sofa with the bowl of popcorn between them and a couple of sodas sitting on the coffee table, Will dove into a subject he generally preferred not to think about, much less talk about. But he'd do this for his daughter.

"Um, Kylie?"

She frowned at his odd tone and he didn't blame her. He pushed on. "I know you've been thinking a lot lately and I was wondering… Do you have any questions about your mom?"

Kylie's gaze flashed up at him and her mouth dropped open. For a moment they stared at one another and somewhere, deep down, Will had a feeling that he was about to walk a tightrope. He was right, but it wasn't the one he was expecting.

"Maybe." She pressed her lips together for a moment, then blurted out, "I'm adopted, right?"

CHAPTER ELEVEN

"ADOPTED?"

"Yeah," Kylie said softly, her dark gaze clinging to his.

He moved the popcorn to the coffee table. "Why would you think you were adopted?" His mouth was dry and he had a hard time getting the words out.

"I don't look like my mother."

Relief washed over him. "You look just like your mother."

She sent him an incredulous look. "I have her picture. She's beautiful."

"So are you." He pulled her close then and hugged her tight, rejoicing that this was easier than he'd thought it would be.

"My face is all roundish and hers isn't. She has cheekbones." She spoke against his chest.

"In that picture, your mother was about eight years older than you are now. Someday you're going to look so much like her you'll be amazed." He expected to feel her relax, but she didn't. She pulled away to look up at him.

"Then what about my eyes?"

He frowned. "What about your eyes?"

"They're brown. We learned in science class that two blue-eyed people can't have a brown-eyed kid."

For a moment he was speechless. Tears were welling up in those brown eyes and he automatically reached out to wipe them away, but they only came faster, running silently down her face.

Words jumbled together in his mind. He wanted to tell her there were exceptions to genetic rules, but it felt too much like a lie, so instead he gave her an undeniable truth.

"Kylie, I was there when you were born. My name and your mom's name are on the birth certificate. I'll show it to you."

"Really?"

He let out a breath, surprised at how shaky it was.

"Really."

"I don't need to see it."

"Maybe I'd like to show it to you. Wait here."

A few minutes later he came back with the colorful certificate, and sat beside her while she looked at it. It listed the hospital, the doctor, the parents—Desiree Rose Bishop and William Trenton Bishop. Time of birth, date of birth, baby's name—Kylie Marie Bishop. Will remembered how shell-shocked he'd been when he'd helped the nurse fill out the details. He hadn't wanted anything to do with the birth, but he'd been there for his wife's sake—still hoping that maybe, once they had the child, she would settle down and they could try to work through the mistakes they'd both made.

As to being a father? It was a concept he couldn't begin to fathom, especially under the circumstances in which he found himself. He'd assumed he'd play an emotionally distant role, as his father had played in his own life, and hadn't counted on falling in love with the squalling pink bundle the nurse placed in his arms. He hadn't known it was merely a reflex action that made Kylie clamp onto his thumb with those tiny fingers. To him it represented the beginning of a lifelong bond and he knew then that he would try his hardest to make his marriage work, if for no other reason than to give this little miracle a decent life.

Unfortunately, Des hadn't been able to make the same commitment.

He reached out now to stroke his

daughter's hair as she held the certificate, intently reading every word. And then she handed it back.

"Thanks, Dad."

"No problem, kid."

"I, uh, don't really feel like popcorn."

"That's okay."

"I think I might just go to bed."

"Sure." She gave him a quick hug and started toward the hall. "Kylie?"

She turned back.

"You should keep that photo of your mom out where you can see it."

She shook her head. "Not yet."

As soon as she was gone, Will sank back onto the sofa, spreading his arms out along the back and tipping his head up to study the ceiling. He'd always had a feeling this day would come, but he'd tried to tell himself it wouldn't.

There was no denying what it said on the birth certificate, but there was also no denying the color of his daughter's eyes.

He just hoped, with all his heart, that Kylie would be satisfied by the birth certificate. He'd worked so hard to give her a stable life, to protect her. It would kill him if it all started to unravel now.

TREV SWUNG BY the next morning, just after the school bus had left. Kylie had been subdued as she got ready for school and Will was uneasy. He didn't know if he'd convinced her, didn't know what else he could do but ride out the storm and hope for the best.

"You want some coffee?" Will needed a healthy dose of caffeine after yet another long night.

"Are you all right?" Trev asked as Will started to dump generous scoops of coffee into a filter basket.

Will knew, if Trev felt the need to comment, he was looking bad, so he added one more scoop for good measure. "I'm fine."

Trev didn't say another word until Will finished making the coffee and turned to lean back against the pine cabinets. "What time do you want to leave?"

"I have to bring Kylie's horse home after jumping class, so I'll meet you at six."

"Sounds good. It'll give me time to trim that horse Madison just bought. His feet are a mess."

Kind of like my life, Will thought.

WILL STAYED for the jumping class. He watched for a while, then paced, watched, then paced some more, his hands shoved deep in his coat pockets. It was cold in the arena. Madison didn't have the blowers on, but Regan didn't think that was why Will was pacing. Something was wrong—something more than their small blowup.

Regan hugged her arms against her chest and walked over to give Sadie advice on her seat. Will turned and paced toward the door. Regan forced herself to focus on her class as they gathered their things and headed for the door themselves.

Her car was close to Will's trailer. Too close, really, but she'd parked there first. Will was opening the rear door as she approached.

"Cold today," she commented, refusing to let herself walk by without acknowledging him. Too small a community for that. And the weather was a safe topic for passing conversation—much better than anything else they'd discussed recently.

"Yeah." He didn't look at her as he led the horse inside.

She drew in a breath, debated. Common sense lost.

"What's wrong?" If he was still upset about the other day, she was ready to have it out again, and maybe—grudgingly—ready to make peace.

"Blue eyes," he muttered from inside the trailer, in such a low voice she knew she wasn't supposed to have heard. He exited and slammed the door shut, hooked the latch.

"Excuse me?"

"Nothing." He made an effort to sound civil as he edged between her car and his trailer. "Good lesson today. You have a knack with the kids." A cardboard speech, delivered to placate her and send her on her way.

Regan frowned after him as he walked to his truck and got inside. A second later the trailer was pulling away.

Two seconds later, Regan had an epiphany. *Blue eyes...*

Will was unloading the horse when she pulled into his driveway. She parked beside his truck as he released the gelding into the pasture. She had no idea what to say, but she knew she had to say something.

He latched the gate as she stopped a few feet away from him. For a moment they stood staring at one another. "Is this a parent-teacher visit?" he finally asked.

"In a way."

He set his jaw. Waited. Regan felt a sense of trepidation.

"Does Kylie's mom have blue eyes?"

He didn't answer, which was confirmation enough for her. Kylie had dark eyes. Her parents both had blue eyes. Regan had really hammered on about blue eyes during her genetics lesson.

She felt sick to her stomach.

She should have told the class that it was possible in rare cases for two blue-eyed people to have a dark-eyed child. Kylie was obviously one of those cases. Regan could only imagine how upset the kid must be.

"I had no idea…"

"How could you have?" Will asked bluntly before she could tell him she'd rectify the mistake the first chance she got.

"I'd appreciate it if you didn't, you know, let on about this. I don't think too many people know, and, well, Kylie…" He broke off, glanced away.

Regan stilled. "What are you talking about, Will?"

A swirl of frigid wind hit them and Regan hunched her shoulders against it. Will was now staring at her, apparently oblivious to the cold until she shoved her hands deeper into her pockets. "You want to go in the house?" he asked gruffly.

"Yes."

He started across the drive and Regan followed, pulling her coat tightly around her.

"Trev'll be here soon. We're going to Reno for a peace-officers' training course." He held the door open and Regan stepped into the warm of house.

As soon as he closed the door she said, "First thing on Monday, I'll explain to the classes that blue-eyed people can have dark-eyed children. It's not a true brown, but…"

"Kylie doesn't have a blue-eyed father. She has a brown-eyed father." Will leaned back against the counter, looking at her with his blue-gray eyes. "You can see why I have issues with Brett and the fact that he's back?"

There was a long, uncomfortable moment of silence, then Regan nodded. She remembered how interested Brett had been in Kylie and suddenly it took on a whole new meaning. Will's reaction to her going out with Brett had a new meaning, too.

"Has Kylie figured it out?"

"She's working on it. I don't quite know how to handle this." Will looked up at the ceiling and she knew he was barely holding on. She took a step toward him, but he put up his hand.

"Parent-teacher," he said softly.

"Screw parent-teacher."

"You need to make up your mind here, Regan."

He had a point, but she didn't back away.

"I'm sorry," she said in a whisper. Then they both heard the sound of a truck pulling to a stop. "That's Trev."

The screen door squeaked as it opened a moment later.

"It'll be okay," Will said. He swallowed. "It'll work out."

"Yes," Regan agreed, as Trev gave a perfunctory knock before pushing the door open.

She wished at least one of them could believe that.

REGAN HAD A MESSAGE waiting on her phone when she got home. It was from Cheryl at Learning Tech. She would appreciate it if Regan would return her call on Monday, concerning an opening they had. Regan exhaled as she hung up the phone. Her mother must have contacted Cheryl. Or, at the very least, somehow let her know that Regan was looking. Which she was not.

Regan went out to feed Toffee and fume a little. She liked being four hundred miles away from Las Vegas. Arlene was crazy if she thought Regan was going to move back.

She put Peanut Butter inside the fence before she started tossing hay. He no longer wandered over to the neighbor's place when he escaped, but instead seemed content to graze on the dry grass just outside the pasture. He and Toffee had developed a bond and if the little guy wandered too far away, the Thoroughbred called until he came back.

The two now happily shared a pile of hay, PB only chasing the bigger horse away when it got down to the last bits. Regan leaned her forearms on the fence and watched them eat, but the usual sense of peace she felt was marred by her mom butting into her life and by what she had learned from Will that afternoon. Her heart ached for him—and she had a hard time with the fact that, in a backhanded way, she was responsible for Kylie being closer to a truth her father didn't want her to have to deal with.

All in all, it had been a rotten enough day that she decided it was a perfect time to call her mother, confront her about the job and tell her to back off. Tactfully, of course.

Arlene liked nothing better than a full frontal assault, so Regan avoided that approach. But when Arlene answered the phone, she was using the strained tone of voice that indicated something—usually something major—was amiss. What had Claire done now?

"What's wrong, Mom?"

"Nothing."

"Nothing?"

"It's Stephen. He's being unreasonable."

Regan pressed her lips together, feeling the beginning of a headache coming on. This was worse than a disagreement with Claire. This was how things had begun the previous two times Arlene's marriages had disintegrated. Her husband had become "unreasonable." He wanted his wife to spend at least a portion of her time with him, instead of devoting one hundred percent of it to her career.

"Maybe counseling, Mom."

"Counseling? Why?"

Regan closed her eyes. "It might help you communicate with Stephen. Then you can discuss your needs and his needs and actually hear what the other is saying."

"I'm hearing just fine, thank you. He wants me to delegate important decisions to underlings and I simply do not have anyone competent enough to take over right now."

"You might want to find someone, Mom. It might be important."

"You sound just like Claire."

"Because maybe Claire knows what she's talking about."

Arlene hung up a few minutes later, leaving Regan feeling even more unsettled than before.

She reached for the phone. Claire hadn't called with a problem in more than a week, but if she had one, Regan figured now was a good time to hear about it.

THERE'D BEEN FEWER PARTICIPANTS than expected in Will's second peace-officer's training session, so by working through the meals, they'd been able to finish a good half day early. When Will picked up his truck from the USDA parking lot it was 8:30 p.m. and he was tired. He headed for the Grants' place.

It had been a long two days, made longer by the fact that he was worried about Kylie. He couldn't tell her the truth. He knew, in his gut, Kylie would feel hurt and betrayed beyond measure and it would forever change their relationship. He wasn't prepared to face that.

Especially when there was no reason for it.

Brett was aware Kylie was his, yet he'd never made a move to acknowledge the fact. It was the one decent thing he'd done in the years since their falling out.

When Will finally pulled into the Grants' driveway and knocked on the door a few seconds later, he was beat, physically, emotionally. All he wanted to do was pick up his daughter, go home and crash.

"Will?"

Beth seemed surprised to see him.

"Is Kylie still up?" It was a dumb question. Kylie was always up at nine.

Beth turned pale. "Kylie's not here, Will."

"What?"

"Is she supposed to be here? I mean, we assumed she was only staying Thursday night—last night."

Will shook his head, trying to get a grasp on the situation. "She was supposed to ride the bus home with Sadie this afternoon, too. Spend one more night. She'd told me it was all set up."

Kylie had always made the arrangements to stay with Sadie—Will hadn't even thought of double-checking. But then, he'd always been able to trust his daughter.

Maybe she was home. Maybe she'd misunderstood. But even as the desperate thoughts rattled through his brain, he knew she'd understood him perfectly.

Beth turned and shouted, "Sadie!"

The girl appeared, took one look at Will and turned white. "Hi. I thought you were coming back tomorrow afternoon."

"I finished early."

"Where's Kylie?" Beth demanded.

Sadie swallowed hard. "She…she went to find her uncle."

"She what?" Will's heart stopped for a moment.

"She had this idea… She just wanted to know the truth, without hurting your feelings. She thought her uncle might know."

"What truth?" Beth demanded, bewildered.

"When did she leave?" Will interrupted. "How did she go up there?"

"Bensons' cattle truck. She left this morning with Zero. She told him she was meeting you up there."

And Zero was just dumb enough to believe it. Will bit back a furious expletive. "How the hell did she plan to get back?"

"She checked the trucking schedule at the feed store," Sadie replied, tears spilling down her cheeks. "They're shipping from the Friday Creek Ranch tomorrow, too. She

thought she could catch another ride with
Zero either today or tomorrow. Tell him you
hadn't made it, after all. She wanted to get
back before you got home." The last word
came out on a sob. "She figured if that didn't
work, then her uncle would help her out."

"Of all the stupid…" Visions of what could
happen to his child out there, who the hell
knew where, alone and unprotected, blazed
through his brain.

"I tried to talk her out of it," Sadie said, her
voice quaking. "She told me I owed her."

"You should have told *me*." Beth sounded
as if she was on the verge of hyperventilating.

"I didn't know she'd actually done it until
she wasn't in class this morning. She called
me when she got there."

Okay. Thank the Lord for that. She got
there. Now all he had to do was get her back.
"Do you have a phone book?"

Beth yanked open a drawer, pulled out a
phone book and gave her daughter a furious
tight-lipped look. Will flipped through the
pages and found the main number for the
Friday Creek Ranch. It rang and rang. He
was about to hang up when someone finally
answered.

"I need to talk to Brett Bishop."

"I was just going to call you."

"Brett?" He recognized the clipped tones now. "Is Kylie there?"

"She's here." Relief slammed into Will.

"Is she all right?" Any other time and he would have reflected on how odd it was to talk to Brett after so many lost years. Right now he didn't care, didn't feel anything except relief that Kylie was with someone he knew, not alone on the highway somewhere.

"She's fine."

"I'll come get her."

"We're already loaded up. I'll be there in an hour and a half."

"Brett…"

"Hour and a half." And then he hung up.

Will wanted to smash down the phone, but instead he set it carefully on the cradle and turned to see Sadie cringe a little.

"She's on her way back with my brother. I'll head home and wait for them."

"I'm sorry." Sadie's voice was little more than a whisper.

"I know," Will said. And he wished "sorry" was enough to fix things.

He walked to his truck, feeling numb. He could hear Beth lighting into Sadie as the door closed behind him.

It looked as if he and Brett were finally going to continue that discussion they'd started thirteen years ago—before the sheriff had broken it up and hauled Brett off to jail for drunk-and-disorderly.

Will wondered how Kylie was going to deal with this. Hell, he wondered what *this* was. He had no idea what Brett might have told her or not told her.

And he wondered, when it was all said and done, whether he'd still have any kind of a relationship with his daughter.

Will was on the porch pacing when the lights turned into the drive. He stopped and walked to the edge of the walk, his heart hammering.

The truck pulled to a stop. Both doors opened. Kylie got out of one side and Brett out of the other.

Will had no idea what to expect and so he just stood there, his heart thumping against his ribs, waiting for a sign from Kylie. He got it. In spades. She rushed for him and threw herself against his side, hitting him with a sturdy thud.

"I'm sorry," she mumbled against his shirt.

"It's okay," he said quietly, clamping an arm around her.

"I know I scared you."

"Yeah." She had no idea how much she'd scared him or how deeply grateful he was that she was there, hugging him, acting as if she still loved and trusted him.

He met his brother's eyes then.

"Brett…"

Brett shook his head, his expression set. He got back into the truck. The door slammed and he put the rig in Reverse.

Will's arm tightened around his daughter as he watched his brother drive away.

I still have my kid.

The thought tumbled through his mind.

"Don't ever do anything like that again."

"I won't. It was stupid."

Kylie pulled in a shaky breath, then eased herself away from her father.

"Dad, I'm so sorry I didn't believe you."

"Come on," he led the way in through the kitchen and down the hall to the sitting room. "Tell me what happened."

"I hitched a ride with Zero. I told him you were going to meet me at the Friday Creek to do the brand inspections. Once I got there, I told the guys at the corrals that I wanted to see my uncle."

"What happened then?"

"It took a while because he was out gathering, but when he got there I knew who he was because he looks just like you."

"He looked really surprised when he saw me. Like he knew who I was, too. Maybe he had pictures." She raised her eyes. "Did you send him pictures?"

He shook his head, knowing that Brett had recognized her simply because she looked so much like Des.

"And then he looked mad or scared or something and asked what I was doing there."

"What did you tell him?"

Kylie swallowed. "I— What I was doing seemed so stupid, once I was there. It was a lot easier in my head. In my head I thought he would be nice."

"What happened?" Will asked gently.

"Okay... Don't be mad?"

"I promise."

"I looked it up on the Internet and I shouldn't have brown eyes, Dad. I just shouldn't. I thought maybe you were just trying to protect me or something." She dropped her gaze. "I thought maybe he'd tell me the truth and you'd never need to know. I tried to call him at the Friday Creek, but he never called back, so I decided to go see him, because I just had to know."

She bit her lower lip and Will held his breath, waiting for the rest of the story. "When I asked him if I was adopted, he got all pissed and asked me if this was the way to treat my father? To run away and ask stupid questions. He was really mad, Dad. *Really* mad."

Will didn't know what to say.

"He told me that my brown eyes were just a freak of nature, and even if they weren't, it didn't matter where I came from. I had a home and I was loved and that was what was important. And then he told me to get in his truck, because he was taking me home."

Will laid his head back against the sofa cushion.

"I'm real sorry, Dad."

"Yeah."

"Uncle Brett is kind of scary. He talked a little on the way home, but it was mostly about my being grateful for what I have." She dropped her own head back against the cushions. "He did ask me whether I rode as well as you did."

"What'd you tell him?"

"I told him yes," she replied matter-of-factly. "That was the only time he smiled." She wiped the back of her hand over her forehead. "I'm tired."

"Me, too."

"How long am I grounded?"

"You know, I think we'll just let it go this time."

"You can ground me."

"I know. But I'm thinking that you won't be doing anything like this again."

"Never," Kylie agreed quietly. "Not ever." She looked him directly in the eye. "I love you, Dad."

"And I love you, kid."

WILL SAT UP late that night, sipping good whiskey, thinking about the past and feeling deeply grateful that Kylie was on the other side of her bedroom door, sleeping in her own bed. The greatest gift of his life had come from the same man who'd perpetrated the greatest betrayal of his life. A man Will had convinced himself he hated.

And now he didn't know how he felt. He and Brett had been close as young boys, but after their mother died, their old man had delighted in pitting them against each other. He particularly liked to hold Will's achievements up as a benchmark for Brett. No matter what Brett did, it wasn't as good as what Will had done. Will had hated being the favored son, but after a while it didn't do any good to talk to Brett, because Brett had stopped listening.

Maybe what had happened had been inevitable. If it hadn't been the deal with Des, it would have been something else. Brett had wanted desperately to show up his older brother.

It was done. It was past. He now knew, for certain, that Brett was not going to try to butt into their lives, claim his rights as Kylie's biological father. From what Kylie had described, it sounded as if Brett had been frightened at the mere idea of admitting paternity. Or felt guilty. Or both.

Will finally put the whiskey bottle back in the cabinet and went to bed, stopping on his way down the hall to look in on Kylie. Stubby was asleep across her feet. The collie opened one eye, then closed it again as he adjusted his chin over Kylie's ankles. Will felt a swell of emotion as he eased the door shut and continued down the hall to his own room.

He still had his kid.

The phone rang at four-thirty, beating the alarm clock by half an hour. Will half stumbled, half jogged out to the kitchen.

"Yeah." Early morning calls weren't always bad news, but somehow he knew this one was.

"Will?"

He recognized the sheriff's baritone. "Yeah, Ernest. What is it?"

"Your brother. We just found him."

CHAPTER TWELVE

WILL'S HEART STUTTERED. "What do you mean *found him?*"

"Lying in the road at the turnoff to Claiborne Canyon. He's in bad shape. From the tracks around there, it looks like he tried to intervene in a stock theft and someone beat the shit out of him. There's an ambulance in transit from Elko. You need to go to the hospital, Will."

"That bad?"

"Could be."

Will hung up the phone and glanced at the clock. He couldn't take Kylie with him and he wasn't going to take her back to the Grants—not unless he absolutely had to. They had a few issues to work out with Sadie, without Kylie being in the middle of things, making matters more tense.

He reached for the note card stuck to the fridge and dialed Regan's number. Too damn early, but not much he could do about it.

"I need a favor."

Less than twenty minutes later, he was steering his stubborn daughter up Regan's front steps. Regan held the door open for Kylie, but her eyes were on Will.

"Thanks for doing this." He set Kylie's small suitcase, still packed from her disastrous stay at Sadie's, just inside the door.

"I'm glad to help." Regan was pale. A small part of him still wondered just how attached she'd become to his brother.

"They've taken Brett to Elko. I'll call when I know something." Kylie had flopped down on the couch and was staring straight ahead. She'd insisted she should come with him, but he wouldn't let her.

"Keep an eye on her, would you?"

"Don't worry."

But he knew he was going to. Even with the small amount he'd told Kylie, he knew she was blaming herself for Brett being in the wrong place at the wrong time.

"She's thinking this is her fault."

"I'll take good care of her. Honest." Their gazes held for a moment and then Regan stepped forward and put her arms around him, pressing her cheek against his chest.

Will hugged her tightly, inhaling her scent and wishing life weren't so damned complex.

"You'd better get going," she finally said, as she eased herself out of his arms.

"I'll call when I know something."

"Do that."

He turned and jogged to his truck, getting in without looking back. Kylie was in good hands. He'd deal with everything else later.

KYLIE SAT ON THE SOFA, her arms wrapped around her waist, staring blankly. Regan had no idea what to say to her. She was fine with kids, in a teaching capacity. But with this kind of stuff… She decided to offer some hospitality.

"Would you like to get a little more sleep? I have a guest room."

Kylie shook her head.

"Something to eat?"

"No, thanks," she murmured, hugging her arms a little tighter. Regan gave hospitality one last shot.

"Television?"

Another shake of the head.

"All right. Well, I'm going to have coffee. Let me know if you get hungry."

Regan kept an eye on Kylie through the doorway as the coffee brewed. The girl didn't move. Finally, Regan gave up and went to sit on the couch next to her. She figured they might as well be miserable together.

"This is my fault," Kylie said as soon as Regan sat down. The girl focused across the room, a pillow hugged tight to her middle.

"How could it be your fault?"

"If he hadn't brought me home…"

Regan had no idea what she was talking about, but she was relatively certain that Kylie was not responsible for Brett getting beat up.

"I've spent a lot of my life thinking that various things happened because of what I did or didn't do. And it's taken me a long time to figure out that just wasn't true."

"But this *is* true. My uncle would have been on the ranch if he hadn't driven me home."

Driven her home? Regan didn't like the sound of that.

"Why don't you tell me about him bringing you home?"

A few minutes later, Regan almost wished she hadn't asked. She was never teaching genetics again.

"So," Kylie said, misreading the expression on Regan's face as an indication of blame, "you see what I mean?"

"No," Regan said firmly. "This isn't your fault."

Kylie looked away.

"Kylie."

The girl refused to turn her head. A tear spilled down her cheek. Regan went into the kitchen and got a box of tissues, which she set on the end table next to Kylie.

"I need to feed Toffee and Peanut Butter. Why don't you come with me?"

Kylie grabbed a tissue and wiped her eyes, then got to her feet without a word.

So far, so good. Regan led the way out the back door.

"Would you put the hose in the water tank?"

She got a mute nod in reply. Kylie submerged the end of the hose and Regan turned on the water.

"I think maybe we should cancel jumping lessons today."

"Yeah."

Regan cut the strings on a bale of hay. "Two flakes for Toffee and one for PB. Spread them far apart."

"Okay."

The feeding was done in no time. "You want to go grocery shopping with me? I usually go early."

"Can we stop by my place on the way back?"

"Why?"

"Dad didn't have time to feed the horses. Maybe we could do it."

"All right."

It took Kylie almost twenty minutes to feed all the animals. She saved Skitters for last, walking into the corral and wrapping her arms around the mare's neck before she went for the hay. The mare nuzzled her.

"Dad won't let me ride her, except in the round pen and the arena. She's blown up with him a couple of times out in the desert, but I know she wouldn't do it with me." She turned to look at Regan. "Maybe with Toffee…?"

Regan shook her head. "I'm not going to let you ride her, kiddo." Not even if it took her mind off her uncle.

Kylie pressed her cheek against the silvery mane. She pulled in a deep breath. Her entire body shuddered when she let it out.

"I'm afraid we're going to have to can her," she said, her voice cracking. "Because she's not trustworthy."

"If your dad sold her as a riding horse, she might hurt someone."

"She wouldn't hurt me. She makes me feel better."

"Maybe he could sell her as a broodmare."

"Can't. She has a tipped uterus." The clinical assessment sounded odd coming from someone Kylie's age.

Regan reached out and touched Kylie's shoulder just as the phone in her car began to ring. Kylie ran for it, barely getting the gate closed behind her.

Regan latched it. She tossed Skitters' hay into the feeder, then followed Kylie to the car.

"Really?" she heard the girl say. "Honest?" Kylie kept her gaze down, a frown of concentration drawing her dark brows together as she listened. "All right. Yes, I will. Okay, I'll tell her." She glanced up at Regan, then down again. "When? I'll tell her. Thanks, Dad. Thanks."

She pushed the end button.

"Uncle Brett is going to be okay. Dad says he'll call later, but right now he and Trev have to do something." The smile suddenly faded and her mouth started to quiver. She squeezed her eyes shut, pressed her lips together. Regan couldn't hold back any longer. She stepped forward and pulled the girl into her arms. Kylie collapsed against her, choking on deep sobs of relief. Regan held her until the sobs had turned to hiccups, by which time Regan's shirt was soaked.

"I'm sorry," Kylie said at last. She pulled back and Regan smoothed her hair away from her damp forehead. "I was really afraid."

"So was I."

"You didn't act like it."

"It's an adult trick."

"I usually figure those out."

"I know, but you're working at a disadvantage today." Regan steered Kylie over to her car. "Come on. Let's go back to my place for now. We can make some lunch, and you can tell me what your dad said."

Kylie sniffed and wiped her nose on her sleeve. "All right."

"WHAT ARE YOU DOING for Thanksgiving?" Kylie asked half an hour later, after helping Regan make turkey sandwiches for their lunch.

"I'm going to Vegas to visit my sister and my mother." Or actually just her sister, since Arlene would be off on a reluctant vacation. If she and Stephen were still together.

"It's funny thinking about a teacher having a mother."

"Well, we're not hatched from eggs."

Kylie smiled. "I was kind of thinking that

you could have spent Thanksgiving with us, but I guess you gotta go see your mom."

Gotta being the keyword there. "Trust me, I'd much rather spend it with you guys." Regan was more than a little surprised at the offhand invitation, after Kylie had warned her away from Will more than once.

"Really?"

"Really," Regan replied adamantly.

"What's your mom like?"

Regan almost said "stressful," but she caught herself. "She's...nice. She's successful in business. She wears clothes I hate. Blouses with bow ties and suits—things like that." Kylie giggled and Regan left it there.

"I think I did okay without a mom."

"You have a terrific dad."

"I know."

Kylie hesitated, then said, "You want to see a picture of my mom?"

"Yes. I would." She wanted to see the woman Will had married. The woman who'd had Will's brother's baby.

Kylie went to her suitcase and pulled a framed photograph from under her clothes.

Regan's first thought upon seeing the picture was that Kylie's mom was young. Very young and very beautiful. Kylie was almost a clone.

"How old was she here?"

"Dad said, when this photo was taken, she was eight years older than I am now, so I guess about twenty. She was a year older than Dad." Her mouth tightened. "Maybe that's why it didn't work out."

"I doubt that," Regan said softly. "It was probably just the fact that they were so young."

"That's what Dad says."

"Do you miss her?"

"No. It's like she's not real. She's just this…picture."

Regan thought that was sad, but it showed what a job Will had done, being both mother and father to the girl.

REGAN SETTLED DOWN to grading later that afternoon, even though her concentration was nil. Kylie amused herself going through the bookshelves.

Will had called again, this time to talk to Regan. He reported that Brett had been beaten almost beyond recognition. He had a battered, swollen face, a fractured wrist, a couple of cracked ribs and a helluva concussion. He was being kept in the hospital for another two days, to be monitored for possible internal injuries, but he was expected to recover. Kylie didn't know the extent of his injuries—only that he was going to pull through—and she was feeling much better.

"Look at your hair." She pulled Regan's junior high yearbook closer, wrinkling her nose as she studied a picture.

"Don't rub it in."

"If the kids saw this…"

"I'll know who showed it to them. I'm going to count my yearbooks when you leave."

"Yes, but you have a scanner on your printer."

"And I also have your grade under my control." Regan got to her feet. She was antsy and so was Kylie.

"Let's make cookies."

Regan wrinkled her brow at the suggestion. "I don't have any dough."

"That's probably because you have to make it first," Kylie replied.

"From scratch?" Regan bought her dough ready-made. Less chance for error that way.

"Yeah. Dad taught me. We make Christmas cookies in the summer sometimes. His mom used to do it with him, before she died."

"I don't know about Christmas cookies, but if we're going to make any kind of cookies, we'll have to go to the store again."

Kylie looked at her as if she were from Mars. "You don't have flour and butter and eggs and baking powder and salt?"

"I have eggs and salt and butter."

"No flour?"

"Get your coat. We'll go buy some."

They'd just returned from the store when Sadie's mother called. They had been shopping in Elko when they heard about Brett, and so they'd stopped by the hospital and offered to let Kylie spend the night with Sadie. Will had agreed.

"We're on our way home now. I think we should be there by six or so."

"I'll call before I bring her over."

"We'll stop by and pick her up."

Kylie was blatantly eavesdropping. "I was kind of hoping to stay here," she said when Regan hung up.

Regan was touched—and just a little concerned. It probably wouldn't be good if Kylie got too attached—although Regan sensed she was stepping over that line herself. "Well, I wouldn't mind, but I really think this is important to the Grants. I think they want to prove they're trustworthy, and that they won't lose you again."

"I guess I can see that."

"They *won't* lose you again, will they?"

Kylie smiled ruefully and shook her head.

Kylie and Regan spent over an hour making cookies. Kylie'd found a recipe on the Internet, but then had to scold Regan for not having the proper baking supplies. Regan talked about the beauty of improvising, though in reality the ability to improvise was one of her weaknesses. She liked things planned and wanted to know exactly where she was going, exactly what was expected of her. Then she could deal with things and relax.

Unfortunately, she couldn't think of many aspects of her life that fit those parameters at the moment.

Almost seven hours later, she pushed aside her grading. Kylie had gone home with the Grants and the house was quiet without her. Regan was no longer able to focus and she was ready to call it a night, when headlights swung into her driveway. Her pulse jumped. It had to be Will. Who else would be stopping by her place so late?

Pete.

Totally mystified and more than a little wary, Regan went out onto her porch, shutting the door behind her. It was close to ten o'clock and extremely chilly, but she had no intention of letting the man into her house. And the look on Pete's face when he stepped on the illuminated walkway told her that she could dispense with the pleasantries.

"Pete." She acknowledged his presence with the single word.

"Miss Flynn."

"What brings you here?"

"I want to give you some career advice."

At ten o'clock. This couldn't be good.

"What kind of career advice?" Regan hugged her arms around her midriff as a gust of wind blasted them. Pete didn't seem to notice the wind. Or maybe he had so much insulation that it didn't bother him.

"They're desperate for warm bodies in the classrooms down in Vegas and you're homesick. I suggest you apply for one of the many semester openings there. If you do, I have it on good authority the school board will release you from your contract with no hard feelings."

Regan had to fight to keep her jaw from dropping. Talk about putting the cards on the table.

"You seriously think I'm going to do that?"

"If you don't, you'll wish you had."

"Another threat?"

"Another threat?" he echoed mockingly. "Think about it. If you transfer out of here, your career is intact. If you don't, well, you might not be the only one hurt when I bring my concerns before the board. This is a small community. Word travels."

She must have reacted then, because Pete smiled.

"Kylie Bishop," he said softly. "Don't you think she's going to find this embarrassing?" His expression hardened. "Although, frankly, the kid could use a little embarrassment. Maybe it would shut her up."

"Get off my property."

Pete bowed his head in a condescending salute. "Make a careful choice, Miss Flynn. It could affect your career, as well as a little girl's peace of mind."

It was all she could do not to chuck one of her empty clay flowerpots at the back of Pete's fat head as he walked down the dimly illuminated path. Instead, she pulled in a deep breath then blew it out as she stood. She watched until the jerk reversed out of her driveway. She wanted to make certain he was truly on his way and not setting up surveillance cameras before he left.

And speaking of which, a movement in the

window of her neighbor's house caught her eye. The place was dark, but the yard light lit up his place like daylight and the curtain had definitely moved.

Was her manure-toting neighbor spying on her for Pete? Or was he just a nosy old man?

WILL WAS ON HIS WAY OUT of the hospital for the night, when Trev showed up.

"How's Brett?" Trev looked patently uncomfortable, though he'd barely set foot in the foyer. He hated hospitals.

"Better. They may move him out soon."

"Good." Trev waited a moment before he said,

"I think I have something."

"What's that?" They started moving toward the exit.

"I talked to the kid who found Brett. He didn't tell Ernest everything."

"Why?" Will pushed the door open and they stepped out into the cool night air.

"Because he's a Stanley. You know how they feel about any branch of law enforcement. Or government. Hell, we're lucky he phoned at all. Anyway, a truck passed him driving in the opposite direction just before he found Brett."

"Who was it?"

"Charley Parker. And there's something else. He says he saw Charley's truck carrying a load of panels up Claiborne Canyon a few days ago. Like he was going to gather."

"He doesn't have any cattle up there to gather. In fact, there shouldn't be any cattle on that allotment right now."

"But there were, according to the kid. Just ten to fifteen head that should have been somewhere else, but weren't—and I think that's why the kid talked to me. I have a feeling that he'd planned to do a little cattle thieving up there himself and he's torqued that Charley beat him to it."

"We might have to do something about this."

"We already are. I told the Stanley kid I'd make it worth his while, *if* we could catch old Charley in the act. He was agreeable."

"It takes a thief to catch a thief?"

"Yep."

BRETT WAS MOVED out of the ICU the next day. He gave a statement to the sheriff, who in turn passed it on to Trev, which was of no help since Brett didn't recall anything after turning onto Claiborne Canyon Road. And he flat-out refused to see Will.

Will wasn't surprised and didn't push the matter. He left the hospital after the last round of visiting hours, then came back the following morning. Brett remained stubborn. So did Will. He hung around until early afternoon, when he met up with one of the guys from the Friday Creek Ranch.

"Listen. Just tell him…" Will hesitated, not wanting to pour too much out to a stranger, then decided to hell with it. "Tell him that I kind of miss having a brother."

On the way home, he phoned the Grants, talked to Kylie and asked her to stay put. She could ride the bus home from school the next day and, yeah, her uncle was fine.

As fine as he could be after having the daylights beat out of him, anyway.

Will really wanted to do something about that.

Trev called just as he was pulling back into Wesley. "Where're you at?"

"Main Street."

"Is Kylie with the Grants?"

"She is."

"Great. Meet me at the USDA office."

Ten minutes later they were on their way back down the highway in Trev's official SUV.

"Let's just say it was an abbreviated call,"

he said as they pulled out of town. Will understood. The Stanleys had never been big talkers. No one cared, because they were kind of scary.

"All he said was, 'Take a look at Willow Creek stone corral, and you'd better do it soon.' I don't know if he meant tonight, tomorrow or couple-of-days soon. And he hung up before I could ask."

"I'd like to check tonight." Will knew they might well get out there and find nothing, but he was glad to be doing something—anything—constructive. He was beyond edgy after spending so many hours cooped up in the hospital. He'd had too much time to think and now he needed to be doing something.

Willow Creek was forty miles out of town on a gravel road that spurred off the state highway. It was not a high-use area, so when they crested the last hill and saw taillights in the distance, Trev accelerated without saying a word.

Will propped his arm against his window as Trev negotiated the washboarded road, keeping his eyes on the rig ahead of them. The truck and trailer were at least two miles away, well past the Willow Creek Road, but it was entirely possible they had turned out of there.

The truck and trailer maintained a constant speed as Trev approached. Will's eyes narrowed as he got his first good look at the outfit.

"I think we should check paperwork. That's the same rig Regan and I saw in the high country." Will had a pretty strong hunch that this driver had no paperwork to prove that the cattle he was hauling were his own.

"Call Ernest, will you?" Trev turned on his light as he spoke.

It took a few seconds before the rig began to slow. It finally pulled to a stop and Trev parked at an angle behind it. The light on the top of the SUV was still flashing as Trev headed toward the driver's window, wearing his business face.

The road was raised a good two to three feet above the desert floor, in order to protect it from the spring floods. There was a steep gravel embankment on either side, and Will only had about eighteen inches of level ground between the trailer and the drop-off. He climbed up on the aluminum running boards and peered into the openings just under the roof.

The trailer was fully loaded, sagging on its springs. The cows inside were tightly packed, shuffling against one another, and the smell of urine was strong. It'd been a while since this trailer had seen a pressure washer. Will instinctively held his breath and jumped down. Fifteen head. He started edging his way toward the passenger side of the truck when the trailer suddenly started rolling backward.

"Hey!" Will shouted, automatically stepping back to the edge of the road.

The driver hit the accelerator hard.

Will jumped sideways, losing his footing and falling down the steep embankment as the trailer jackknifed. He looked up in time to see it smash into Trev's vehicle, crumpling the hood and pushing it almost completely off the road. Radiator fluid sprayed from the SUV, coating the back of the trailer, whose rear wheels had slid just far enough over the edge of the embankment to bring it to a grinding halt. The cows bellowed and smashed against the sides as the trailer tilted.

The truck lurched forward again, its tires spinning as it strained to pull the loaded trailer back up onto the road. Gravel flew, but the trailer didn't budge. Suddenly the passenger door of the truck swung open and a man jumped out. He dashed to the back of the trailer and started yanking on the latch of the damaged door, which was now slick with green radiator gunk.

The bastard was trying to let the cows go, dump the evidence, lighten the trailer and make an escape.

"Trev!" Will shouted as he scrambled up the embankment. He could hear sounds of a struggle on the far side of the trailer over the noise of the cattle—grunts and thuds, followed by a crash as something hit the side of the truck hard.

A woman started screaming and Will moved faster. He couldn't see what Trev was up against. The worst-case scenario was two against one, possibly with weapons, but then it became obvious he had his own problem. The guy at the back of the trailer abandoned the latch when he saw Will coming and charged straight at him, growling with rage.

Will dodged sideways and grabbed the man's coat as he made contact, pulling him off balance and somehow managing to block a wild punch in the process. He hung on, hindering the man's movements until they both lost their footing and tumbled back down the embankment.

Will made a lunge for his opponent, who'd broken free during the fall. He managed to get hold of the coat again, but the other guy twisted free, scrambling away on his hands and knees.

A split second later he sprang to his feet and charged, tackling Will and taking him down.

But he hadn't counted on the number of years Will and Brett had spent attempting to beat each other to death. Will shifted into fighting mode.

His opponent was wiry and strong. He got in a couple of good body shots before Will finally connected with a solid fist to the jaw and the man toppled back, collapsing on the ground. He lay on the half-frozen mud, moaning.

The cows were still thrashing inside the trailer, as Will slowly straightened, working to catch his breath. With the exception of the cattle, there was now an ominous silence.

Will cautiously started for the embankment, half-afraid to call Trev's name. He could see the woman working on the damaged trailer door, trying to free the jammed handle, but he had no idea where the driver was. He was almost to the top of the berm, when a bullet zinged over his shoulder.

Instantly, he froze, his brain refusing to acknowledge what had happened.

The driver, a man Will did not recognize, stood in the middle of the roadway with a gun in his shaking hand. Trev was on his hands and knees, gasping, a few feet away. The driver's chest was heaving. Will took a slow step backward. The man lifted the gun and coolly fired again, barely missing him. "Hold still," he screamed, and then he glanced at Charley Parker's wife, who was also standing frozen, her mouth gaping open. "Get that damn door open," he growled. The words were barely out of his mouth when Trev executed a crouching tackle that even Pete would have been proud of. The driver's head hit the edge of the trailer with a sickening thud and he lay still.

"You bastard," Charley's wife shrieked, stumbling forward toward the fallen man. Will pulled her back.

"Look," Trev said, still gasping for air. He pointed in the general direction of Wesley, and there in the distance, they could see headlights.

"Damn," Will muttered. "I hope those are good guys."

CHAPTER THIRTEEN

IT WAS LATE when Will left the sheriff's office. He took the loop to Regan's house without pausing to think or analyze.

He wasn't going back to a lonely house. He'd spent too much time alone. Today. Yesterday. The past decade.

He pulled into the drive on autopilot. If Regan was awake, he wanted to be with her. He could still feel the sensation of that bullet whizzing past and see the man he now knew to be Charley's brother-in-law pointing that gun at him again. He was no coward, but confronting your own mortality did have a sobering effect.

He drew in a deep breath and got out of the truck, his sore muscles protesting the move. His boots felt as if they weighed fifty pounds each and clunked hollowly as he walked up the front steps.

Regan opened the door, a quizzical expression pulling her brows together. Then the color drained from her face as she got her first good look at him. "What happened?"

"Long story." He tried for flippant but just ended up with weary.

She took him by the arm without another word and steered him toward the open door. "You look like hell," she muttered, pushing the door shut behind them.

"You should see the other guy."

There was a fire burning low in the wood-stove. She led him closer to the warmth, then bent to open the damper so that the flames grew brighter.

"What happened?" she repeated.

He gave her an overview, which consisted of "We found some people stealing cows and arrested them." He left out the part where he could have died.

"Do I know them?"

"Charley Parker's wife, her brother and one of his friends. We still don't know if Charley was involved."

He turned back to the stove, watching the light play through the little glass window. Regan stood a few feet away, watching him watch the flames.

"It was bad, wasn't it?"

"Yeah."

For a long moment the only movement in the room was that of the flames, twisting and curling; the only sound was the pop of the log as the heat intensified. Will put his fingers to his temples. His face was sore. Dirt flaked off his sleeve when he dropped his hands back to his sides. He stared down at his filthy clothing, surprised at how dirty he was.

The fire popped again.

"I wish you would come over here."

He looked over at her. "Dirt and all?" he asked quietly.

"Dirt and all."

He moved toward her. When he got close, he awkwardly put an arm around her pristine blue robe, aware of how grimy he was. She brushed at his chest, flaking more dirt off onto the hearth tiles.

"It's hopeless."

"Yeah." In many ways. But he was alive and he was here with her.

Regan leaned her head against his chest. He managed not to wince as she came upon a bruise. And then the pain evaporated as other sensations began to take its place.

He touched her face lightly with his free hand. She glanced up and he bent his head to touch her lips. Softly. Savoring the sensation of tasting her.

She was the one who deepened the kiss, pushing her fingers into his hair, dislodging bits of mud and debris before letting her hand slide back down to grasp the edge of his shirt as she pressed her body against his. And this time he felt no pain, at all.

His breathing was unsteady when their lips parted. "Should I go home?" he asked. Because if he didn't go soon, he didn't think he'd make it out the door.

"Why'd you come here?"

"So I wouldn't be alone."

"Then, don't go. Just for tonight, Will. Don't go." Her expression was so serious that he knew she meant it. A brief sidestep from reality. A celebration of being alive, when he very easily could have been dead.

Damn, but he wanted her.

He pulled her against him, kissing her hard. She cupped his sore face in both hands.

"The shower is back here. Come on."

He followed her down a short hall, knowing there would be no going back. But deep down, he'd known that from the second he pulled into her driveway.

She snapped on the bathroom light. When

he saw himself in the mirror, he was shocked that she had let him into her house, much less kissed him.

When he turned away from his reflection, Regan reached up and undid the top button of his shirt, biting the edge of her lip in concentration. He didn't move. She undid another button. His hands came up to cover hers. She raised her eyes.

"Regan…"

"Yes?"

"I don't have anything to wear after I shower."

"I'll wash your clothes."

And it would probably take a while for them to dry.

She went to the shower and turned on the water.

He eased out of his clothes, extremely aware of her standing there still dressed, watching, and of the fact that he was almost fully erect. Pushing the shower curtain aside, he stepped into a blast of blessedly hot water. Mud spiraled around his feet.

Regan picked up his clothes and he heard the bathroom door close as she slipped out. A few minutes later the water pressure bumped, telling him she'd started the washing machine. Then the door opened again. The curtain shifted a second later, sending a draft of cold air swirling in as Regan stepped into the far end of the tub. She held a net scrubber in one hand and a bar of soap in the other.

"I thought maybe I could help."

As Will ran his gaze over her, almost-erect became fully, enthusiastically erect. He was certain that teachers hadn't looked like that when he'd been in school. If they had, he would have paid a lot more attention.

"Turn around," she murmured after a perusal of what he had to offer. He turned and a moment later she was soaping down his back and shoulders, her touch light enough not to hurt too much, her strokes long and sensual. She rubbed down to the small of his back. His erection pulsed.

"I think you understated the extent of your activities tonight. You are on your way to becoming one solid bruise."

He was surprised he had enough blood left to even make a bruise. It all seemed to be ending up in another part of his body.

He ducked and let the water pour straight onto his head, but it didn't help him think any more clearly.

The scrubbing stopped. Will felt a moment of disappointment, until she put her palms flat on the muscles of his back and began to slowly rub circles in the lather. She slid her hands around Will, over the muscles of his chest where the cascade of water instantly rinsed the suds away. And then she pressed herself against him, her breasts flattening against his back.

He closed his eyes. It had been way too long since he'd done this.

He took her hand and pushed it lower, so that her fingers could encircle him. She sighed as she took hold of him. He was astonished he didn't come right then. But what a waste that would have been.

He turned, pulling her close. She lost her balance and he caught her, his hand cupping her buttocks, pressing her more firmly against his erection.

"This is dangerous," she said with a laugh.

In many, many ways. But he was not interested in assessing the danger. For once in his life, he was going to go with the moment. And to celebrate the decision, he kissed her again. And again.

"The water is getting cold," she pointed out a few minutes and many deep kisses later. "I have a small water tank."

"You should see about getting a bigger one."

She smiled, water streaming down her face. "I'll talk to the landlord."

He turned off the water, and Regan pushed the curtain open to reach for the one towel on the bar. A few seconds later she led him to her bedroom. She turned at the doorway to touch her finger to his lips in a soft caress.

"Last chance for sanity," she murmured with a raise of her eyebrows.

He was not surprised that she knew exactly what he was thinking.

"Screw sanity," he said gruffly. "At least this once."

ONCE WAS NOT ENOUGH. They made love twice. The first time was wild and needy—a long overdue release for both of them. The second time was languid and tender. Afterward, Will held Regan against him, their bodies pressed almost as closely together as they'd been while making love.

And Regan was dealing with the aftermath. Making love to Will was different than making love to anyone else. She didn't know why. She was afraid of knowing why.

"You all right?" Will murmured.

She laughed softly against his chest. "I'll survive."

"Me, too." And his voice was just intimate enough to spark her desire yet again.

This could easily become a habit, making love with him. She needed to get her feet back on the ground. Work her way back to reality.

"Where'd you meet your wife?" she asked softly, thinking this was about as real as she could get.

"Rodeo circuit. She was a barrel racer." He spoke matter-of-factly, so she chanced another question.

"And you married young?"

"Too young, but neither of us really had any family left. Her mom had dumped her with a cousin when she was just a kid. And my dad didn't have a lot to do with me after I had left home. Brett and I weren't too close, by then."

"Were you married long?" Regan propped herself up on one elbow. This was really none of her business, but she wanted to know what had happened.

"Almost three whole years," he said, with a measure of sarcasm. "We had issues from day one. Money was one of the biggest. It costs a lot to rodeo and I was tired of being broke all the time. I wanted to get a real job and try to buy a place of our own, but Des loved the rodeo. She wanted to stay on the circuit as long as we could." His lips curved humorlessly. "She wanted to party while we were young. We agreed to do one more season before we decided anything, one way or the other, and then I got beat up pretty bad by a bronc halfway through. I came home to mend and Des kept racing. She was pissed about being alone on the road. And I was pissed she wouldn't come home with me."

Regan found herself holding her breath, knowing what was coming next and not really wanting to hear it because she knew how deeply it had hurt the man beside her. She lowered her head to the pillow.

"I started hearing rumors about her and Brett. And then," his mouth tightened, "she came home pregnant. There was no way the baby was mine." Will rolled on his side to face her, then, settling his arm over her and drawing her close. She snuggled against him.

"I don't understand how Brett could do that," Regan murmured, her voice a whisper.

"He was only eighteen, which was something I hadn't given a lot of thought to until I was pacing at the hospital the other night." Will brought a hand up to touch her hair, his fingers sifting through the layers. "Brett and I had a pretty bad fight after I found out Des was pregnant. He said she'd told him we were separated." Will let out a soft, scornful snort. "If she did, she was only referring to the distance between us. But I knew I'd screwed up by leaving her on the road. There's no doubt how she'd screwed up. We agreed we'd try to make things work, for the kid."

"It didn't work?"

He shook his head. "Des wasn't cut out to be a mother. It was almost as if she lacked the confidence to take care of someone other than herself. I think she was scared. One day she just left. She didn't sneak out or anything. She just told me she couldn't do it, handed me Kylie, walked to her truck and left."

"And that was that?"

"That was that. I hated her for a while. Okay, more than a while." A muscle worked near the corner of his mouth. "But I don't hate her anymore."

Regan pulled the blanket over them and cuddled closer to Will's side, telling herself to stop thinking.

REGAN WASN'T SURE exactly when they'd fallen asleep, but she had a feeling she'd been the first to succumb. She awoke when Will gently eased away from her.

"I've got to go," he said softly. His voice was intimate, stirring things inside her. He did a little more damage by pressing a kiss to her temple.

"What time is it?"

"Nearly five."

She pushed herself upright. He gently brushed the hair away from her cheek. "Stay here. I'll let myself out."

She heard him dressing in the clothes she'd put in the dryer after they'd made love the first time. A few seconds later, the front door opened and closed, then she heard the rumble of his truck's diesel engine. She pulled the blanket around her shoulders more tightly, missing his warmth. Missing him.

And once again she felt not quite in control, even though she'd made it clear they were only going to be together for that one night. It alarmed her.

She consoled herself with the thought that they both understood the situation. This was a one-time thing, meant to be healing. And that was that. She was not taking a lover.

Not even Will.

"PETE'S LOOKING FOR YOU."

Regan had barely put her coat away when Tanya stuck her head into her classroom.

"Thanks." Regan opened her bottom drawer and put her purse inside.

"There you are." Mrs. Serrano peeked in next to Tanya. "Mr. Domingo would like to meet with you before classes." She gave a gentle, unreadable smile and disappeared.

"What do you think?" Regan asked Tanya.

"I think we'd better plan on a wine-cooler night."

"I hope not," Regan said, as she put on her professional face and headed down the hall.

Pete was waiting in his trophy-studded lair.

"Please close the door."

Regan closed it and moved to the chair, but she didn't sit.

"I'll need you to sign this," Pete said, pushing a student transfer form toward her. "You won't need to collect the texts. The next teacher will get them back to you at the end of the year."

Regan stared at the paper and then her gaze shifted to Pete.

"Why is Kylie being taken out of my classes?"

"For her own well-being."

Regan's mouth dropped open. Pete gave her that cold smile of his. "Miss Flynn, when you spend the night with someone, you shouldn't let him park his vehicle where everyone can see. It gives rise to speculation."

Regan had no defense.

"Please don't take Kylie out of my classes. She won't understand."

"I guess you should have thought of that before. I did warn you." He tapped his pen on the desk, next to the paper she had yet to sign. "You know, there are still quite a few semester openings in your old hometown. You may want to think about applying."

"Or maybe I'll just stay here and see how this all plays out. You aren't principal yet. You're an interim." She managed to make the last word sound satisfyingly derogatory.

"I'm still writing your evaluations."

"Yes, and while you're doing your best to make me look bad here, you're also making it darned hard for me to go elsewhere. Think about it."

She could see he hadn't considered that point.

"I'm not signing that," she said. "Do whatever you do when a teacher refuses."

"So, HOW BADLY did I mess up?" she asked later, as she and Tanya and Karlene, who was still dressed in her gym clothes from teaching PE, settled into Tanya's overstuffed chairs with their wine coolers. Pete had written her up for professional insubordination, for refusing to sign the transfer request. He'd sent a copy to the superintendent, and she could only imagine what else he'd told the boss. Regan had a feeling her days in the district were numbered. She hadn't quite realized how much went on behind the scenes in a smaller district, how many people owed each other favors.

And then, to add insult to injury, word had come down that the school board had approved a district transfer procedure for administrative jobs. When the principal's job was announced in March, it would be open to transfer, prior to being advertised. The only reason they would have done that was if Pete had already been slated unofficially for the position. Regan knew, without a doubt, that her life would be a living hell if she stayed. Pete Domingo was not a forgive-and-forget sort of guy.

"How'd Kylie take being moved out of your classes?" Tanya asked, pushing her

blond hair back over her shoulders. It immediately fell forward again.

"She thinks I had something to do with
it. I never got the chance to explain. Not
that I'd know what to say." There really
wasn't much she *could* say, considering the
situation, and she despised Pete for putting
her in that position. "Has this ever happened before?"

Karlene and Tanya exchanged glances.

"It has, but never like this. If it was known
that a parent and a teacher were…friendly,
shall we say, then the registrar wouldn't put
the kid in that teacher's class," Tanya explained. "To avoid conflict of interest."

"So they don't automatically enforce that
rule Pete threatened me with? The one concerning parents and teachers?"

"I think the only morality thing they
actually enforce, without exception, is the
moral-turpitude clause and you have to get
pretty wild for them to employ that."

"But," Karlene said carefully, "Pete
could justify taking Kylie out of your class
if he had to."

"How?" Regan asked, wanting to know
Karlene's take on the matter. She was a native

of Wesley and had worked in the district for more than ten years.

"By saying that being in your class is detrimental to Kylie. That it affects her academic performance. That she is embarrassed by the rumors and that he's only thinking of the good of the child."

Regan held up a hand. "I get the picture." Pete could very well say all those things— whether they were true or not—and look like a child advocate in the process. "You know this district, Karlene. Can Pete make much trouble for me? Concerning Will, I mean?"

Karlene wrapped one of her brown curls around her index finger. "Under normal circumstances, nobody would dream of saying anything about you and Will. It would be your own business. You know, like it is in real life. But if Pete decides to make a big deal of this…" She sucked air through her teeth and left the rest unsaid.

"The school board is conservative and it looks like they're impressed by Pete," Tanya said as she followed Karlene's line of reasoning. She leaned forward, her expression sober. "My feeling is that if Pete decides to push the matter and get loud about it in the name of protecting morality and decency and peace of mind, the board will do what looks best. As near as I can tell, appearances are more important than reality with public boards."

"And you did annoy the Taylor family and there's a Taylor on the board," Karlene pointed out with a tilt of her bottle.

"Thanks for reminding me," Regan muttered. "So what do you think they would do, if Pete made a big deal?"

"Probably give you an official reprimand and a warning," Karlene said. "They won't fire you or anything, but it would go on your record. And I'm sure they'd put a letter in your file, documenting the incident."

"That doesn't sound good." Prospective employers would want to read her file. Regan set aside her wine and slumped lower in her chair. She hadn't really thought about how much politicking she was up against.

"It's not good. Rumor travels fast. And sometimes one letter in your file can lead to another."

"And since Pete hasn't been laid in a decade," Karlene added, "he can make a big sanctimonious deal with no fear of repercussion."

Well, that didn't sound too good, either. Especially in light of the fact that the board had adjusted hiring protocol to make it easier for Pete to slide into the principal's position.

They sat quietly for a moment.

"So," Regan summarized, "what you're both saying is that Pete can definitely make trouble for me one way or another."

Both of her friends nodded.

"Lovely," she murmured. "So glad I got on his bad side." She picked up her wine, took a healthy swallow and set it back down on the table with a hollow thump.

Karlene shifted in her chair. "Do you want to stay? Here in the district?" she asked, reaching down to catch the lavender afghan that had started to slide off her chair when she'd moved.

"I like this district—except for Pete. I don't want to go back to Las Vegas." But she would, if she had to; in fact, she was already taking steps in that direction, just in case. She not only had herself to feed now, but her horse and pony, too, and she wasn't giving them up. She hoped. It would be expensive to board a horse and a pony in Las Vegas, unless she got roommates to help with her rent. Or moved in with Claire. She wasn't certain she could take that much drama. She seemed to be generating enough of her own lately.

"Well, I, for one, don't think we should let Pete push Regan around," Tanya said, draining the last drops of her wine.

"And what do you, for one, think we should do about it?" Karlene asked.

"I say we show a united front, make a point of the fact that our private lives are just that."

"That's the problem," Regan said softly. "If we do that, my private life won't remain private." And she wasn't going to put Kylie through the embarrassment. She'd been through enough lately. "I'm going to handle this alone, although I'm not sure how just yet. Pete's clever. Everything he does in public shows him to be a guy focused on fulfilling his administrative duties."

"Taking the hard line," Karlene muttered. "Running a tight ship."

"He has the board impressed," Tanya added, quietly.

"Because they aren't teachers. They don't have a clue." Karlene drained her glass, then looked at her watch. "I have to go meet Jared."

Regan and Tanya looked at her with surprise.

"Yes," she said briskly, picking up her jacket, "we're skirting the school fraternization rule, which is a real rule," she added with a glance in Regan's direction. "But, he's only a sub, so I'm not sure it applies."

"It will, if you annoy Pete," Tanya pointed out. "Is Jared still considering the Barlow Ridge job?"

"Too far away, but," Karlene smiled, "Mrs. Biggs is finally talking retirement and that would open up a third-grade job. That's what we're hoping for. That way we'd be at different schools and we could come out of the closet." She zipped her coat with a flourish. "Think good thoughts for us, okay?"

"DAD, IT WAS AN ACCIDENT." Kylie's lower lip was quivering. He leaned closer to look at the nasty bruise blooming just above the top of her cowboy boot. Skitters had come unglued when a loose paper had blown into the arena and even though Kylie had ridden her out nicely, the mare had smashed her leg against the arena rail.

Kylie gulped a breath. "Give her another chance."

His expression must have told the story. The mare could have broken Kylie's leg. Accidents happened in riding, but there was no sense helping them along. There were too many other good horses out there, to keep one that wasn't trustworthy.

"It isn't her fault," Kylie said from between her teeth. "She's reacting."

As if he didn't know that. The only problem was, Skitters' frears were so deeply ingrained that no matter how much Will worked with her, he knew he'd never trust her. Her self-protective instinct was too strong. Whatever had happened to her was too much a part of her.

"This stinks," Kylie muttered, before she turned and limped toward the house, her back stiff. "First Regan, now you."

Regan. No longer Miss Flynn after their days together, although Will was certain that she still called her Miss Flynn at school.

Or would have, if Regan had still been her teacher.

Kylie was damned upset over that one. He couldn't blame her, and he couldn't explain what had happened, either.

Regan had called just before Kylie'd gotten home to warn him about the transfer. She was at school, so the conversation was, of necessity, short, but it wasn't hard to deduce that their mutual "going with the moment" the night before was producing consequences neither of them had foreseen. With his daughter bearing the brunt of them.

It made him angry. And now it looked as though he was going to have to do something about Skitters.

If the horse stayed, Kylie would insist on riding her. She was convinced that she could break through the animal's fear. And Will was afraid of what might happen if she kept trying. He was going to have to help Kylie face reality, and that was going to hurt, too.

Will was beginning to feel like a damned failure as a father and protector.

AS SOON AS REGAN GOT HOME, she went to her closet and pulled out her interview suit, checking it over to see if it was ready for action or if it needed a quick trip to the dry cleaners. She had not grown up with Arlene Flynn Duncan Bernoulli at the helm without learning a thing or two. First, cover yourself— have a safety net in place before you act. And that meant being prepared in case the worst happened and she had to leave Wesley. She loved her job, but she was not going to stay in a position where she had to answer to a bullying principal. Life was too short.

With that in mind, she'd spent her prep

period that day contacting the central district office in Las Vegas, Learning Tech and even her old school. She'd signed off to let her personnel file, complete with Pete's less-than-complimentary evaluation, go south if a prospective employer wanted it. And they would. As Pete had said, they needed warm bodies in the classrooms in Las Vegas, so she knew she'd be offered a position—whether she wanted to go back or not. Unfortunately, Las Vegas was the only place with jobs available midyear. She feared that Pete might be able to do her so much harm if she stayed until the end of the school year that she would have a hard time getting a job anywhere. If she was going to take a stand, she had to be ready to retreat.

And she was honest enough to admit to herself that maybe she was looking for a reason to retreat. An easy way out that allowed her to leave before she had to face the fact that she and Will were not going to be able to live in the same place and ignore one another. Will had a daughter to protect and the level of relationship he needed was far beyond what she thought she wanted or was even capable of. She needed to get out, before she hurt any of them more than she already had.

As part of her campaign to make Pete accountable, Regan had submitted a written request for a meeting with Pete and their immediate supervisor, which in this case happened to be the superintendent of schools. She knew exactly when Pete had learned of her request. He'd stalked into her classroom and stood at the rear, glowering at her under the guise of informal observation. Regan kept her cool and added to the documentation she'd spent the previous weekend compiling. It was probably too little, too late, but she was determined to take a stand. She knew enough about bullies to know that Pete was never going to let up on her, but at the very least, she'd go down swinging.

She received word late the next afternoon that the meeting would take place in three days. She was encouraged to have representation, if she so desired. Regan did not "so desire," even though she knew Arlene would think she was making a rookie move. She wanted to keep things as private as possible.

She contacted her friend Cheryl, at Learning Tech, as she drove home, to explain the so-so evaluation that Mrs. Serrano had already faxed her. Cheryl assured her it was only a small part of the overall selection process and that, frankly, Regan was exactly what they were looking for.

Regan hung up, knowing she should feel elated, but instead she felt depressed.

When she got home that afternoon, she fed her horses and decided it was time to have a chat with her neighbor. The old guy now waved at her when he pushed his wheelbarrow down the drive, but he didn't seem to have a lot to say. It was possible, though, that he was more vigilant than verbal.

Regan headed across her property line, being careful to stay on the path and out of his garden beds, and quickly discovered that her neighbor, whom she was to call Chet from now on, was more than happy to respond when asked direct questions.

Yes, Pete Domingo had stopped by once, but Chet had no idea that Pete was anything other than curious when he'd asked a few questions about Regan. He didn't even know Pete was her boss. He thought he was the football coach and Will's friend. In fact, his excuse for stopping was that he was looking for Will.

Regan knew that Will would love that. He and Pete. Friends.

And it turned out Chet did remember the night Pete's car had pulled in so late. He also remembered the other night when Will's truck came late, too. And stayed. Chet was a very vigilant neighbor.

Regan thanked him and promised him full access to all the fertilizer her horses could produce. She added to her documentation as soon as she got home, then wondered if Chet was watching when Will knocked on her door later that night.

No matter. She pulled the door open, but she was unprepared for the powerful emotions that swept over her when she came face-to-face with the man she had to admit she'd been avoiding.

CHAPTER FOURTEEN

"I HAVEN'T SEEN YOU in a while, so I thought I'd stop by. You know… So we could talk in person." Will knew they were both remembering the last time he'd "stopped by." With some difficulty, he shifted his attention back to business. "I want to know why Pete took Kylie out of your class." He had a pretty good idea, but he wanted confirmation.

Regan stepped back, politely allowing him to enter the house before she answered. It was hard to believe they'd made love, passionately, not that long ago.

"Someone saw your truck here the other night," she said after closing the door. "And Pete's making the most of it."

"Regan," Will reached out, but she took an automatic step back. He let his hand fall to his side and felt something close up inside of him at the distance she put between them. "I would never have stayed if…"

"Hey, I knew what I was risking, and I'd do it again." But she spoke so calmly, he wondered if she meant it.

"What's going on with the job?"

Regan's mouth tightened. "It's becoming clear that I can't work for Pete and it's possible I'll be taking a job elsewhere at the end of this semester."

She was leaving? He hadn't been ready for that. "Kind of drastic, don't you think?"

She moved to the sofa, idly running a hand over the fleece blanket lying along the back. "It's pretty certain, according to those in the know, that Pete will become principal—the school board is paving the way. He'll be looking for ways to get rid of me and I don't want to work under those conditions."

He hated the cool, straightforward way Regan was presenting the facts, although he knew it was her defense. "Is leaving your only option?"

"I have a meeting with the superintendent, but I don't think it's going to do a lot of good. Pete has the home-field advantage." She folded her arms. "It's probably for the best, considering everything involved."

"Meaning me?"

"Yes."

He took a couple of steps forward. "Look, Regan, I know you've had some bad experiences with relationships." She smiled tightly, but said nothing. "And I have Kylie to think of. But maybe if we take things slow, stay sane about it."

Regan shook her head. "We've complicated things enough being just friends. Let's not complicate them more."

He studied her for a moment. Her defenses were a mile high. She was running on instinct and he knew there was no sense in trying to communicate with her now. He'd have to wait until she quit running. Then maybe he could help her move past the fear.

Damn, he hoped so, because this was ripping him apart.

"Then there's not a hell of a lot more to say, is there?"

"No, Will, there's not."

THIS TIME IT HURT. Every other time Regan had eased her way out of a situation that had been getting too close, it had felt uncomfortable yet inevitable—something that had to be done.

Not this time.

And the bizarre thing was that she and Will had barely even started a relationship.

One night couldn't even be called a relationship, which only drove home the point of how important it was to end things now before they got crazy.

She spent the rest of the evening trying not to think about Will and instead concentrating on her upcoming meeting with Superintendent Zeiger and Pete. She didn't have much luck.

The next school day passed all too fast and Regan's stomach was in a knot, but she was as ready for her meeting as she was ever going to be. Pete might end up with a Regan Flynn–free district, but he was going to have to work for it. Regan was not going down without getting in at least a few pokes at him.

"We're going to keep this informal," Superintendent Zeiger said, pointing Pete and Regan toward their chairs.

Like her, Pete had dressed in his administrative best and he did look rather impressive in a bullfroggish way as he lowered his well-tailored bulk into a chair. "Neither of you have opted for representation, so let's see what we can do about this situation." He put his hand on Regan's sheaf of papers. "Miss Flynn has some concerns that she has documented here. Apparently some friction has developed between you two, starting with a student prank involving lab materials, followed by some question of athletic eligibility?"

"I'm not certain what Miss Flynn has *documented,* but I assure you, I've done everything by the book." Pete straightened his striped tie importantly as he spoke.

Regan barely kept her mouth shut.

Zeiger leveled a questioning look at Pete. "A home visit at ten o'clock at night? Apparently witnessed by Miss Flynn's neighbor?"

Pete's mouth popped opened, but he immediately clamped it shut again. "I had reason to believe Miss Flynn was looking for a new position. I stopped to tell her about one I had heard of."

Of all the flipping flat-out lies. Regan's jaw muscles tightened as she struggled to maintain her composure. She could almost hear her mother whisper: *Don't show weakness.* It helped.

"It didn't seem professional to mention it at school," Pete continued. "I thought it would be more appropriate in a private setting. I didn't realize she'd try to twist a perfectly innocent incident, one in which I was trying to help her."

Pete began folding and creasing one corner of the manila folder in front of him, then caught himself. His fidgeting subsided as he raised his double chin and announced, "Miss Flynn opposes me whenever possible. In fact, I'd say whatever complaints you've had are in retaliation for me simply doing my job."

"So, you're saying there is some friction, Pete?"

Regan held her breath as she watched him search for an answer. Finally, he settled for a succinct yes. He couldn't very well say anything else, with her sitting across from him, ready to contradict him. "But it's her fault."

Zeiger nodded. "Would you be willing to undergo peer counseling to work it out?"

Pete's eyes widened. "I don't think that would be necessary."

"I do," Regan said. Pete sent her a killer look. "Pete?"

"Mr. Zeiger, she is doing this just to make me look bad at a sensitive time in my career."

"If that's the case, we need to deal with it. Whether you're principal or not, Pete, you and Miss Flynn will be working together."

Regan could tell from the way Pete was staring at her that as far as he was concerned there was no way they'd be working together in the future. He'd get her for this.

"You know I'll do whatever it takes to help in the smooth running of my school," Pete said.

"Good. We'll set something up."

The meeting ended shortly thereafter. Pete stalked out through the main office. Regan was almost to the door when Zeiger called her back.

"May I take another moment?"

"Sure."

"I called your former principal this afternoon."

Regan's heart skipped a beat as she once again took a seat. She'd had her share of head-to-heads with her former boss. He'd been a weak administrator, but she'd no longer call him a poor one. Working under Pete had put an entirely different spin on the definition of a poor administrator.

"We had a chat. I asked him if he would hire you again. He said he'd hire you in a heartbeat."

Regan let out a silent sigh of relief, glad to have at least one point on her side.

Mr. Zeiger carefully put back his pen in its ornate holder. "I'd hate to lose you as a teacher. I've talked to parents and students over the past few days. They like what you're doing. They think you're excellent, in fact."

"That's gratifying."

"So, that's why I hope you'll take the peer counseling seriously. Pete has some areas to work on, granted, but he's a good man and I think he'll be an excellent administrator with time."

Regan nodded. "Maybe so, but… You also might want to take an informal survey among those who are currently working for him."

"Change is never easy, Miss Flynn. Pete runs a tighter ship than Mr. Bernardi, but frankly, the school needs strong leadership, strong discipline. Things will settle."

"If Pete gets the job."

"If Pete gets the job," Zeiger agreed, but the way he spoke made Regan believe it was a done deal.

WHEN A VEHICLE pulled into her driveway after dark, Regan's heart began to race. She hoped it was Will. She hoped it wasn't. Damn. She crossed to the door and pulled it open. It wasn't Will.

"Do I want to know?"

"I'm giving Mom a time-out." Claire looked around as she stepped inside, suitcase in hand. Regan's eyes widened as she took in the size of the suitcase. "This is cute," her sister said. "A little isolated, but cute."

"Isolated? I have a neighbor close enough to spy on me." Regan closed the door. "How'd you find the place?"

"I just asked at the convenience store. They were very helpful." Claire dropped her bag and walked into the kitchen, taking inventory as she went. She'd had her hair redone since Regan had last seen her and now had a short geometric cut that went well with her retro sweater, clunky jewelry and leggings.

"Well?"

"Not quite the same as your old place," Claire said as she picked up an issue of *Western Horseman* from the kitchen table. She wrinkled her nose before she set it back down.

"Yes, but so much more me."

"Probably so," Claire agreed. She opened the fridge and pulled out a bottle of white wine. "Glasses?"

"I'll get them."

"Actually, I wanted to get out of town and I thought you might need a little moral support, stuck out here in the wilderness." Claire unerringly opened the drawer that contained the corkscrew and lifted it out with a flourish.

"Thanks."

"I'm serious." Claire plunged the corkscrew into the top of the bottle through the foil and twisted. A few seconds later, she eased the cork free.

"You know there's not much shopping here to clear the head," Regan said, accepting a glass of wine.

"I noticed. This will be kind of like an adventure for me. You know, roughing it? I'm looking forward to meeting your animals."

"How long are you staying?"

"Just a day or two. Then I have to get back for classes."

"So, what happened?" Regan asked after they had settled in the living room with the wine and a bowl of pretzels on the table between their chairs.

"Well, I'm dropping out of engineering."

Regan almost dropped her glass. "Mom will have a cow."

"She already did." Claire smiled before she popped a pretzel into her mouth. "It was a boy." Then her expression sobered. "I don't want to be an engineer yet. Maybe sometime. Right now I want to do something more… people oriented."

"Don't you dare use the phrase *people person*."

"Mom is not happy with my choice." Claire stared down into her wine and gave it a swirl. "I've always wondered why people undervalue teaching as a career choice. I mean, what could be more important than shaping kids?"

Regan smiled. Claire would be a good teacher. She was just crazy enough that her students would never know what was coming. And she was sharp.

"There's nothing more important," she agreed. "But," she tilted one corner of her mouth, "you need to know that it isn't like in the books—or the college classes, for that matter. These kids are not empty vessels, waiting to be filled. They fight you tooth and nail sometimes."

"You don't think I'm up to it?"

"Of course, I think you're capable. But engineers make a lot more money, with a lot less yelling."

"That's exactly what Mom said." Claire drank the rest of her wine in one gulp. She put the glass down on the arm of her chair, keeping her fingers wrapped around the stem.

Regan couldn't help her smile. "Heaven forbid I sound like Mom. That's not supposed to happen until I have kids." She leaned over to pour more Riesling into her sister's glass and to top up her own.

Claire looked at her, her expression shrewd. "Are you ever going to have kids, Regan?"

"Well, I'd probably have to find a husband first."

"And you're probably not going to do that, are you?"

Regan stared into her own wine. "Maybe not."

"I didn't think so."

"Why do you say that?"

Claire looked at her like she was kidding. "Oh, come on, Reg. You only date walk aways.'

"Walk aways?" Regan frowned at her sister.

"You only date men that you can walk away from, when the time comes."

Regan shook her head. "Not true." She didn't think... She'd really liked all of the men she'd dated seriously. In the beginning, anyway.

Claire gave her a superior look in response. "Let's take a look at your most recent beaus. We'll start with Jeff. He was a nice guy. Fun, good-natured, but just needy enough that he wasn't husband material—unless you wanted to help him with every decision of his day, from choosing his shirt to what time to go to bed. You probably liked the fact that he didn't try to control anything, but you couldn't really respect him, could you? So you had to…walk away."

Regan's expression grew somber. "Go on."

"Tyson. *Very* good-looking. Intelligent, fun to argue with…" Claire smiled reminiscently. "But his needs always superseded yours. I knew you wouldn't put up with that for long. The control thing again, you know."

"And Daniel?"

"Ah, Daniel. Perhaps the best of the bunch. Also good-looking, personable. Supportive. And a liar and a cheat."

"But I didn't know he was a liar and a cheat. He appeared to be almost perfect."

"Why did you date him?"

"He appeared to be almost perfect. He gave me space when I needed it."

"Did you have any intention of growing old with him?"

"No."

"Which was why he was perfect. You could eventually walk away." And she smiled in that maddening way she had.

"I don't…" Regan broke off abruptly, compressed her lips.

Claire rolled her eyes. "Regan, did you ever notice that whenever a guy got to a point where he could have a say in your life, you'd end it? I'm talking about before Jeff. Back when you were in college and maybe still believed in true love?"

Regan didn't answer, but she knew exactly what her sister was talking about.

"And then I think you just started dating guys who would cause the least amount of pain when you had to end things. Ones you weren't all that attached to." Claire smiled ironically over her empty glass. "Do you think Mom has anything to do with that behavior?"

"Of course Mom has something to do with it," Regan replied with a scowl. "I know I have control issues. So have you." She rallied a defense. "What's wrong with just dating, without having serious intentions?"

"Nothing. You get companionship. Sex."

"Exactly."

"You have a facsimile of closeness, without risking anything."

That wasn't exactly what Regan had been getting at, but it summed up her relationship with Daniel perfectly.

Claire continued her assessment without noticing Regan's expression. "You get to do what you want. Be what you want. No one has much say in your decisions."

Regan nodded, thinking that all sounded just a wee bit selfish and empty.

"But you lose something, too, Reg."

And that was where the *facsimile* came in. The relationship looked real, but it wasn't.

Regan stared into her wine for a moment. "Have you been reading self-help books?" she finally asked.

"Campus counseling center. I've been a regular since you moved. It helped me put my relationship with Mom in perspective and it's also why I haven't been calling so much." She ran a finger around the top of her glass, making the crystal sing. "I suppose you could send them a tax-deductible donation as a thank you for your quiet evenings."

"So why are you hiding out here?"

"Hey, even counseling has its limits." She smiled. "I miss you and I wish you'd come home."

"You may just get your wish."

Claire leaned forward. "What happened?" she asked.

"Job troubles."

"Tell me about it."

"I have a boss who wants to get rid of me," Regan said wearily. "He is not a person of reason."

"What man is?"

Regan smiled, then told her sister the entire story.

"That doesn't sound good," Claire said, once Regan had finished. "But tell me about the guy. Will."

"I don't really want to discuss it."

"That doesn't sound good, either."

No, it didn't, because there had never been much that Regan wasn't willing to discuss with her sister. But the situation with Will…it was going to remain private. This was something she had to figure out alone and she knew she had some thinking to do. That *facsimile of closeness* comment bothered her. A lot.

The phone rang. The sisters exchanged glances.

"If it's Mom," Claire said adamantly, "you haven't seen me."

Regan sucked in a breath and picked up the phone. There was no one she wanted to talk to right now.

"Cheryl?" Regan had spoken to her only hours ago. "Do you need any other information?

"Yes," her friend said in a sardonic voice, "if this is a bad evaluation, what do you consider a good evaluation?"

WILL SETTLED the saddle on Skitters's back, trying not to think about the tense evening he'd just spent with his daughter, telling her how things had to be. Maybe he should have waited until the spring or just sent the mare on her way without telling Kylie. But he couldn't bring himself to lie to her and every day he kept the mare was just going to make it harder for Kylie to let go. Ultimately, he decided it was best to get it over with, so his kid could start healing on this front, too. The sale-yard truck was coming tomorrow and Skitters was slated to be on it when it left.

The mare stood stock-still, as she always did when he tightened the cinch, but Will could feel the energy vibrating through her body. A coiled spring, ready to go off at any moment.

One last ride, he told himself, even though he was not a sentimental man. He was almost hoping she'd explode again, to validate the decision he'd made.

Damn it, it was the right decision. He rubbed the mare's neck, felt the muscles start to give a little and then they pulled tight again.

Some horses could take a lot and forgive. Others learned their lessons quickly and they stuck. Skitters was certain that pain was never far away from the human touch. No matter what, that lesson was lodged in her brain. No amount of TLC was going to make her trustworthy with his daughter. Or anyone else for that matter.

The mare moved out as they headed across the river meadows. Will kept his attention on the ride, even though part of his mind kept edging toward thoughts of Regan.

Skitters went willingly, ears forward, moving out, almost as if she sensed these would be her last moments of total freedom. They crossed one low pass over the hills behind the house and then another. Will felt himself relax, his mind again began to wander, but he caught himself.

Maybe he should keep the mare.

For Kylie, as a pet.

Couldn't do it. He had trouble making ends meet, as it was. Adding five more tons of hay a year for an animal that Kylie would almost certainly insist on riding was not going to help either his budget or his peace of mind.

The mare suddenly put her head up. Will pulled her to a stop.

In the distance was the mustang herd, heading for the water hole. Skitters blew through her nose. Will gathered the reins, but she didn't move. She watched.

Will watched, too, as the distant animals walked single file to the spring. Skitters put her nose higher in the air and whinnied, the shrill sound cutting the air.

He could feel the energy again and so he did the sane thing. He stepped off the mare and stood beside her holding the reins, studying her perfect head, her deep brown eyes, which should have been soft, but weren't—except when she was around Kylie. She quivered and whinnied again.

Will flipped one stirrup over the seat of the saddle and undid the cinch tie. Then he pulled the saddle off, dumping it on the ground.

Think, Will.

He unbuckled the throatlatch; the mare didn't seem to notice. One quick move and the bridle slipped off. Will caught the bit automatically, so it wouldn't clack against her teeth. She stood for a split second, then tossed her head and took off for the herd, kicking up divots of sod with her hind feet as she galloped.

Will watched her go, a golden blur, thinking that it was too bad he hadn't had the tools with him to pull her shoes.

But they'd come off with time. They always did.

He pulled the sweaty blanket out from under the saddle and shook off the debris. He folded it and laid it over the back of the saddle. And then he looped the bridle, hung it over the horn, gathered the cinches and secured them over the blanket, finally hefting the saddle to his hip with one hand. He started walking back.

IT HAD BEEN a long time since Will had walked so far in cowboy boots. He'd topped the second-to-last rise before he could see the house when the rider appeared. He'd seen his brother in the saddle often enough to recognize him at a distance.

"Taking your saddle out for some air?" Brett asked when he was finally within speaking range. The first time they'd spoken face-to-face in years and Brett was his old flippant self. Which meant he was hiding emotions.

Will cocked a hip to support the weight as he looked up at his brother, who was riding Kylie's old gelding. "Helping yourself to my stuff?" Probably not the best thing to say, considering their past, but Brett didn't flinch.

"I wanted to find you." He nodded at Stubby. "This little pup knew exactly where you were. I'd almost say he's more tracker than cow dog."

"Are you healed?"

"For the most part." Which was something of a lie, because he still had bruises on his face. Brett placed both gloved hands on the saddle horn, one on top of the other. "I wanted to tell you that I'm pushing on."

"What about Kylie?"

Brett pushed his hat back. "You've done a good job with her. I like her."

"She's my world."

"I know. And I wouldn't interfere with that."

Will swallowed before he spoke. "Thank you." His voice was slightly uneven, but Brett pretended not to notice.

"You want to tell me where your horse went?"

Will smiled a little. "Yeah, I'll tell you. I'm breaking the law for Kylie." He gave his brother the story.

Brett shook his head when Will was done, then dismounted stiffly and pulled the reins over the horse's head. "Why don't you load your saddle on?"

Will swung his saddle up on top of Brett's and tied the strings of the two saddles together, securing them.

"You'll get blisters walking in those new boots," Will pointed out. "At least mine are broken in."

Brett smiled. "Maybe I should take them off. Remember when you convinced me to do that?"

"You always were easily led."

"At least I wasn't all pushy. Is Kylie much like Des?"

Will was not surprised by the rapid-fire change of topics. He started to walk and Brett fell into step, leading the horse.

"She has the fire, but I think you've seen that. She isn't so desperate for the attention." He walked a few more paces, then said the bravest words of his life. "You could get to know her better, you know. Be part of her life."

Brett immediately shook his head. "Wouldn't be good for anybody." He raised his chin, his eyes fixed on the horizon. "Nope. I've got a job waiting in Idaho and that's where I'm going. I'll be back to testify, if I remember anything. Which brings me to saying thanks for going after the guys who beat me up. I guess you fight a little better than I do."

Will didn't answer. It didn't seem like there was much he could say.

"Kylie called me."

Will's heart gave an extra thump. "Yeah?"

"She's worried about you. Says you're lonely."

Will swore under his breath. He hated that his kid noticed, hated that she'd tried to do something about it. But he had to admit, she succeeded where he hadn't. Brett had at least taken her calls.

They walked the miles home in silence, which seemed to amplify the sound of their boots clunking over the rocks, the saddles creaking as they swayed in tandem on the horse's back.

"You're crazy if you let that woman go," Brett said after they'd unsaddled the horse.

"You don't understand the situation."

Brett simply lifted his eyebrows. "One of us doesn't," he agreed. He hesitated, then took a step forward and gave his brother a quick embrace. "Don't know when I'll see you again."

Will nodded and watched as his brother walked alone back to his truck.

REGAN STOPPED at the district office at 4:30 p.m., as per the superintendent's e-mail request. She was ushered directly into his office when she arrived.

Zeiger gave her an ironic smile as he waved her to a seat.

"I received an interesting fax this morning."

Regan nodded.

"You are aware of it, aren't you?"

"Only that the evaluation Learning Tech received was glowing and I know the one in my file was not."

"There's no proof that Pete substituted the evaluation, you know. The signature pages have not been tampered with, so anyone could have inserted the middle pages."

The message was clear. "Pete's going to be principal, isn't he?"

Zeiger gave a slow nod. "All I can give you is an opinion, but, yes, I'd say it's almost a given."

"Then I'd like to transfer to Barlow Ridge."

Zeiger couldn't hide his surprise at her blunt statement. "Have you ever been to Barlow Ridge?" he asked flatly.

"No." But it seemed like a solution.

She'd come up with the idea just that morning. Barlow Ridge was seventy miles away—a rugged seventy miles, from what she'd heard—but it wasn't Las Vegas. She wouldn't be within Pete's sphere of influence and she could keep her horses. Plus, she'd be fairly close to Will while she tried to figure things out and she'd still have her own space.

And damn, but she had a lot to figure out. She was entering unknown territory here and she was scared. But she also sensed that she and Will had the beginning of something that shouldn't be abandoned simply because of a knee-jerk fear.

"You need to take a visit, first," Mr. Zeiger was saying. "Find out what you'd be getting into. Do you have a truck or an SUV?"

"I have a car."

Zeiger winced. "You'd better go soon, before the weather changes." He put his pen back in its holder. "Do you mind if I ask why you want to transfer to Barlow, rather than just go home to Las Vegas?"

"I'm going to face my fears," she said matter-of-factly.

"Miss Flynn, I don't know what you're talking about, but if you end up taking the Barlow Ridge transfer, I wish you all the luck in the world."

CHAPTER FIFTEEN

THE BUS PULLED TO A STOP and Kylie tumbled down the steps, barely staying on her feet. She raced toward Will, skidding to a stop in front of him. He'd known that she would see Skitters' empty pen from her bus window and assume the worst.

"It's okay, Kylie. You don't need to worry about Skitters."

"It's not Skitters's," she said imperatively, barely sparing a glance for the empty pen. "It's Regan."

"Regan?"

"She's leaving. I was in the office—I wasn't in trouble—and I heard Mrs. Serrano talking to Miss Prescott. She's leaving!"

Will didn't say anything and Kylie stared at him in thunderstruck silence. "You know!" she finally blurted out. Her mouth worked for a moment, then she said, "Well, you need to do something about this."

"Like what?"

"Like…like marry her or something."

Will barely kept his jaw from hitting his boots. "Marry her?"

"Yes. If you guys got married, then she would stay. Marry her." Will frowned at his daughter, started to shake his head. "Oh, come on," she said impatiently. "You guys *like* each other. It's only obvious."

"Kylie. Kid. Even if we do like each other, neither of us is going to jump into marriage. Regan doesn't want to get married."

"Get engaged, then. That'll give you some time."

Will rubbed his forehead with the tips of his fingers. How to explain this one? The fact that Regan was afraid of committed relationships. "Even if we got together, it would be a long time before we got engaged or married. And," he settled a hand on his daughter's shoulder, "even if we did get together, there is no guarantee it would work out."

"But it might."

"Yeah. It might. But it might not."

"I'd be willing to take a chance. Why aren't you?"

"Regan has plans, Kylie." Will swallowed. "And it hurts when things fall apart. It'd hurt me and, more than that—since you like Regan so much—it'd hurt you."

"It hurts right now, Dad."

"It'd hurt more later."

"Well, you know what?" Kylie blurted, her eyes filling with tears. "I don't care. *I'd* take the chance."

The tears started to roll down her cheeks and she lifted her chin. "If you don't do something, I will."

"Kylie."

"What?"

Will knew he had to prepare them both, just in case he wasn't able to break through Regan's defenses. "Sometimes it's better not to have something than to lose it."

Kylie gave him a pitying look through her tears. "No offense, Dad, but that's just plain dumb."

PEANUT BUTTER was grazing peacefully on the lawn when Will drove up. He automatically caught the pony and led him back to the corral.

"Stay put," he said sternly, as he latched the gate.

"Like that's going to help."

The woman standing on the porch was not

Regan, but the resemblance was unmistakable. And now he knew what Regan would look like if she dyed her hair blond and cut it into a short choppy do.

"I'm looking for Regan."

"She isn't here."

"Do you know when she'll be back?"

"No."

Will put his hands on his hips, took a moment to regroup. "It's important."

The woman wrapped her hand around the newel post. "You're Will, aren't you?"

"Yes. And you are…?"

"Claire."

"Nice to meet you, Claire." Will faked a smile. It disappeared instantly. "Where is she?"

"She's on an interview."

Damn. "Where?"

Claire gave him a long, hard look. "You're just going to hurt her if you chase after her, you know. She isn't interested in happily-ever-after."

His mouth tightened. "Right now Regan isn't the one in danger of being hurt."

To his surprise, Claire suddenly smiled. "Tell me, cowboy. How are you going to handle a woman who's afraid of commitment?"

"I'll start by telling her how I feel."

"Like that's not going to turn her inside out." Claire took a moment to study Peanut Butter, who was idly mouthing the gate latch. "What do you know about my sister?"

"That she cuts and runs when she's scared and that I want to talk to her about it."

Claire looked impressed. "She went to visit a school."

"What school?"

"Some Ridge place."

"Barlow Ridge?"

"Possibly."

REGAN SAW THE TRUCK coming for miles across the wide valley. She'd crossed two mountain passes to get to Barlow Ridge, separated by wide expanses of…nothing. The country was beautiful, wild. The kind of place where you didn't want your car to break down, because it would be quite a while before another vehicle passed by.

And she was suffering from a slight case of culture shock.

There was no shopping here, except for one tiny mercantile. No place to eat, except for the local bar. The main street was six blocks long. But Toffee and Peanut Butter would probably like it. She'd never been to a place where the ranches literally butted up onto the town streets, and the term *street* was loosely used.

The truck neared and Regan suddenly recognized both the vehicle and the silhouette of the man at the wheel. She automatically slowed, pulling off the side of the road as far as she dared.

Will was out of his vehicle by the time she opened her door.

But they stayed on opposite sides of the road, regarding one another across the expanse of frozen rutted gravel.

Neither spoke. Regan breathed in the frosty air, wondering who'd be the first to break the silence. It was Will.

"What are you doing out here?"

"Exploring my options." Somehow she managed to put a wry spin on the words.

"At Barlow Ridge?"

"Are you familiar?" she asked, buying time.

"My great-grandfather homesteaded there before he moved to Wesley. You have to be dedicated to live in Barlow Ridge."

"I don't want to go back to Vegas. I can't afford to keep my horses there."

"Quite a sacrifice, for horses."

"It isn't all for the horses." Regan edged

closer to the truth. "What are you doing out here?"

"Coming to find you."

Regan's heart thudded against her chest wall.

"Here I am," she said softly.

"And don't I know it," he replied. He took a slow pacing step forward. "I met your sister."

"What'd you think?"

"That she must be exhausting to live with." Regan smiled.

A breeze swirled past, blowing frost crystals in a small cyclone. Regan waited for it to pass, thinking this was about as far from the Vegas heat as she could get and still remain in Nevada. And yet she preferred it.

"Why are you doing this, Regan?"

She swallowed before she said matter-of-factly, "I realized that I've never before been afraid of ending a relationship before it started." She focused on the gravel instead of looking at him. It was hard to think, with those blue-gray eyes looking directly into her soul. "Which makes me believe this one is different. It scares me."

There was a beat of silence.

"So your solution is to move to Barlow Ridge?"

"I have two options, because of Pete.

Barlow Ridge or Vegas. Barlow Ridge is seventy miles away. Las Vegas is four hundred miles away."

And four hundred miles was a lot farther away from Will than she wanted to be. She pushed her hair behind her ear. "I figured that this way I can keep a job with the district and still be within fairly easy driving distance." She shook her head as she regarded the potholed, washboarded road. "Obviously, I'll have to rethink the 'easy' part."

"Obviously."

"At least it'll give me some thinking time."

"Yeah." Will agreed. He turned to look down the miles of road she had just traveled. "How much time are you going to need?"

She didn't understand what he was getting at, so she slowly shook her head.

"This road. It's hard on tires. I'll need to calculate it into my budget."

Regan almost smiled. Somehow, now that he was here, it was easier to believe that everything would turn out all right.

But in reality, she knew there was more involved than the two of them simply taking a risk on each other. "I don't want to make a mistake, with Kylie involved. I wouldn't hurt her for the world."

"And I think I'm finally beginning to understand that protecting Kylie from situations where people might leave doesn't guarantee she won't be hurt." He took another step toward her, his hands still in his pockets. "And I want to give Kylie a chance to see what it's like to love and be loved. I didn't realize it, but I'd been shielding her from that, too."

Regan drew in a breath and went for full disclosure. "I can't guarantee anything, Will. One of us—all of us—may end up getting hurt."

He looked surprised. "I'm not asking for a guarantee. I'm asking for communication and trust." He took another slow step toward her. "We can deal with just about anything else if we've got those. And as to getting hurt, it's no fun, but a person heals. I know."

Regan's heart started beating even harder as he neared. This was for real. Not a walk away.

"So what do you say?" he asked, his expression intent. "Will you consider the possibility of trying to make a life with me and Kylie?"

She cleared her throat and went with her heart. "I'd kind of like to try."

And the next thing she knew she was in his arms. He swung her around, and when he finished, her feet still weren't on the ground. But her lips were on his mouth.

He slowly lowered her toes to the ground as the kiss deepened. And then he brought his forehead down to touch hers, their frosty breath mingling. It was so cold, the air was starting to burn her cheeks, but she didn't care. She pulled back a little, her expression serious.

"I have to take the job in Barlow Ridge, Will. I can't stay where I am. Maybe I can transfer back to Wesley later."

"I can live with that," he said in a low voice. "It'll be hard on my truck," his expression softened, "but I can live with it."

Regan laughed as she took his face in her hands. "You're a good guy, Will."

"I can get even better," he murmured near her ear. "Come on. It's a long way back to town. We'd better get going." He pressed a kiss to her temple and Regan shivered, but it wasn't from the cold.

"I love you, Will." And she was surprised at how free she felt, saying the words.

"I love you, too. And the way I see things, that's a pretty good start."

Passion. Power. Suspense.
It's time to fall under the spell
of Nora Roberts.

2nd January 2009

6th February 2009

6th March 2009

3rd April 2009

The Donovan Legacy
Four cousins. Four stories. One terrifying secret.

FREE!

2 Books
and a surprise gift!

We would like to take this opportunity to thank you for reading this Mills & Boon® book by offering you the chance to take TWO more specially selected titles from the Superromance series absolutely FREE! We're also making this offer to introduce you to the benefits of the Mills & Boon® Book Club™ —

- ★ **FREE home delivery**
- ★ **FREE gifts and competitions**
- ★ **FREE monthly Newsletter**
- ★ **Exclusive Mills & Boon Book Club offers**
- ★ **Books available before they're in the shops**

Accepting these FREE books and gift places you under no obligation to buy, you may cancel at any time, even after receiving your free shipment. Simply complete your details below and return the entire page to the address below. You don't even need a stamp!

YES! Please send me 2 free Superromance books and a surprise gift. I understand that unless you hear from me, I will receive 4 superb new titles every month for just £3.69 each, postage and packing free. i am under no obligation to purchase any books and may cancel my subscription at any time. The free books and gift will be mine to keep in any case.

U9ZEF

Ms/Mrs/Miss/Mr ....Initials ....
BLOCK CAPITALS PLEASE
Surname ....
Address..
....
....Postcode ....

Send this whole page to:
UK: FREEPOST CN81, Croydon, CR9 3WZ